EYE OF THE SEAHORSE

Also by Virginia McCausland

Death's Ferryman Rides A Harley

Eye of the Seahorse

Virginia McCausland

First Paperback Edition: May 2024

Book and Cover Design: Virginia McCausland
Cover/Title Page Images: Deposit Photos
Interior Chapter Image (Celtic Seahorse): Shutterstock

Author Photo: Ray Hudson

Paperback ISBN: 978-1-7776778-2-4
E-book   ISBN: 978-1-7776778-3-1

Website: www.virginiamccausland.com

*"Did you ever think the eye would not be the
eye without the I? They sound the same but the I
cannot see without the eye." ~Kieran*

Chapter One

Brannon

Ballycastle, Northern Ireland - 1929

Every day it grew stronger. It crept across the land like a smothering vine, and at every harvest, there was more rot, diseased sheep, soured milk, and sick children. The day of the fair, I smelled it, like the sour stink on Granda when he'd been out fishing. It tasted like morning breath, no worse, like rotten fish. It seeped into our minds, kindling fights for no reason. It got Granda, and it got me. It made us say and do things we didn't want to do, and if I hadn't gone to the fair looking for the sweet toffee known as Yellowman, Peter would still be alive.

Yellowman. I'd waited all summer for it, and the tinkers had the best recipe. I found their barrel-shaped wagons at the edge of the fair near loud-voiced vendors bartering chickens, sheep, and horses. Fiddle music soared over the din of squealing pigs, horse traders, and a girl singing and dancing in front of the pub.

"Hope your teeth are tight, or the tooth fairy will be visiting you tonight." The tinker's mouth wrinkled into a smile over toothless gums. "Lost one of me own yesterday. Serves me right for eating toffee with a wobbly tooth, but if it's Yellowman you want, you won't find any better at the fair."

There were so many things I wanted to buy at the fair, but I had only enough money for one treat. It had to be Yellowman, the sweet honeycomb toffee that tasted like sunshine and heather.

I licked my lips as the old woman hammered off the golden nuggets and packed them into a paper cone. Before she could pocket my coin, I had eaten the biggest piece of toffee I could fit into my mouth.

"Good?"

"Oh aye," I said through stuck teeth.

I popped another piece of toffee in my mouth and turned around to look for my ma, whom I'd left to buy vegetables at a nearby stall. I called and waved my cone of toffee in the air, but a boy darted out of the crowd, bumped me, and knocked the cone from my hand. The devil be damned if it didn't fall into a heap of sheep shit.

"Connor!" the old tinkered hollered.

Connor stood an inch or two taller than me, but I didn't care about that. I grabbed a fistful of hair before he could get away and spun him around. "Watch where you're going, you stupid knacker. You ruined my Yellowman, and you're gonna pay for it." I raised my fists and braced for a fight.

"Get out of my way, you eejit." Connor spat a gob of chewing tobacco in my face before shoving me onto the tinker's craft table. It snapped, and I sank to the ground on top of woven sea-grass baskets, rugs, sweaters, and shawls.

"Connor!" the tinker shrieked as Connor jumped over me to get away from Anrai McKinley, the village silversmith who blocked Connor's escape on the other side of the table.

McKinley lunged and grabbed Connor's arm. "You little thief," he growled.

"What's he gone and done now?" the tinker asked.

"Me knife! I saw him take it," McKinley said. "Chased him clear across the fairgrounds, I did."

Connor pushed McKinley's hand away as he tried to reach into Connor's pocket. "I don't have it, you lying old crabbit." He turned his pockets inside out to prove it.

"Watch your tongue, you good for nothing hellion, or I'll clip you," McKinley snarled.

"I'm telling you. It wasn't me. It was him."

Before I could stop him, Connor's hand darted in and out of my pocket. With a satisfied grin, he held up a small knife. "See, what did I tell you? He had it all along."

I clenched my fists. More than anything, I wanted to pound Connor's head soft as shit, but my ma called to me as she pushed through the crowd that had gathered to watch us fight.

"What happened?" She had a firm grip on my arm.

"He put it there," I said before anyone could accuse me. "He put the knife there when he knocked me over."

McKinley snatched the knife from Connor and put it in his pocket. "You bloody buzzies," he grumbled. But before he vanished into the crowd, Connor had slipped his hand in and out of McKinley's pocket and taken back the knife. It happened so fast that McKinley didn't notice. Neither did Ma, or the old tinker, for that matter.

The tinker shook her finger at Connor. "Look at what you gone and done, you dirty little urchin. You're giving us good folks a bad name with your thieving ways, and I ought to slap you on the napper for setting this poor boy up for a lot of trouble. Get yourself cleaned up. You'll not get in my wagon with sheep shit all over your shoes and trousers."

I plugged my nose and feigned a look of disgust. Connor glared and shook his fist at me before ducking under the wagon.

"I'm sorry," the old one said. "I know you didn't do it, and I hope your ma knows too."

I searched Ma's face for a sign she believed me, but she was looking at the woman, whose eyes filled with tears.

Ma's hand rested on my shoulder. "He's a good boy. That I know."

The tinker pursed her lips and blinked away the tears dotting her eyelashes. "And a fine-looking lad at that. I'd heard you had a son, Molly, and by god, I hoped that one day we would be back this way again. It's been so long."

"What brought you this far north?" Ma's eyes watered too.

"The blight," Etain said. "We needed supplies that have grown scarce elsewhere."

"You know Ma?" I asked.

"This is Etain," Ma said. "I used to buy Yellowman from her wagon when I was a little girl." Ma picked up one of the shawls knocked on the ground by my fight with Connor. "Brannon, look how beautifully she blended these colors to look like an autumn sunset." She folded the shawl and placed it on the wagon steps.

"Oh aye, the earth does marvelous and daring things with color," Etain said as she filled cones with Yellowman for a group of children gathered around her stall. "But I've noticed that each year there are more and more brown tones than red or gold. The wildflowers don't smell as fragrant, and it takes more herbs to spice the stew. Some peppers have lost their bite altogether. Oh, and the quality of the wool has been poor lately, too. Sometimes it won't take the dye. If it does, it comes out too dark or too light. I've heard that the sheep have a strange sickness. No one knows what it is."

"The crops, too," Ma added. "I heard some farmers talking. Too many storms and too much rain just before the crops are harvested. The cycles are off. They're worried about another potato famine."

"It's a blight for sure, and it's going to touch more than the potatoes this time," Etain said. "I fear it'll be in everything."

"The apples too," I said. "They're rotting before they fall. There're a few good ones at the top of the trees, though."

"You like apples, do you?" Etain asked.

"Oh, aye, but I like Yellowman best." I glanced at my toffee and the golden nuggets trampled in the shit by the fairgoers.

"Ah, it's spoiled," Etain said. "You can't eat it now." She scooped some nuggets into a fresh cone and held it out to me.

I shook my head. I had no more money, and I couldn't ask Ma.

"Take it," Etain said. "I'll make that scallywag pay for it. You'll see."

Before Ma could say no, I took the cone, put a piece of toffee in my mouth, and let it melt in the hollow of my cheek. "Thank you. Yellow's my favorite color. I like how it tastes and blends with other colors when I'm painting."

"You're an artist, then? Like your ma?"

"I'm teaching him," Ma said. "When he listens, he learns. When he doesn't—"

"He still learns. Yes? Ah, that's the way of it." Etain removed a blue gemstone from the folds of her shawl, attached around her neck by a silk cord. "Brannon, what does this star sapphire remind you of?"

If only I hadn't looked at it. Peter might still be alive, but the gem pulled me in, and I stood mesmerized by the six-rayed star flickering white in the center of the stone. It reminded me of two crisscrossed swords glinting in the sunlight under a summer sky, but I couldn't say so. It was as if a piece of toffee was stuck in my throat and choking my words. The fairgrounds blurred around me as the light drew me to the center where the blades intersected. I blinked, and all at once, I was standing on the seashore with the roar of surf breaking upon the rocks.

Scenes flashed before my eyes: dawn's sky, the smell of snow to come, the smell of fire. A small bird, a pipit, winged up from a burning wagon. A boy's face framed by fire and blackened wood. His hands on fire. Searing pain. The nauseating smell of charred flesh, putrid and steaky. My hands burned from the heat. The toffee slipped from my fingers.

I screamed and reached through the star-shaped gateway that appeared before me. I felt a silken cord entwined in my fingers, a salve against the burns. I yanked on it.

Sounds from the fair came crashing around me: horses clip-clopped down the street, children laughed as they chased a ball, a dog barked, two men argued in the nearby pub, and lovers whispered in the alley behind the shoemaker's store. I opened my eyes, and to my surprise, I had a choking grip on the silk necklace around Etain's neck. My ma was screaming at me to let go. The cord snapped, and the gem fell into my hand. The sapphire felt like a small creature snuggled warmly in my palm.

"No!" Ma shouted and grabbed my wrist. "Give it back to her. Give it back now."

If I had obeyed her, Peter would still be here, but I didn't. I couldn't. In a strange way, the gem felt like a part of me, and giving it back would be as painful as hacking off a finger or a toe. Now, I'd be happy to give an arm or leg for Peter's life.

Before Ma could take the gem from me, I yanked my hand from her grip and closed my fist tight around the gemstone. The urge to keep the sapphire was overwhelming. I wanted it more than I wanted Yellowman. It made me feel strong, and not even a slap across the back of my head would make me give it back.

"There, child, let him go." Etain blocked my ma's next blow and covered Ma's hand with her hand. Ma had never hit me before today.

"I'm sorry," Ma said. "I promise you. He'll be punished."

"There's no need. I'm afraid I've only myself to blame for his strange behavior. I didn't know it would affect him so." She placed her hand over the awful welt around her neck.

My face burned with shame as I crouched behind the wagon wheel. It was a dumb thing to do, as Connor had gone there to hide and was waiting for his chance to get me. His fist shot out and punched me in the face. Clutching the sapphire, I raised my arm for protection against a second blow, but Connor slammed his body into mine and knocked me onto my back under the wagon. His punches were quick and fierce. I kicked him between blows, once on the arm and once in the stomach. The women watched from opposite sides of the wagon.

"If you don't come out now, Connor, I'm gonna beat the lard out of you," Etain threatened.

"It's mine. Give it to me," Connor kept saying over and over.

I scooped up a handful of dirt and flung it into Connor's face. He fell back, spitting dirt from his mouth and wiping his tearing eyes. Without thinking of the harm I could do, I kicked Connor smack in the middle of his forehead with my boot. Connor fell backward and clunked the back of his head against the rear axle.

It was a terrible sound, his head hitting the iron. I feared the worst and rolled onto my knees and crawled toward him. My heart lay crossways to see him lying so still. I nudged his arm, but he lay as if dead.

"Brannon, what's going on? Come out from under there, right now." Ma knelt on the ground to watch.

I hunched over and listened for Connor's breath. Nothing. Not even a wee puff. I leaned closer, almost nose to nose with him. He smelled of tobacco and horse manure. As I turned, Connor woke and whacked me in the jaw. I bit my lip. Blood pooled under my tongue and dripped down my chin. I forgot about the sapphire and dropped it as I lifted my hands to protect my face from a second blow. We both scrambled for the gem, but before Connor could scoop it up, I got it, clutched it tight in my fist, and rolled out from underneath the wagon.

My ma grabbed my blood-spattered shirt by the sleeve and shook me so hard the stitches popped one at a time. It was favorite shirt, not my Sunday best, but the one I wore the most.

"There now. He's just a boy. No harm done." Etain coughed.

I felt terrible to have harmed her.

"He's old enough to know better." I'd never seen Ma look so angry.

I turned away to spit blood from my mouth. "I'm so sorry," I said and wiped my mouth with the back of my hand.

"Give it back," Ma said.

Halfheartedly, I opened my hand. The gem sat bloodied in my palm. Etain closed my fingers over it. "It's a talisman now, son, washed in your blood. Keep it and use it well."

"No, it's not for him," Ma said.

I put it in my pocket before she could take it. "Please, Ma. I'm sorry. Let me keep it."

"Why would you give this to my son? You, of all people, know what it can do." Ma pulled my hand out of my pocket. "Give it to me."

"The gem is meant for him." Etain placed her hands on my shoulders. "I'm pleased you're sorry, and it was wrong of you to take something that didn't belong to you, but I understand why. Now tell me, what did the gem show you?"

"A burning wagon like this one and a boy surrounded by flames." I'd never get that steaky smell of burned flesh out of my nose.

"By everything holy." Ma covered her mouth.

"Just as I thought," Etain mused. "Brannon, you have a gift. You see, that sapphire was only a pretty stone to me, but your blood has made it a talisman. Now you must keep it, but be warned. Such gifts can lead you on a path of light or dark. In the end, you must choose, and it won't be easy."

"No!" Connor scrambled from under the wagon. "You said I could have it."

"I told you, when the time is right, you'll have your own talisman. Such gifts are earned, not given."

"But he's done nothing to earn it," Connor said.

"You don't have the eye to judge such things, Connor."

"I know a Ginny Ann when I see one," Connor spat.

At that moment, I leaned toward the darker path and clipped Connor's nose with the same fist that held the sapphire.

"Brannon," Ma scolded. "This isn't like you." She gripped my arm and pulled me away before Connor could give me back some of my own.

She was right. I had struck Connor without thinking, and I wasn't the kind of boy to go out of my way to cause a fight. I should have been shaking in my boots as I watched the blood run from Connor's nose to his lip. Instead, I was itching to get in another whack. Maybe loosen a tooth or two. With the back of his hand, Connor wiped the blood away, smearing it from his cheek to his ear. Large eyes, bluer than any I'd ever seen, glared at me through matted sandy locks.

"One day, when you're not looking, I'll get you and that talisman too," Connor said.

"None of that now." Etain handed him a rag. "Get yourself cleaned up and help me tidy up this mess."

"How could you give it to him?" He squashed the rag into a ball and shoved it into his pocket. "The little shit doesn't even know what it really is or even how to use it." He stomped up the three steps to the wagon door.

"But I do," Ma said, "and I don't want him to have it. Give it back, Brannon."

"There now." Etain placed the shawl, which looked like an autumn sunset, around Ma's shoulders. "We can't take the gem back now. You know that." She spoke to her in Shelta, the tinker's language, and to my surprise, my mother answered in the strange tongue. At first, Etain's words were soothing, but then Ma became angry. I didn't understand what they were saying, but I knew by the way they looked at me that it was about the talisman.

"What did she say, Ma?" I asked as she took my arm to lead me away.

"What one generation failed to do, the next must complete," Etain shouted after us. "He's been called to right a wrong. Will you stand in his way, Molly?"

"What does she mean, Ma, I must right a wrong?"

"No more questions. She's a silly old tinker. It's time we started home, and you'd better be praying all the way that I don't tell your da about this."

No worries there. She'd never tell Da or Granda—especially Granda—that she knew a tinker or that she could speak their language or that Etain had given me a special stone.

I glanced over my shoulder and saw Connor standing on the wagon steps with a glint of something in his hand. The knife.

Chapter Two

Brannon

I leaned my head against the bedroom wall and sat cross-legged on the floor beside my bed. My head hurt. It always did when Ma pulled me awake from that place where I'd go to do my art. I knew it scared her to find me away from myself, but I couldn't stop it from happening. Some people walked in their sleep, and some talked. I drew pictures. All over the floor, my drawings rustled in the breeze from the open window.

"You think I do it on purpose, but I don't." I stretched and pushed my sketchbook off my lap and sat on the edge of the bed.

Ma picked up the sketchbook and flipped through it. "It's not the drawings I'm worried about." She placed the sketchbook on the desk by the window. "It's the wind. It's un-natural. I fear for your da and the other fishermen. You called it, didn't you?"

The winds could be strong at this time of year. Nothing unusual about that, so why did she think I called it? True, sometimes I could get the wind to do my bidding, but not always. Ma had an uncanny sense, though. She always seemed to know when I was up to no good, so there was no point lying about it. "I only wanted the wind to knock the apples down, the good ones I couldn't reach, the ones untouched by the blight."

While holding onto the talisman, I'd given a little extra effort to the summoning, for I was sure there was magic in the gem Etain had given me. The wind came stronger than expected. It ripped our gate from the fence and tore our clean clothes from the line. I hadn't meant the wind to be that strong or dangerous to the boats at sea. Now, the wind was out of control, knocking not only the apples from the trees but snapping the branches in half and sending them banging against the house.

"I've told you before. Terrible things can happen when you summon the elements. What if someone died tonight, your father, a friend's father, or a brother? Then how would you feel?"

The thought of someone dying because I'd only wanted a few apples horrified me, so I left the talisman, rolled in the sheet, and slid off the bed. "Away now," I said and slammed the window shut.

Ma drew the curtains aside. "Be gone with you," she whispered, but the wind couldn't be stilled so easily. It rattled the shutters and tore a piece of thatching from the roof.

A thump on the bedroom door startled us. I scrambled to the door and held it shut with my toe so Granda couldn't see the mess in my room.

"Jaysus, what's that blasted noise?" Granda pushed the door wider. His girth filled the entrance.

"It's only the wind," I said.

"Gave him a fright," Ma added.

"Aye, 'tis a terrible one." Granda shook his head. "And look at this pigsty. What did you break in here?"

"Nothing broke, Granda. Was only the window slamming shut."

"Then away to your bed before I come in there and give you a beating for waking me out of a fine sleep. And you'll get more than a slap if this room isn't cleaned by the time I get up in the morning." Granda yawned and closed the door.

While Ma gathered my paintings and sketches off the floor, I picked up my charcoal pencils and watercolors. She looked at each picture before placing it in a pile on my worktable. One painting, a watercolor, made her pause.

"It's Manannan." I took the picture, tacked it to my wall, and stood back and admired it. The Lord of the Sea wore a cloak adorned with scales of mother-of-pearl and turquoise. His fleet of horses, great muscular beasts, blended into the white-crested waves as he steered his boat, Wave-Sweeper, without oar or sail. At his side, he wore his deadly sword, The Answerer.

A portrait of Etain lay face down on the floor. Ma picked it up and turned it over. "Ah, Brannon, the likeness. The stroke of white lightens her eyes, and the red streak shows the curve of her lips. Your skill is so mature for one so young." She smoothed the wrinkled paper and placed the portrait on the worktable.

"How do you know her?" I knew she was hiding something from me by how she talked to Etain at the fair.

"One day, I'll tell you, when you're older."

I tossed my pillow onto the ruffled bed and lay down. The sapphire rolled from the crumpled folds onto the floor when I pulled on the sheet. Before Ma could pick it up, I hung my head over the bed and snatched it from under her fingers. "I promise I won't call the wind again."

"And I'll hold you to that promise." Ma sat on the edge of the bed. "I don't understand why Etain would give a boy without training a talisman."

I rolled the gem between my palms. "What's a talisman?"

"Well, there are many kinds of talismans. Some answer prayers. Some will keep you safe."

"Like the rosary?" I had seen Ma pray with her rosary from time to time when Granda wasn't around.

"Yes, but different. A talisman can have a will of its own, so you must promise me you won't use it until you've learned how to control it. Calling the wind to get a few apples is one thing. Causing someone's death is another."

"How can I learn control without practicing?"

"You need someone to show you, someone skilled in using a talisman. I know someone. I hope that one day you'll meet him. The sooner, the better, I think. Now, promise you won't try to use it again."

"Ma, don't worry so. It's just a stone."

"Brannon, a talisman is never just a stone. I'd take it from you now if I could, but—"

"But what?"

"If you're meant to have it, it will only find its way back to you."

"Ooh, it's magic then." I held it tighter.

"Holy Mother, I wish Etain had never given it to you. Now go to sleep." She turned down the lantern and left me lying in the dark.

Sleep wouldn't come. Thoughts swirled in my mind: the tinker Etain, Connor, the boy who fought me for the talisman, and the strange vision of the young man in the burning wagon. I crawled out of bed, sat at my worktable, and held the gem in the moonlight.

I hoped no one would die tonight just because I'd wanted a few apples. "Talisman, can you keep Da safe?" I asked aloud.

The star sapphire glowed and filled the room with a pale blue light. My eyes felt sleepy, so I slumped over my worktable, and with my cheek pressed against the drawing of Etain, I fell asleep.

The sound of someone playing a haunting melody on a harmonica woke me. When I opened my eyes, I was standing on the deck of *The Zephyr,* my da's fishing boat.

A dream? A vision? I couldn't be sure, yet I could smell the brine, feel the north wind's chill, and see my da leaning against the gunnels playing his harmonica. Like the vision at the fair, I found myself in two places at once, on the deck and in my bedroom. I checked my pocket and felt the talisman warm against my fingers. I knew it had come alive. I hadn't meant to use it again. It was an accident this time. I'd only made a wish, and wishes seldom came true. I hoped my ma wouldn't find out.

Sturdy waves lifted and set the boat up and down in a steady rhythm. "Da, a terrible wind is coming," I said.

My da stopped playing, pocketed his harmonica, and walked past me to check the lines. He paced the length of the deck two more times before rechecking them. There was fear in his eyes as he muttered prayers to Manannan to take pity and send the catch they desperately needed.

"Da," I tried again. "Can you see or hear me?"

Da pulled a flask of whiskey from his jacket pocket, and took a swig. He sighed from the warming effects of the liquor and leaned back against the gunnels.

It was that magical hour before dawn. Starlight flickered on the water, but it wasn't the stars' reflection that caught my eye. It was the sudden swell and the twinkle of silver. A shoal of herring rippled the ocean's surface. Da saw it too.

"Manannan, be praised!" He scrambled to the cabin door, flung it open, and called to his mate, who was resting on a bunk. "Evan! Get up! Get your arse up here. It's coming. Hurry!"

Da steered the boat before the wind and across the tide. Evan flew onto the deck and cast the net over the boat's quarter. It wasn't long before I felt the tug of a full net on the boat. But I knew the storm was coming. I could see it gathering on the horizon.

Da cut the motor and helped Evan haul in the net.

"Da, look. A storm," I said.

He didn't hear me, but Evan saw the signs and cried, "Bloody hell!"

For a minute, both men stood, cursing the mist gathering in the distance. "It's gonna be a dirty one," Da shouted over the waves, knocking against the boat. "How long?" he asked.

"Hard to say, but by the look of those cats' paws, within the hour or sooner," Evan said.

They worked as fast as they could, pitching the herring into the hold and setting the net for a second and a third load. Just before landing their fourth catch, a vicious gust sent the boat plunging into a flat-bottomed trough one moment and slowly rising on the face of an enormous swell the next. I held the guardrail to keep myself from being tossed overboard as the boat rose with the wave and dropped again. I wondered what would happen if I drowned. Would I wake up in my bedroom or Tir na nOg?

Evan took the helm and angled the boat into the next swell, but the vessel pitched and stood suspended at the crest of a twelve-footer before plummeting. The engine stalled.

"Jumpin' Jaysus!" Evan spat.

Their catch had become a deadly noose dragging behind them, causing the boat to toss and bob like a cork in the water. The boat rocked back and forth with each swell. With a queasy gut, I reached for the toerail to steady myself. Evan turned the engine over once, twice, three times before the boat dipped into the next trough. Like a demon, the blackened ocean threw itself against the boat until it rolled broadside to the waves. The net, attached to the boom, pulled the boat over starboard. The boom snapped and fell across the deck and into the water.

Da raced to drop the sea anchor over the bow. Evan grabbed the ax and, in a single swipe, cut the cable and released the net that held the boat in its death grip. The boat rolled to port, sending Da and me skidding down the greasy deck.

I glanced over my shoulder and saw Evan set the ax in the remains of the boom. He grabbed Da by his jacket as he slipped by, stopping him from colliding with the gunnels or, worse, being swept into the churning waves. I grasped the rigging and held on.

Evan hollered something above the wind, something about a pen board coming loose. Now the herring had shifted in the hold. An unstable boat was a death ship.

With shovel in hand, Evan jumped into the hold and pitched the fish from one section to the other. An oncoming wave washed onto the deck and swept Da into the hold. Da gagged and picked himself up out of the mound of herring.

"Hang on, mate, don't heave at me now," Evan said. "It's bloody nasty in here as it is."

Fish, still in the throes of death, writhed beneath their boots. As hard as they tried to balance the boat, the more futile it became, with water filling the hold and herring jumping from pen to pen.

"Sweet Jaysus, help us. We need a bloody miracle here. Can't you see we're shittin' our cacks?" Evan knelt to secure a pen board. "Should have known it was too late in the season to be chasing the herring this far out, especially in this rotten can of piss. It should have been broken up and burned long ago."

The Zephyr had been in our family for generations and almost every inch of it had been mended or rebuilt.

A miracle. They needed a miracle, so I took the talisman and held it before me. "Manannan, great lord of the sea," I said in a voice not my own. "Take pity and calm the winds that bear upon this boat and threaten the lives of your faithful servants."

Sapphire light filled the hold. Both men stopped pitching fish and stared.

"Lord Almighty," Evan whispered, "do you see that now?"

"Where's it coming from?" Da's eyes were wide with fear. He couldn't see me, but he could see the sapphire's light.

The winds dropped, and the boat righted with a jarring lurch. Evan bumped into Da and sent him sprawling headfirst onto the deck at my feet.

"Sorry, mate." Evan offered his hand and pulled Da to his feet. "But think on the bright side. We got our miracle, and this can of piss is still floating."

While Da heaved over the rail, Evan half-cursed and half-pleaded with the engine to turn over. Finally, the engine hiccupped and engaged. "There's a good lass," Evan cooed. "I won't have any more mean words for you now. I know you're an old lady, and you're doing the best you can."

The storm had taken half their catch, net, and boom, but at least I still had a da. I thanked Manannan as I felt myself pulled away from the boat and finally waking at dawn in my bedroom.

Chapter Three

Connor

Thoughts of Brannon, the eejit who stole my talisman, kept me up most of the night. Brannon and the blasted wind that is. The wind tore through the camp, clanging pots, pans, and anything else it could lift from the wagons. Blustery weather came and went as surely as night and day, but this storm had come out of nowhere without a murmur of warning. And it carried the scent of something unnatural. It reminded me of the banshee's death call I'd heard last winter when a child in our camp died suddenly in his sleep. Horses knew when things weren't right, and their frightened whinnies kept me on the edge of sleep until daybreak, when the storm vanished as quickly as it had come.

I yawned and led the horses to the meadow to graze. I kept thinking about Etain and why she would give the talisman to that brat. What was so special about Brannon that Etain would give him such a gift? The only reasonable explanation was that Etain knew him. How she knew him was the mystery I needed to solve, because I was determined to get that gem back.

My favorite mare, Epona, a cream piebald with chestnut markings, twitched the ends of her tail across the ground. She was restless today, staying close to me and not going to graze with the rest of the herd. I brushed a comb through her mane, smoothing it over her crest and down her shoulder. The feathering on her legs extended from her knees to cover her hooves in a plume. She tossed her head and snuffed the air.

"Aye, I know you're feeling it now." I brushed a forelock from her eye.

I felt her foal kick as I eased my hand over her swollen flanks. It had grown more in the past few days than it had in months. When I stroked her muzzle, she pinned her ears, lifted her head, and nipped my finger. I yelped, pulled my hand back, and slapped her on the loins. Not a hard slap, just enough to let her know she'd pissed me off. She wheeled away and galloped to the middle of the pasture to join the other horses grazing on coarse grass.

My thumb throbbed where she'd broken the skin. I took a handkerchief from my pocket and squeezed blood from the wound to prevent infection. It troubled me that Epona had taken to sudden bursts of temper. When I complained to Etain, she smiled and said, "You have much to learn about women."

Etain was right. I'd hurt Tara's feelings at least twice in the past week. I didn't expect her to bring me tea this morning like she usually did, so it surprised me when she rustled beside me, bringing the faint smell of lilac and wild rose. No tea, though.

Her unbound hair blew into her eyes. Her skirt, fringed with burrs and forget-me-not seeds, swished around her legs.

She shivered and hugged herself inside her sweater, her fingers disappearing inside the wool sleeves. Lately, Tara's moods have been as unpredictable as Epona's. Tara was changing faster than an oak leaf in autumn. When her hair wasn't braided, she looked older, more like a woman. Now Tara had secrets she shared with only the other girls. It scared me when she looked at me the way some girls looked at boys they liked. Not that I didn't want to kiss her. I did, but Seanán, Tara's da, said he would skin me alive if I didn't watch my ways. He'd pulled me aside a few weeks ago when he caught us wrestling on the grass. We weren't doing anything bad, but I noticed for the first time that Tara's shape had changed. She was rounder and softer than before, not the skinny stick I had grown up with.

Sometimes it was easier to keep my promise to Seanán, like when Tara wouldn't speak to me or when she was chattering so fast that I couldn't get a word in. On other days, when she was pretending to be a famous actor and making me laugh in that teasing way, I felt the urge to take her in my arms and kiss her. Ever since we had snuck in to see *Romeo and Juliet* at the Belfast Theatre, Tara had wanted to be an actor. Her singing and dancing always attracted a crowd at the fairs and a shower of coins.

"Epona bit me," I said, breaking the silence, which was more annoying than her chatter.

She took my hand and untied the cloth. My rough hand rested on her soft one. I didn't dare pull it away and hurt her feelings again. Besides, I didn't want to. Her touch soothed the pain.

"It doesn't look that bad. It'll heal." She let my hand drop to my side. Strange, my finger didn't hurt anymore.

"Epona's been so cranky lately," I said, "and she's getting bigger."

"Her foal will be a big girl, that's for sure." Tara trampled through the long grass toward the mare.

"Girl?" I said, rushing to catch up.

"The foal will be a filly. That I know." Tara stooped to grab a handful of long grass and offered it to Epona.

"You might be wrong."

"I'm never wrong. Human, horse, sheep, or pig, I always know before it's born if it's a boy or a girl."

"Maybe you should follow in Etain's footsteps," I said. "Maybe you should be a midwife."

"That's not funny." She looked cute when she pouted.

I took her hand, and together we watched Epona nuzzle Malachy, the stallion who had fathered her foal. When Malachy tried to nuzzle her back, she raised her lips and showed her teeth. Poor Malachy. One moment Epona would be affectionate, and the next, kick dirt at him whenever he tried to get near her. "She's not feeling very well," I said.

I led Malachy away from Epona while Tara stroked the mare's muzzle and hummed a lullaby. Her voice calmed the horse into nibbling the grass again.

"I think she'll foal early," Tara said.

"I hope not. She has at least a month to go."

"That's a long time to wait. That's a long time to wait for anything when you're hurting." Tara sat on a rock, pulled off her shoe, and shook out a stone. She slipped the shoe back on, stood up, and, without saying another word, turned and left me standing in the meadow. I debated letting her go this time, but I wanted to talk to her about what had happened at the fair. I ran after her, overtook her, and tugged the edge of her sweater. She stopped and spun around.

"What did I do now?" I asked, confused by her walking away without an explanation.

As she waded through the long grass toward the camp, I fell into step beside her. The smell of fried bacon and tatties made my mouth water.

"Sometimes I wish I lived in the village like a normal girl," she said. "I'd like to go to school and study music and dancing."

I thought about the village girls and the one who had been my mother. She didn't want no tinker's child. My da didn't want me either. But blood or no, Etain had taken me in and raised me as her own. "What's wrong with being who you are? You look normal enough to me."

"I don't want to spend my life chasing brats, getting old, and not doing anything with my life. I don't want to be normal. I want to be special. You know what I mean?"

I knew what she meant. I wanted to be special too, but I didn't dare tell her, or she might run away like some other girls who left to look for something better than family and friends.

"You're only fourteen."

"You're not much older, and you've been talking about leaving. Admit it. You tell me every day that you want to travel like Kieran."

"I don't want to end up a silversmith like your da, shaping metal for the rest of my life." I wished that Kieran, instead of Tara's da, had taken me on as his apprentice.

"What's wrong with being like my da?" She turned away and walked toward the camp.

"I didn't mean it like that." I ran to catch up with her. "You know I'm grateful for what Seanán has taught me."

"Da said he's got lots of work for you to do when you finish tending the horses," she said.

I groaned. I'd wanted to spend the morning carving, but Seanán would be angry if I didn't show up. I took a silver bracelet braided into a Celtic knot from my pocket. I'd seen Tara admire one like it at the fair. Perhaps now would be a good time to give it to her. Maybe it would make her happy. I stepped in front of her. "I have something for you." She tried to go around me, but I stopped her, took her hand, and placed the bracelet on her wrist.

The bracelet didn't make her smile. It didn't make her squeal and reach out to hug and kiss me. Instead, she frowned and slipped it off her wrist. "You stole it. Didn't you? Don't you see? This is what I hate. This is what everyone expects of us. They don't want us in the towns. They don't want us anywhere. You don't have to be like your da." She handed me the bracelet.

Her words stung. "I'm not like Da, and I didn't steal it. I made it. It's a copy of the one you liked at the fair. Your da helped me. He said I had a talent for shaping silver, and I knew you wanted the bracelet but didn't have enough money to buy it. I wanted to surprise you." I put the bracelet in my pocket, turned, and ran back toward the horses. Taking Malachy's reins, I pulled myself onto the horse's back and coaxed him into a gallop.

"Wait, Connor. I'm sorry. Wait, will you?" Tara's footsteps fell away as Malachy gathered speed. She'd hurt my feelings. Now it was her turn to stew about how to say sorry.

Skirting the edges of the marshland bordering the lake, I took the road toward the round tower. I passed the witch's stone, a large boulder with two shallow hollows on its flat surface. Everyone believed an angry witch threw herself off the tower's roof and landed so hard she left the imprint of her knee and elbow in the stone. Since then, water has always filled the hollows. Witch or no, I had never seen the cup-like dimples dry.

I rode Malachy toward the tower, which rose at least ninety feet into the air. Topped with a conical cap, it had windows facing in all four directions. The mid-morning sunlight streamed inside the east window and out through the western window in a way I had never seen before. Curious, I drew closer. I wondered how the Tuatha could calculate the exact alignment to allow the sun to stream through windows like that. They believed the round tower trapped and stored energy from the earth and the stars.

The Tuatha fashioned the entranceway high off the ground to discourage raiders of old and curious people like me from going in. Not impossible, though. I could reach the doorsill if I stood on Malachy's back. But should I?

Kieran warned me to keep out of the tower. Etain too. They said the round towers weren't safe, and many intruders had perished inside them. How they died was a mystery. Tara said the round tower was haunted. If I went in, I would bring bad luck to all who knew me. Superstition, that's all it was. Still, I could sense a presence, and to be sure, it hung around the tower as thick as morning fog over the bog. Heck, that wouldn't stop me. Besides, my curiosity was greater than my fear, so I stood on the stallion's back and leaned against the pebbly wall to get my balance. I grabbed the ledge, pulled myself up to the doorsill, swung my legs over, and jumped to the dirt floor.

Stone steps, some chipped and crumbling with only a small foothold, led to the tower's cap. I climbed the steps to a light-filled chamber. Sunbeams streaming through the two narrow windows crisscrossed over the altar, which sat in the center of the chamber. As I circled the room, I sensed an uncanny presence. I brushed my fingers over runes and symbols etched into the stone slab, including the triple spiral, the symbol of Manannan, and the three realms: earth, air, and sea. It was the same symbol I had used to fashion Tara's bracelet. I took the bracelet out of my pocket and held it to the light. The bracelet attracted particles of dust twirling in the sunlight like iron pyrite to a magnet. With my thumb, I brushed the dust particles from the silver and placed the bracelet on my wrist.

It felt warm, then hot. White hot. Searing heat flickered up and down my arm. I yelped, pulled the bracelet off my wrist, and dropped it, but it didn't fall. Instead, it floated suspended in the sunlight streaming through the window. The air crackled with energy. Lightning bounced off the granite. As it gathered momentum, it became a ring of fire clinging to the tower walls. Before it could descend upon me, I ran to the doorsill, slid through the opening, and onto Malachy's back. Light-headed and nauseous, I kicked Malachy into a gallop. Struggling to keep from fainting, I watched the ground rise in a blur of brown and green. Malachy's mane brushed my cheek as I wrapped my arms around the horse's neck and passed out.

When I awoke, I was straddled across Malachy with my head hanging over the stallion's shoulder.

Tara tugged my arm. "Connor, this isn't funny. I said I was sorry. Don't do this. You're scaring me."

I lifted my head, aching and feeling heavier than the witch's boulder. The trees, the horses, and Tara's face looked blurry. If I moved too quickly, I would puke, so I slid off the stallion and sat on the ground with my head between my knees.

"What's wrong with you? Are you sick? And what's this on your arm?" She held my hand and examined the mark circling my wrist. "Did you burn this into your skin because you were mad at me?"

"No. Do you think I'm stupid or something?" I pulled my hand away while feeling bad that I snapped at her.

"It must hurt. You'd better get Etain to put some salve on it." She bit her bottom lip before continuing. "I'm sorry I accused you of stealing the bracelet. Da told me you made it. He's proud of your talent. If it's still all right, I'd like to have it. Where is it?"

"I lost it."

She twirled a piece of grass around her finger. "I guess you don't want to give it to me now. I can't blame you. I haven't been very nice to you lately." She looked at me hopefully.

I had to say something. "I lost the bracelet because it caught on fire and disappeared. Crazy, I know, but that's the truth."

"Connor, if you don't want me to have it, just say so."

"It's true, Tara. Believe me this time, will you?" I thought she would go away mad again, but instead, she looked toward the tower where the tip of the conical roof rose above the trees.

"While you were gone, the sky darkened for a while. There was thunder and lightning. It didn't last very long, but I thought I saw lightning strike the tower." Tara offered her hand and pulled me up. "You don't look well."

"A bit shaky is all, and hungry. I think I'll faint again if I don't eat soon."

"You're always hungry." She slapped me on the back. "It's a good thing Ma saved us breakfast. Later, we can go back to the tower and see if we can find the bracelet. It must still be there."

"I don't know if we should. What happened in the tower scared the bejaysus out of me. I wish Kieran would come home."

"He's home now. He came in late last night but went into Ballycastle early this morning. Ma said he'll be back later today."

I whooped and, forgetting my worries about Epona, my troubles with Tara, and the strange experience I had at the round tower, headed off toward Tara's wagon. After breakfast, I planned to finish, as fast as possible, all the work Seanán had waiting for me. I didn't want to spend the whole day in the smith's shop if I didn't have to. It had been three months since I'd last seen Kieran, and I couldn't wait to tell him what happened in the tower and show him Manannan's mark on my wrist.

Chapter Four

Brannon

I held the cutty knife over the loaf of bread, golden, warm, and perfectly peaked, having risen with the sun. If I snitched a piece, I'd be in trouble, but I couldn't wait for it to cool. I glanced out the kitchen window and saw Ma plucking laundry off the hawthorn bush. The wind snatched the clothes from the line and scattered them all over the yard. Last night she'd told me to bring in the clothes before the dew fell. But I forgot. Now her tea towels were hanging from the fence, and Granda's undershorts were probably down at the Grainger cottage. Those two old sisters would get a fright to see them hanging there on their apple tree. I laughed and then thought of my own knickers. I hoped they had stayed in the yard.

Heck, I'll be in trouble for not bringing in the laundry, so I might as well have a piece of bread and be in trouble for that, too. Besides, I couldn't resist the smell of yeast and flour rising in the oven. It was better than the scent of crispy fried potatoes, apple pie, or the wind blowing off the sea. And I did love the smell of seaweed, but nothing compared to the aroma of fresh-baked bread, doughy, soft, and sticky.

Even with a sharp knife, I couldn't stop the bread from squishing into the shape of a boat as I made the first slice. But no matter, the shape of it didn't change the taste. I dropped a knob of butter in the center and waited for it to melt before slathering it up the sides. With my eyes closed, I took a bite and lost myself in the buttery softness. The second piece was a boat, too. Before stuffing half of it in my mouth, I rocked it in the palm of my hand like a ship tossed on the high seas.

I couldn't shake last night's dream and the sound of the waves drumming against the boat, the timbers creaking, the snap of the boom, and the terror in my da's eyes. I felt in my pocket for the talisman. Had it been a dream, or had Manannan heard my plea and stilled the wind? I hoped so. Still, I felt anxious to get to the pier this morning to meet Da's boat. I pushed the front door open and almost knocked the laundry basket from my ma's arms.

"Where're you to in such a hurry?" Ma said.

"Da's boat's coming in."

She pointed to a tea towel caught in the apple tree.

I shoved the rest of the bread into my mouth. "I'll get it," I said through doughy mouthfuls. Swinging from a lower branch to a crook in the trunk, I climbed until I reached the towel flapping in the breeze. After tugging it free, I swung to the ground and dropped the towel into the laundry basket.

"Sorry, ma, I forgot about the laundry."

She shifted the basket to her other hip. "Aw, Brannon, you little scallywag. You didn't slice the bread, did you?"

"But it's my birthday."

"Aye, and I was making you a special breakfast, but by the looks of it, you've already gone and eaten it."

"Do you think Da brought presents?"

"You know there won't be money for that, but come in now, and I'll fry you up some eggs and tatties."

"But I want to show him this." I took a sketch from my pocket, unfolded it, and held it up. An ebony horse with an arched neck and burning red eyes rode the white crests.

"Don't be drawing them pookas, son. It's not wise to be calling on the beast himself on Pooky Night."

"Aw Ma, you know it's not."

"It looks like a pooka to me, with them red eyes."

"It's just a stallion."

"Don't be showing it to Da. He won't like it."

I ran down the steps, dragged my bike from under a rhododendron, and was halfway down the road before I heard my ma calling me back.

Everyone knew the pooka existed only in the minds of the old ones like Granda, who used it to scare the heebie-jeebies out of me when I was little. He'd say, 'If you don't go to bed, the pooka will get you, and if you don't eat your tatties, then the pooka will come and carry you away.'

Besides, some old pooka wouldn't scare Da, even if it was Pooky Night. Ma had raised me to believe in the wee folk right along with Jesus, but Da's faith in the otherworld reached only as far as Manannan.

Still, thoughts of the shape-shifting pooka filled my mind: a goat, an eagle, and a black horse rising out of the sea. It was Ma's fault for putting the silly ideas in my head, but I couldn't stop them. What if I had conjured up the dreaded beast after all?

I swerved to take the shortcut that led toward the coast. The narrow path between a rocky cliff on one side and a jagged hedge on the other was being hogged by Seamus O'Reilly. I slowed almost to a stop behind the wagon. I could squeeze by if Seamus moved over a tad. But no, the old farmer pigheadedly steered his donkey and milk cart in the middle of the road as if he owned it.

Seamus O'Reilly traveled this road twice daily to take his fresh milk to the creamery. He coaxed his scruffy old mule up the steep slope by tapping its hindquarters with his shillelagh and whistling to the rhythm of the donkey's hooves, clicking on the cobblestones. No one in the county could whistle like Seamus O'Reilly. His gift far surpassed any fiddler or piper around. Usually, I enjoyed listening to his songs, but today I was in a hurry and didn't want to wait for Seamus to reach the flat stretch where I could pass the wagon.

I rang the bell, but the old whistler couldn't hear it or chose to ignore it. Impatient, I banked up the side of the cliff and just missed colliding with the cart. Gravel tumbled toward us. Startled, old Seamus dug his knobstick into the rocks to avoid falling over the cliff. Milk tanks clanked, the donkey brayed, and Seamus cursed and shouted, "You selfish little urchin. You could have killed me. Wait till I tell your Da. He'll give you a good kick in the arse for scaring the bejaysus out of me."

I glanced over my shoulder. Fortunately, Seamus had caught his footing, and not a drop of milk was spilled. "Sorry," I called, but there was no point getting any closer to Seamus O'Reilly and his shillelagh, not if I didn't want to get a beating with it. It didn't matter that everyone knew that the old one was loopers. If Seamus tattled on me, I'd get a thumping for more than snitching the bread this morning. Besides, I'd done a stupid thing and almost caused a terrible accident. I couldn't blame Seamus for wanting to give me a good whack with his knobstick or for all those curses upon my soul. I deserved every single one of them and more. What if the old one and his donkey had slipped over the cliff and died on the rocks below? As I steered my bike down a cow path to the shore, I pushed the terrible thoughts from my mind.

The surf boomed louder as I neared the coast. With every crash against the cliff, my excitement grew. The seagulls were feeding inland, which meant another storm was on its way. This one wouldn't be my fault, though, not like last night's storm.

I left my bike at the top of an incline and climbed over the rocks to the beach. Mussels clung in great dark clumps to the smooth sea-weathered boulders. The sun sparkled against the surface of the waves, surging up and down, still agitated by last night's storm. I shielded my eyes. On the horizon, *The Zephyr* moved toward the shore.

I thought I saw a heron circling the ship but then noticed the bird's outstretched neck. It was a crane, not a heron. I'd never seen a crane, except in pictures. Cranes became extinct in Ireland hundreds of years ago so from where did the crane come?

I climbed onto the rocks and stood for a moment on the beach. After washing my hands in the surf, I sprinkled the salty water over my face while silently thanking Manannan for bringing my da home safely. The ocean swelled as if in reply. A wall of water broke against the shore, showering the rocks with a fine mist. Fleeing back toward the cliff, I tried to outrun the waves, but the sea-foam nipped at my heels, soaking me right up to my knees before retreating and leaving a wealth of sea treasures at my feet, presents for my birthday. The ocean, like the wind, was my friend, and I never feared it would take me and swallow me up like some of the unlucky fishermen who tried to save their catch from sudden storms.

The sand sparkled with broken shells and quartz pebbles. I sifted through the glitter for the prettiest spire shells, periwinkles, purple tellins, moon shells, and peach-striped scallops. I weaved in and out of the tide pools with my pockets bulging. Broken oysters were everywhere. They were too common to pick up and save.

The crane I'd seen circling in the sky landed on a barnacle-covered boulder with an oyster in its mouth. It placed the oyster on top of the barnacles, squawked, and flew up to perch on a rock outcropping. I had seen gulls smash oysters on the rocks and dive to devour the muscle inside, but this shell was already splayed open. I leaned over the boulder and picked it up. Cradled inside one-half of the shell was the largest pearl I had ever seen. Not cream, white, or pale pink, but blue.

The crane squawked and scraped its beak against the rock. A gift from Manannán's sacred bird was a gift from the sea-god. How lucky, and on my birthday too. With reverence, I picked up the shell and fingered the pearl. "Oh, thank you. It's a beauty."

The crane's wings blocked the sun and created a feathered shadow as it swooshed over my head. Shading my eyes, I watched it fly over the water until it became a sliver in the sky. Then, I closed the oyster and put it in my pocket with the rest of my treasures.

What a lucky day, I thought, as I squatted to watch sea anemones in a tide pool. Trapped with the anemones was a seahorse about the length of my palm. The seahorse, camou-flaged greenish yellow to hide from the hungry sea anemones, would be lucky to survive until the next high tide. If the sea anemones didn't get it, a razorbill or cormorant would. I cupped my hand and picked it up with enough water to keep it alive. It was a maned seahorse with fleshy spines that ran down its neck, giving it the appearance of a horse's mane.

The seahorse gripped my baby finger with its tail as I raced along the shoreline and down the pier. *The Zephyr* had docked, and my da was unloading the fish onto the dock.

"Da! Da look! Look what I found!" I opened my hand to show him the seahorse, now reddish-brown.

Da blinked his pale eyes and gently touched the seahorse with his finger. I cringed to see Da's fingernail missing and a black bump in its place.

"Ah, a wee seahorse. Put him back in the water, or he'll die. You don't want Manannan mad at you for catching one of his own," Da said.

I shivered. I hadn't thought of that. With a silent apology, I leaned over the pier and dropped the seahorse into the ocean. "It's my birthday." I hoped Da remembered.

"Is it now? Last night's storm took most of the catch, son, so I hope you're not wanting gifts."

I couldn't help but slump at the news. I had only myself to blame. I hadn't meant to call a storm, only the wind. I'd only wanted a few apples.

"Look, Da," I said, taking the pearl from my pocket. "I found this too." I held the oyster in my hand and carefully opened the shell.

Evan whistled through his teeth. "Oh, aye, that's one mighty big pearl, and look at the color."

Nearby, other fishermen looked up to see what Evan had whistled about, and local folks, who had come to the pier to buy fish, gathered around to get a look too.

A man wearing a black suit, like he'd just come from a funeral, strolled over with his hands thrust in his pockets. His open jacket flapped in the breeze. He looked like the kind of man who was awkward in a suit. A neatly trimmed beard framed his face, but his auburn hair, streaked with a tinge of blood-red, looked unkempt, a little too long, and shaggy. His face had that tanned look from hours in the sun and wind.

"May I see?" The man cradled my hand in his, gloved with black lambskin. Worn over the glove on his middle finger was an unusual gold ring engraved with a symbol I had never seen before. "Where did you find it?"

"Washed up on the shore. A gift from Manannan for my birthday," I said.

"By all the gods, there're not many pearls that size or color. They're very rare. I found a pearl identical to this one when I was your age." The man's hand shook as he plucked a monocle from his pocket, held it to one eye, pulled my hand closer, and examined the pearl. "I'd be willing to buy it from you."

I closed my fingers over the pearl. The man's grip grew tighter. For a moment, I couldn't breathe and yanked my hand away. The man took out his wallet, fat with bills, removed a ten-shilling note, and waved it in front of my face.

"Ach, we all know it's worth more than that," Evan said. "If I were you, Brannon, I'd keep it. Right, William?"

"I'm the boy's da, William Mac Lir." He offered his hand to the man, who hesitated before shaking it.

"Faolan Gallagher," he said. "You must be Molly's husband"

"How's it, you know my Molly?"

"I guess you could say I'm a relative of sorts," Faolan said.

Da frowned. "She never told me she had kin around these parts."

Faolan was silent for a moment. "No, I suspect she wouldn't have mentioned me."

"Ma was adopted," I said.

"Oh, but I knew her before that." Faolan added another bill from his wallet. "I can throw in a little extra for you to get something for your birthday. A new bike, maybe? What use does a boy have for a pearl, anyway?"

I shook my head.

"No? You strike a hard bargain, son. How about enough money to help your da pay to fix his boat? I see it needs some hefty repairs."

"True enough," Evan said. "We won't be going anywhere until it's fixed."

"We could use the money, son." Da eyed the cash in Faolan's hand.

"Aw, Da." I held the pearl so tight my fingernails dug into my palm. I glanced at *The Zephyr's* broken boom and torn sails. If only I hadn't called the wind. "I… I guess I could find another one."

"You'll never find another pearl like that one, son." A man stepped up beside me just as I was about to give the pearl to Faolan. The man wore a long brown coat over a wheat-colored suit. His flaxen hair was pulled back into a knot at the base of his neck. His eyes, a golden brown flecked with blue, shone with an ancient light. He was older than my father, but he carried himself with the grace of a younger man.

He faced Faolan. "I'd heard you were living in England. Here on business?"

"This is none of your concern, Kieran," Faolan said. He added more bills to his offer.

"Faolan, this time, the pearl is not meant for you," Kieran said.

Faolan's back straightened. "The purchase of the pearl will help the family. I think the decision is the boy's and his da's."

A silent interchange like a pale light flickering against a red sky passed between the men. I felt the hairs rise on the back of my neck.

Kieran offered his hand to Da. "It's been a long time."

"Mighty long," Da said, shaking his hand. "But selling that pearl could repair my boat and feed us all winter. It sure would be nice to have the money for Molly and my boy here."

"True, a rare gem such as this would probably bring a good price, but if you sell this pearl, your need will increase. You don't want to sell it, William. It's not wise to refuse a gift from the sea-god. Now, I have something to give you that would also bring a good price. It won't bring as much as the pearl, but enough to help repair your boat and some left over for your mate here." Kieran placed a small gold diamond wedding ring in William's hand.

"My brother's ring." Da's voice broke. "I'd thought you'd have sold it by now. Why?"

Kieran put a hand on Da's shoulder. "I promised to save it for you, and since you now have a need, it's yours."

"This ring will help us, that's for sure," Da cleared his throat. "We lost most of our catch in the storm last night."

"Ah yes, a mighty wind like none I've seen in a while." Kieran glanced sideways at me.

I felt my face flush, my stomach flip-flop, and my hands grow clammy. Kieran didn't know I'd summoned the storm, did he? Of course not. How could he?

"Now, there's no need to take Manannan's gift from the boy," Kieran said to Faolan, who put his cash back in his wallet.

"If you change your mind, I'll be on my boat, *Breath of Cerridwen*. I expect to be here for a week or two." Faolan forced a smile and looked me in the eye. Feeling faint, I staggered back to let the man walk around me. Faolan's footsteps rang hollow on the wooden planks as he strode to the end of the pier and boarded a schooner.

"Never mind him, son." Kieran took my forearm to steady me. "Now, I think you need a place to keep that pearl safe." He took a small pouch from his pocket and gave it to me. "Put it in here, for I'm sure you will forget the pearl in your pocket, and it will end up in the wash."

I rubbed the soft fabric between my fingers. "What's it made of?"

"The skin of a crane, Manannan's sacred bird. A fitting place for a gift from the sea-god, don't you think?"

"Oh aye, thank you, sir." I put the oyster in the pouch and placed the crane bag in my jacket pocket.

Kieran turned to William. "Tell Molly I was asking about her. Is she still painting?"

"When she can."

"Good. I'd love to see Molly and her paintings again one day."

"I'll tell her. I'm sure she'll be sad to have missed you."

"I'm staying just outside of Ballycastle, near Ballintoy. Not too far for a visit." With a warm smile for me, he turned away and joined the crowd of locals milling about the pier.

"How did Kieran get Uncle Ian's ring?" I asked.

"That's a long story for another time." Da closed his fingers over the ring.

"I'd like to hear it," Evan said, egging him on.

"Me too."

"Not now, son."

"A story for his birthday." Evan winked at me.

"Tell us, Da. I'd like to hear about Uncle Ian and how you met that man Kieran. I like him. And wasn't it nice of him to give me the crane bag? How does he know Ma?"

"Oh, all right." William opened his hand and touched the ring with his baby finger. "I'd forgotten about this ring and never expected to see it again." He removed a flask of whisky from his pocket, took a swig, and wiped his lips on his sleeve. He passed it to Evan. With a somber look, he began the telling, pausing now and then to find the right words.

"Well, now, I think I was your age, Brannon, when Ian decided he would elope and move to America. I was angry because he was supposed to take over Da's business. Fishing was his passion, but not mine. I had other plans. I'd wanted to be a singer, and I thought I would be the one going to America, not Ian. I didn't plan to spend my life fishing, that's for sure, but what's a man to do? Life doesn't always work out the way you want it. I have no regrets, though.

"Anyway, Ian asked me to help him get to Portrush to

take the ship to America. An hour outside Portrush, the winds came, just as miserable as last night. Large boomers crashed down on us. I tried to turn the curragh into the wind so we wouldn't be sucked into the shore and smashed on the rocks, but as I scrambled to adjust the storm sail, the next violent gust unraveled the sail from the mast sending the boom swinging to the opposite side and hitting Ian in the back. He fell over the gunnels and into the churning waves. "Somehow, I managed to get him back in the boat, but he fell unconscious. I found the ring for his fiancée in his pocket and a tiny seahorse like the one you brought here today. It was still alive."

"Manannan's own," Evan whispered.

William nodded. "I don't know why, but I filled a jar with seawater and took the seahorse home. It died three days later, and so did Ian."

"You know it wasn't your fault, don't you?" Evan said.

"Oh, but it was. When I tied the lines, I didn't use the right knot. I remember noticing I'd done it wrong and hearing Da's voice in my head telling me to do it properly. I guess I was so upset that Ian was leaving that I didn't use the proper knot. And Ian was there with his cases and all narky to get going, so I didn't redo them." Da shook his head as if he still couldn't believe he'd been so careless.

"Aw, mate." Evan placed his hand on Da's shoulder. "You can't be blaming yourself. A man's time is a man's time, and when Manannan chooses to take one of his own to Tir na nOg, nothing can be done about it even if you'd tied them lines tighter than a druid's knot."

"My head knows, but my heart…." He ran his hand across the graying stubble on his chin. "Anyway, years later, when I first met Molly, she was selling some paintings at the Lammas Fair. One of her portraits looked exactly like Ian."

"The painting over the fireplace?" I said.

"Yes. I had to have it, but I didn't have enough money, and when Kieran bought it, I offered him the ring for it. He didn't want to take it from me. He said that if I ever wanted the ring back to find him, and he would give it to me. I never expected to see him or that ring again."

"Well, now," Evan said, "I'm not a superstitious man, but it being Pooky Night and all, I believe some things happen for a reason. Imagine being born on Pooky Night." He placed his hand on my shoulder. The fierce sea wind had etched deep crevices into Evan's hands and face. They matched like a hat and glove, leathery and wrinkled with grime embedded in the creases.

"How old are you now?"

I stood taller. "Thirteen."

"You don't look it." Evan wiped his nose with the back of his hand. "But if thirteen is what you are, then I think you're old enough to be out on the boat helping your da. Ain't that right, William?"

I cast a sideways glance at Da. "Ah, I'm afraid he's useless that way," he said.

"Gotta teach 'em, that's all. You can learn, can't you, boy?" Evan whistled through a gap in his front teeth as he emptied a bucket of fish onto the deck.

I leaped out of the way and covered my nose. A glassy, lifeless eye stared up at me.

"Here, like this." With a grunt, Evan slit the fish in one bold stroke. I stood mesmerized by the eye.

"Whatcha staring at, boy? It ain't gonna bite you now." Evan placed the blood-soiled gutting knife in my hand. The blade, heavier than it looked, smelled worse than the herring and Evan put together. I didn't want to do it with the fish's eye, Manannan's eye, holding me in his sight. I gripped the wooden handle until my knuckles ached.

Da's blustery face leaned next to mine, breath puffing white against the cold air. "Like this." He took my hand, guided it crossways below the gill, and severed the head in one stroke. I hated that sound—the squish. Then Da steered my hand along the central backbone from head to tail, crunching through scales and bone. Entrails gushed, and foul-smelling liquid squirted my face. "There now. That's how it's done. Now you've got the feel of it."

I straightened, dropped the knife, and ran back along the pier to my bike.

Evan laughed. "Where'd you get that one, Willy? Were there tinkers nearby then?"

The wind carried Da's voice. "You listen here now. I won't have you talking about my Molly like that."

"Aw, c'mon now, can't you take a joke? You have to admit he ain't like the rest of us."

I had to escape Manannan's eye and Evan's mean words. I pedaled away from the quay to the top of the hill. I took my feet off the pedals and raised my hands. The bike soared, soothed my soul, and lifted my spirits. Free from laughing voices and staring eyes, I rode the wind, my chariot, to heaven. My squeals rang clear across the meadow. I was beginning to feel like myself again when a water-filled pothole appeared across the road. The bike hit the flooded crater with a splash. I tasted mud as the bike bounced and flung me over the handlebars. I landed on my back near a paddock at the side of the road.

Chapter Five

Brannon

Blood, warm and salty, pooled under my tongue. My lip hurt like the dickens, and my knee, too. I spat blood and wiped my mouth with the back of my hand. After I pulled up my pant leg, I cupped my palm over the scrape on my knee. It felt hot.

I leaned back onto the grass, raised my finger, and traced the pictures formed by the clouds. An old man's beard reached out across the horizon, a herd of seahorses rode the waves, and a hand reached toward me, offering me a sword. Nothing else mattered but the sweet-smelling grass, the sky, and the pictures in the clouds. I let my arm drop and closed my eyes, enjoying the sun on my face.

I almost nodded off when I heard a wee voice say, "Brannon, did you hurt yourself?"

With eyes open halfway against the sun, I saw Mary, Peter's little sister, standing over me in a halo of sunlight. She had a mangy orange tomcat slung over her shoulders.

I squinted and shaded my eyes against the sun's glare. "Jeez, Mary, you just about put my heart crossways, sneaking up on me like that. Did you see me fall?"

"I did. It was funny."

"Where's Peter?"

"Riding his bike. He's looking for you, but I ran away."

"Why? Did you get a beating or something?"

"No. Declan and Da are fighting again. I'm scared to go home. Scared they're going to kill each other. Peter's mad too. The meanness is catchy, making everyone shout."

I gripped the fence post and pulled myself up. "That bad?"

"Worse. Declan hit Ma." Tears pooled in her eyes.

"Aw, he didn't."

"He did. He made Ma cry, and Da got mad and hit him back."

No one liked Declan, and everyone breathed a sigh of relief when he left town a year ago. There had been burnings, stolen cattle, and all sorts of nasty business. Then one night, Declan got into a fight, and someone clobbered his napper. It made him odd as all get-out and left him with a scar that ran the length of his hairline.

Mary shifted the tomcat to her other shoulder. "I've been hiding with the kittens in the barn."

"Can't blame you for that, but what if McNeil catches

you in there?" I scratched the cat's chin. It purred and rubbed its whiskers against my hand.

"They said I could have a kitten. There's an orange one with six toes on every paw." Mary had a slight lisp when she spoke.

"Japers!"

"Really. I counted them all myself. Come see if you don't believe me."

The tomcat squirmed, jumped out of Mary's arms, and flew after a pipit that swooped down on us. The cat growled, crouched, and twitched the tip of its tail. At first, I thought the silly bird was teasing the cat, flying low and making it jump in the air, but there was something odd about how it kept flying at my face. Mary ducked and put her hands over her head when the pipit swooped a second time. It brushed its wings against the top of my head. The tomcat pounced and almost caught the bird in its claws.

Behind a cloud, the sun dipped. The sky darkened, and with it came a bone-chilling gust whirling dirt in all directions. The cat hissed, flattened its ears, and darted into the barn. Mary hugged her arms. She looked across the street at the hillside where the sheep had stopped munching on the grass. They stood as still as porcelain figures on a shelf.

I rubbed the goosebumps on my arms. "Do you feel it then?"

"Oh, aye." Mary wiped the sand from her eyes with the edge of her sweater. "Pooka bird."

"I don't know about that, but it was weird how it attacked us." I felt better when a ray of light spilled from the edge of the cloud.

"Come see the kittens," Mary said as she pulled on my arm.

"Nah, I gotta go. I'll find Peter and come by later and look at them."

"Please." She held my arm tighter.

"I promise. We'll both come to see them."

"Oh, all right then." She pouted and went into the barn.

I didn't mean to disappoint her, but something else had caught my attention. A fine-looking horse watched me through the slats in the fence. The stallion was black except for the speckled tufts of white and gray over each eyebrow. I climbed to the top of the fence and sat on the railing, eye to eye with the mount. I was so close I could see the stallion's nostrils flare and feel the warmth of its breath on my face. Then the pipit swooped down from the roof where it had perched to watch us. It dived again and brushed its wings across the horse's back. The horse snorted, shied away, and galloped to the other side of the field. I wished the cat had caught the wee black nuisance.

With the pocketknife Granda had given me, I etched an outline of a horse's head into the wooden railing. A pooka for Pooky Night.

Remembering my bike, I hopped off the fence, picked it up, and groaned. The front tire was flat and bent out of shape.

Grey wisps grew into a cowlick at the top of Granda's head. His nose, thick and red from the whiskey he liked to drink, turned up at the end like a leprechaun's. He took a flask from his pocket, knocked back a swig, then bent over my bike and pounded the front fender into shape.

While I waited for Granda to fix my bike, I used a stick to sketch a horse in the dirt. "When I grow up, I'm gonna be an artist."

"That you will, me boy," Granda said without looking up.

I stood back and admired my sketch. "I wish we could have a horse."

"Aye, that would be fine." Granda straightened a spoke on the right front tire of my bike.

"Granda? Have you ever seen a pooka?"

Granda's eyes narrowed. "Get away with you now, and don't be thinking about such things."

"But have you?"

He took a pipe from his pocket and stuffed it with tobacco. "Oh aye, it could gallop as fast as the wind and steal your soul with just one look from its fiery eye."

"But where did the pooka come from?"

"Born of the sea and to the sea, it returns."

"But it was a horse?"

"Aye, it was. The pooka can take many shapes, even that of a man, but it likes the form of a horse best. They say only the knights of the Tuatha De Danann dare ride one of them stallions."

"But Granda, how can I be a knight of the Tuatha De Danann?"

Granda lit his pipe and puffed to get it going. "Well, now, I wouldn't be surprised if you didn't have a few drops of their blood running through your veins." A smoke ring floated in front of us.

"Really?"

"Masters they were. Masters of the elements."

"What elements?"

"Why, sea and stone, fire, and wind. Ah, 'tis a mighty force, the wind. No one has ever seen it, except maybe one of the Tuatha De Danann."

"I have seen the wind."

"You have, have you?"

"Yes, it blows the grass in the meadow and steers Da's boat to shore. It moves the clouds in the sky, and I have seen it in the tops of the trees."

With his pipe balanced in the corner of his mouth, Granda leaned his foot on a boulder. "Aye, and what does she look like now?"

"She looks like… um." I turned a full circle. "She looks like… but I have felt her."

Granda's belly rolled up and down as he laughed. He was as wide as he was short. "Aw, never mind, son. Some things are meant to be felt, not seen. Love, for example. You can't see love, but you can feel it." He picked up the bike and pushed it toward me. "There now, 'tis good as new."

"Thanks, Granda."

Tiny scratches and dents tarnished the frame, but the tires were pumped and firm, the squeaky pedal oiled, and the handlebars straightened. I couldn't wait to take it for a ride with Peter, who circled on his bike in front of the house. I waved to him.

Peter waved back and slid to a stop, spraying dirt in the air.

Granda gripped my arm. "Listen to me, boy," he whispered into my ear. "Steer clear of that young Taig—I see him hangin' about. Give him a whipping if that's what it takes to get rid of him. Peter comes from a bad lot, just like his brother, Declan."

Granda didn't like Peter because Peter was Catholic, but I didn't think he'd ever try to hurt him. "Peter's not bad," I said.

"Ach, he's just like his brother. Remember how Declan beat old Seamus for a few coins?"

"But that was Declan, not Peter."

"The blight starts in the potato's eyes and spreads to all of them. There's nothing to be done about it. When one is tainted, they're all spoiled. Now, do as I say."

"But Peter's my friend," I said before stopping myself. I knew better than to argue with Granda, whose temper could foam like the froth on a freshly poured Guinness.

"By the gods, but you've plenty of lip. Is this how you thank your Granda? No Taig will ever be your friend, boy, and don't you forget it. He'll shove a knife in your back if the Pope tells him to."

"Gotta go, Granda." I tried to squirm out of his grip, but he pulled me closer. I smelled whisky on his breath.

"Take my word for it. You can't trust Peter. I once knew a man in the days before the Great War when fishing was easy. In those days, most folks here in Ballycastle didn't care much about home rule. We all got along. It didn't matter who took the money from our pockets. It was Mahoney I was in business with.

"We had two boats, and when the herring ran, we worked together. Even though he was Catholic, he always gave me my fair share of the catch, and I was as honest as the day was long with him.

"We worked together for five years, but then the war came. Some of our lads were drafted, but the Taigs weren't happy sending their sons to fight a war made by the British. So much bellyaching was going on, and fights broke out on the streets. Some supported the British, and others were German sympathizers. The Germans rewarded them by providing the Irish Republican Brotherhood with guns. Damn that Mahoney if he didn't try to make a few extra pounds on the side running guns. One night they caught him and sank his boat. As I was part owner, I had a lot of explaining to do. It's treason, boy. Punishable by death. Did you know that?"

"No, Granda."

"Well, it is, and fortunately, my views on religion and politics were well known, and the constabulary was sympathetic, but that didn't get my boat back."

"What happened to Mahoney?"

"He's rotting in some Belfast jail, and he'll have more than a broken nose if ever I see him again. All those sermons he heard on Sunday morning didn't make him an honest man. So, listen to your granda when he tells you to stay away from them Taigs."

"But Ma's Catholic," I mumbled.

"Aye, but you're an Orangeman like your da and granda. Now go and make me proud." He drew a long puff, sending smoke rings like round eyes drifting toward me. How quickly Granda's mood had changed. Stilled by the hatred in his eyes, I dared not answer him back. Besides, I felt something closing in on us. An evil that made people say and do things they shouldn't. It had taken hold of Granda and turned his mood as rotten as the wet leaves.

I had to get away, away from Granda and the terrible feeling that something bad was going to happen. The air felt humid like it did before a storm. With a queasy gut, I picked up my bike, mounted it, and fumbled for the pedals. Gripping the handlebars, I pedaled hard and fast to catch up to Peter, who had disappeared down the road.

Many paths led off the road, bordered by rhododendrons on one side and a moss-covered brick wall on the other. I knew Peter would hide beneath a bush or in one of the many nooks and crannies. Knowing how sneaky Peter could be, I slowed down to navigate a curve. Still, I jumped out of my skin when Peter hollered and leaped out from behind a shrub. I swerved to miss him, slid on the gravel, and fell under my bike.

Peter pulled the bike off of me. "Hey, you okay?"

My knee throbbed as I rolled and reached out to snatch a stick off the ground. "Nah, bruises are a knight's honor." I stood and swung the branch at Peter, almost hitting him.

"Whoa." Peter jumped back. "Watch it. You could've poked me eye out." He took another step backward.

"If we're gonna be knights, we'll need swords." I swung again.

Peter ducked and ran toward a grove of apple trees. I chased him, but he jumped up, grabbed a branch, swung over my head, and landed behind me. He bent, scooped a stick off the ground, and dodged my attack. I heard a swoosh as his blow landed next to my ear. I grabbed the end and snapped it in two. Peter scrambled to find another branch while I poked him with my makeshift sword. "Take that and that," I said.

Peter grabbed the first stick he could lay his hands on, whirled around, and lunged at me with its forked tip. I laughed at his sorry excuse for a sword, but that didn't stop him. He came at me like a wild boar, barreling into my chest and knocking me on my back. He stood over me with his foot on my stomach and pointed his sword at my heart.

"Devil be dammed. I ain't asking for mercy from no Taig," I said.

Peter moved the sword to my throat and pressed on my Adam's apple. "What did you call me?"

I pushed the stick away. "Ah, it was just a joke. You know I didn't mean it." I didn't know why I said it. It was Granda's voice, not mine. I rolled to my knees and stood up.

Peter whipped me across my hand as I reached for my sword. With stinging knuckles, I chased Peter and whacked him across the legs, sending him sprawling on the ground. I held the stick above Peter's head, about to strike him again when he looked up at me, blinking back tears, and said, "I ain't surrendering to no Prod either."

"Touché." I lowered my sword.

Peter pulled his pant leg up and inspected the welt on his calf, beading with blood.

I winced at the sight of it. "I'm sorry I hurt you."

He smeared the blood with his finger and drew his pant leg back over the wound. "It's all right," Peter said, always forgiving, always thinking the best of people.

"No, it's not. I shouldn't have hit you so hard. I'm terribly sorry." I picked up Peter's stick. "Hey, this looks more like a fork than a sword. Let me fix it for you." After taking my knife from my trouser pocket, I took the branch and shaved off the excess bark and twigs.

"Where'd you get that knife?" Peter stood, favoring his wounded leg.

"Me, Granda. For my birthday."

"I have something for your birthday, too." Peter thrust his hand into his pocket and took out a small piece of flint he'd found while we explored a cave in the rocky outcrops by the shore. The flint had strange markings etched into it, and I'd been envious when Peter found it. We searched until the tide crept dangerously close, but we couldn't find another one.

"Are you sure?" I took the flint and gave Peter his sword, smooth and shaved to a point.

"My da says the writing on it is Ogham, the old Irish alphabet. If it means something, I know you'll work it out. Besides, if I keep it, it'll get lost amongst my stuff or forgotten at the bottom of a drawer."

"Thank you! You'll always be my best friend no matter what Granda says."

"Why doesn't your Granda like me?"

"Cause you're the wrong color."

"Am not."

"You are too."

"I'm the same as you."

"No, you're not. You're green. You really are. You're green, and I'm orange."

Peter pressed the point of his sword into my chest. "I've got you now, Orangeman. Your life is mine!" he teased.

I pushed his sword aside and swung at him, but Peter countered with a series of hard blows that knocked my sword out of my hand. Before I could pick it up and follow, Peter hopped on his bike and pedaled out of sight.

Chapter Six

Connor

Why did the stepping stones on the path up the hillside stay firm under Kieran's feet but teeter under mine? I bit my lip to keep from crying out as my ankle turned for the second time. It didn't matter how I placed my foot. The stone wobbled even though I wore the same sheepskin boots as Kieran and followed exactly in his footsteps. Somehow, Kieran knew how to place his weight without losing his balance or tipping the stones. He moved as if he was born to climb. Limping, I fell behind. I didn't want to call out and ask him to slow down and appear like a Ginny Ann, weak and complaining. I had to keep up, no matter what. Now and then, Kieran disappeared behind an outcrop, only to reemerge to stand on top of a boulder to urge me on.

Feeling out of puff, I dragged on, hoping that Kieran would stop for a break. We'd been climbing up the rocky hillside since midday, and I wished he'd stop soon. My ankle had swelled on both sides like the cheeks of a squirrel stuffed with acorns. The pale sun shone overhead, glistening off the smooth-faced rocks, creating a blinding glare every time I lifted my head to see how far Kieran had gone ahead of me.

I caught the toe of my boot on a jagged stone and fell, sprawling on my knees. My nose narrowly missed hitting the limestone. Cursing, I rolled over, sat up, drew my knees to my chest, leaned against a boulder, and let the heat massage my back. The sun, red behind my eyelids, vanished in shadow. I opened my eyes. Kieran.

"I go away for three months, and you become as weak as a newborn kitten. What have you been doing, Connor? Helping Tara with her crafts?" He sounded stern, but his eyes were laughing. He offered a hand and pulled me to my feet.

I stepped backward and sat on a boulder with my legs dangling over the stone. "It's the rocks." I pulled up my pant leg. Blood dribbled from my kneecap down my leg.

"Oh, I see. It's the rocks' fault, then."

"You climb like a goat. How do you do it?"

"I watch my step." Kieran scraped a clump of sphagnum moss from one of the loose, ankle-turning boulders and placed it over the cut. "Add a little pressure, and it should stop the bleeding. Now, how's that ankle?"

"Sore. You knew I sprained it?"

"By your breathing and groaning and carrying on."

"I didn't groan, did I?"

"You sounded like a cow in labor. I wondered when you'd

ask me to stop." Kieran slung his leather bag from his shoulder and placed it on a rock. He rummaged through it and took out a block of goat's cheese.

"I ain't no Ginny Ann."

"Asking for help isn't a sign of a sissy but of good judgment. Do you have a knife?"

Without thinking, I offered him the knife I had taken from McKinley. Kieran felt the weight and examined it.

I held my breath, hoping Kieran wouldn't ask where I got it. What could I say to distract him? With my hands pressed on both thighs, I looked over at the countryside. Sheep lolled on mist-covered hills to the north, and waves churned against the rocks on the shore to the south. "Nice day." I winced at the sound of my voice, higher than it should be, ringing out with guilt.

"Nice knife. One of McKinley's, I see." Kieran sliced a piece of cheese and offered it to me. "A fine silversmith. His work is almost as good as Seanán's."

"I found it." The words came tumbling out before I could stop them. I would have kicked myself if my ankle wasn't so sore.

Kieran nodded and cut another piece of cheese with my knife.

"He accused me of stealing it, but I didn't. I found it on the ground near his stall." It was stupid to confess, but once again, the words flew from my mouth. I slid down the rock and tried to put weight on my ankle. I winced and sat back down.

"Why didn't you give the knife back?" Kieran asked, not accusing me, just matter-of-factly.

I couldn't look Kieran in the eye. Instead, I looked toward the sea, where the sun's glare off the water caused my eyes to tear. "Because if you find something someone lost, it's yours to keep." It was a lame excuse, but it made sense to me at the time.

"Even if you know who it belongs to?"

"There's nothing on it to say it's his."

"His initials are entwined in the leaf pattern, where the handle meets the blade." Kieran handed me the knife so that I could see the initials.

"Oh. I didn't see that."

"You alone know if it's right or wrong to keep it." Kieran offered me his walking stick. I stepped to the edge of the cliff and tossed the knife over. It landed point down in the sand.

"Why throw it away? Why not give it back?"

"If I do, he'll say I stole it."

"Didn't you?"

"No. Yes. The second time I stole it. The first time I found it on the ground. That's the truth. It was near McKinley's stall, but I didn't think it was his."

Kieran turned to step down the rocks toward the shore. Climbing down the rocky incline was even more difficult than climbing up, but this time Kieran followed rather than led, directing me to the sturdiest stones and steadying me with a light touch to my forearm when I stumbled. I felt like an old man. When we reached the shore, we found the knife, the silver handle shining in the sun.

"I don't want it now." I stepped on the hilt, pressing it into the ground with my boot until the sand covered it.

"Burying your mistakes doesn't erase them." Kieran placed his hand over the spot where I'd buried the knife. It rose out of the ground and into Kieran's hand. He held it by the blade with the hilt toward me.

I took it and put it back in my pocket. "I didn't steal it. I found it."

"Then I guess it's yours to keep," he said.

I turned away to brush a frustrated tear from my eye. I knew right from wrong, but sometimes things seemed right one way and wrong another way. Like the fight I had with Brannon over the talisman. It wasn't right that the boy, a stranger, should have it. It had been in my family for a long time. I couldn't ever remember seeing Etain without it. The loss of it felt so wrong. I felt helpless to explain it. "Sometimes right is wrong, and wrong is right. I don't get it. I mean, sometimes wrong seems right in the moment. I found the knife. It was mine. Then McKinley tried to take it from me, and I felt that was wrong. He thought it was his right to take it back because I'm just a tinker boy. And then Etain gave away the sapphire to a boy at the fair. I just had to have it and would have beaten the crap out of the kid to get it. I wanted it so bad. It felt wrong for him to have it. Do you know what I mean?"

"That is one reason I've been careful about teaching you my craft. You lack good judgment at times."

A crushing weight fell over me. "I don't understand. If Etain had never met Brannon before, why did she give it to him?"

"It was hers to keep or give away as she saw fit."

"But what's so special about him?"

"Brannon is her great-grandson."

I put my full weight on my ankle and cried out in pain. "My cousin?"

"His mother is your da's sister."

I knew my da had a sister, but I had never met her. They had grown up in separate homes when their parents died in a fire, the fire that scarred my da's hands.

"Does Brannon know I'm his cousin?"

For a long moment, Kieran looked out to sea. I watched the surf lap the bottom of his trousers, soaking the hem. "I don't think so. Molly blamed your da for the fire that killed their parents. She ran away, and a Catholic family in town took her in and raised her as one of their own. I found her and tried to convince her to come home, but she wouldn't." From his belt, he untied his slingshot, picked up a smooth pebble, and shot it so that it skipped along the surface of the water.

"But the fire was an accident, right?"

Kieran didn't answer. Instead, he picked up another stone, rubbed it between his thumb and forefinger, tossed it away, and picked up a smoother one. "Do you want to try?"

Japers. Kieran had never allowed me to use his slingshot before. I had never even seen him use it for hunting, only to skip stones. I took the weapon, loaded the leather thong with a rock, pulled back the sling, and fired. The stone flew a short distance before falling into the water with a single skip. I tried several more stones with the same results. Disappointed, I handed the slingshot back to Kieran.

"Keep it and practice. Have patience, Connor. Let your talents unfold naturally. Now, I have something else for you. It doesn't have the beauty of the sapphire Etain gave Brannon, but it's every bit as powerful if you have the eyes to see its value." Kieran took from his leather pouch a piece of oak and handed it to me.

I scowled as if he had given me a lump of coal.

"Magnificent forests once covered Ireland. This piece of wood is from that time. It's cured and ready for carving."

I turned it around in my hand. "Carve what?"

"That's for you to discover, and Connor, don't be in a hurry. You'll know when the time is right for this ugly lump to reveal its beauty."

"I didn't say it was ugly. It's just not a talisman."

"This wood carries special energy. When it's transformed, it will blend the energies of wood, metal, fire, and water. Aren't your gifts in shaping wood and metal?"

"Yes, I guess it's just…." I took a step forward and stumbled. When Kieran caught my arm, I felt his fingers close around my wrist and the tattooed bracelet.

His grip tightened. "What's this?"

I pulled my arm away, and for an instant, I thought of lying to Kieran. Would he be disappointed to learn that I disobeyed him and gone into the round tower, or would he be happy that Manannan had branded me with his mark? Kieran had a similar tattoo around his forearm.

"Did you do this yourself? I know your desire to walk in the old ways is strong, but—"

"I didn't do it. It just happened." I pursed my lips. "You think the gods wouldn't be bothering with the likes of me, but maybe… just maybe, Manannan does."

"Connor, this is the same knot Manannan used to bind the Fomorii when he banished them."

"I didn't know they used a special knot to bind them. I thought Manannan sealed the Fomorii in a cave somewhere along the coast. Why did this happen to me? What does it mean?" I hoped Kieran didn't hear the tremble in my voice or sense my fear.

"It depends. How did it happen?"

I pointed in the direction of the round tower. "Tara and I fought about the bracelet I made for her. She said I stole it because it looked like the one she wanted from the fair. I was so angry I went to the tower."

"You disobeyed me."

I felt his disappointment hit me in the chest. I blinked away tears. "The way the sunlight streamed from the eastern to the western window was magical. It filled the tower with light and energy. I took Tara's bracelet and slipped it on my wrist to look at it. The energy in the tower became attracted to the bracelet and set it on fire. I yanked it off my wrist and dropped it, but it vanished into the light before hitting the ground."

"Let me see." He took my hand in his and leaned over to look closer. "You saw this knot at the fair?"

"Yes, but I changed it a little to make it my own. Tara didn't notice. I didn't want to copy it exactly."

"Yes, the difference between the two knots is subtle, but that's what makes it powerful. This knot is a gift, as it will protect you. I knew this day would come, but I hoped you'd be older and more patient when it did. The good news is that your training must begin, ready or not. I have already given you your first task. Find the beauty in the oak wood. Now, we should return to the camp, as I must discuss this with Etain."

I couldn't be happier as I tucked the piece of oak into my pocket and limped behind Kieran. I didn't know what the carving would be, but I knew it would be magical, and when I had finished carving it, I hoped Kieran would be proud of me.

Chapter Seven

Brannon

Peter gripped a branch and swung up into the apple tree. Leaves, speckled with mold, drifted to the ground. He raised his arms, flexed his muscles, beat his chest, and hollered like Tarzan.

I laughed and sat on the edge of the brick retaining wall at the Bonamargy Friary, the ruins of a Franciscan monastery on the outskirts of Ballycastle. Tilted gravestones jutted from tufts of long, coarse grass. I balanced my sketchbook on my knee, ruffled the pages, and turned to the first blank sheet.

With a final shout, Peter dropped out of the tree and stood among the fallen apples. He leaned against the trunk and buried his hands in his pockets. "Do you want me to pose or something?" Even now, impatient to get on with playing, Peter smiled at me with his head turned to one side. Blond curls framed his face, rosy and plump with cheerfulness.

"No, just hold still." Not a simple task for Peter, who was always in motion.

"Never had my portrait done before," he said, taking another turn around the tree trunk.

I studied his face, wondering how to capture his likeness on paper. An ordinary portrait wouldn't do for Peter: the fastest runner, the most fearless climber, and the best friend in all of Ballycastle.

Peter reached up, picked an apple from one of the lower branches, took a bite, and spit it out. "It's rotten." He threw the apple over my head, then leaned back against the trunk. Peter and trees. He climbed them, swung from them, or sat cradled in the branches, looking as comfortable as a tree spirit.

I'd never seen one of the wee folk, but Granda assured me that not even St. Patrick could chase them away from our land. They existed whether people believed in them or not because the old magic had deeper roots than the new ways. That was it. I would blend Peter's face into the tree trunk.

I brushed my hand across the page, dappled with twig-shaped lines one moment and the shadow of a horse rearing the next. Hooves rose to strike at me through the paper. Startled, I jumped up and dropped the sketchbook flat on the ground.

"Ants in your pants?" Peter picked up the sketchbook and handed it to me.

"I thought I saw something." With a shaky hand, I picked up my pencil.

Peter knew about my nighttime drawings, but he'd never seen me do them. The visions usually came at night, before sleep, not in broad daylight. Sometimes I could fight the strange feelings that overwhelmed me, sometimes not, but I had to try.

Not wanting to scare Peter, I leaned against the apple tree and placed my hands against the trunk, hoping the tree would offer me some stability.

"You sick or something?"

"Dizzy, that's all." I turned and faked a smile.

"What did you see?"

"A horse. I've been drawing lots of them lately. I don't know why. Ma says they look like pookas to her."

"Oooh… spooky pooky." Peter neighed, tossed his head, and galloped around the tree.

I caught him, jumped on his back, and wrapped my feet around his waist. "I'll ride you till you're tame."

Peter bucked, spun, and scraped me against the tree to throw me from his back. My pocket caught on a branch, ripped open, and released the crane bag Kieran gave me. Peter snatched the bag from the ground and dangled it between his fingers. "What's this?"

He was about to open it when I swiped it out of his hand. I took out the oyster, opened the shell, and placed the pearl in my palm. "I found it this morning, a present from Manannan."

"Japers, it's blue," Peter touched the pearl with his fingertip.

"It's quite rare, I hear."

A meadow pipit shrieked. It flew over our heads, narrowly missing Peter, who crouched to dodge the bird before it landed on my hand. I snapped the oyster shut, but the bird hung onto my wrist and pecked at me. I shook my arm. Crying out, the bird flapped its wings, giving me one last nip before flying over the field of yellow gorse across from the friary.

"Did you see that? The darn pipit tried to steal my pearl right out of the shell. It gave me a nasty bite, too." I wiped the blood from the bite on my pants.

Peter ran his fingers through his hair. "Didn't get me, did it?" He leaned his head toward me so I could see the top.

"No. You're clean." I tucked the shell into my crane bag.

"You sure? I felt its wings brush my head. It's bad luck, you know."

Everyone knew the old wives' tale that if a pipit flew over your head, it meant death. On the other hand, if it pooped on your head, good luck would follow. I wished the pipit had pooped on both of us because the darn bird had flown over my head twice today.

"Let's go to the nun's grave and ask for protection against the pipit," Peter said. "If we walk around her grave seven times clockwise and seven times counterclockwise, and if we put our hand through the hole-stone cross and tell her we're praying for her and all the souls buried there, she might let us see her."

I would have gone to Manannan with my request for protection, not the four-hundred-year-old nun, Julia McQuillan, who had died slipping on the seventh stone step in the stairwell at the Bonamargy Friary. Some said it was murder and some an accident, but I agreed to go because it would make Peter feel better about the pipit's curse.

"Do you think we'll see the nun?" I packed my sketchbook into my bag and slung it over my shoulder.

"If you have faith," he said.

I believed in the power of the elements and Manannan, so maybe having faith in the protection of an old spook didn't seem so crazy. I followed Peter down the weed-worn path, through the remains of the gatehouse, to Julia's grave, marked by a hole-stone cross near the entrance to the church. We circled the gravestone both ways seven times and waited. When nothing happened, I thought of using my talisman to call her. I'd promised my ma I'd never use it for summoning again until someone could teach me, but we needed protection. She would want us to be safe, wouldn't she?

I took the sapphire from around my neck. With the talisman dangling from my fingers, I placed my hand through the holestone. "Julia McQuillan, it's Brannon calling you and Peter too."

"We pray for you and all the quiet folks resting here," Peter added.

We held our breath and waited. The wind swirled dry leaves around our feet.

"I guess Julia's not coming." Peter scuffed the ground with disappointment.

I put my arm around his shoulders. "Even if we don't see Julia, I'm sure she'll grant us her protection. Now it's your turn to have faith."

"Ma has some holy water from St. Brigid's well. I'll ask her for some, just in case. I'll ask for both of us." Peter grasped the branch he used for a sword that hung from a loop in his belt as if it could save him from the creatures of the Otherworld.

A visit to the Bonamargy Friary was always fun on Pooky Night, but this year it felt different. It wasn't the quiet ones resting in their graves that worried me. It was something else, a darker soul hovering just beyond my sight.

A sudden gust made us turn around. We saw a woman sitting on the remains of a gravestone, tilted almost parallel to the ground. Her white dress shimmered with silver. Black hair flowed over her shoulder to her waist. With her head slanted slightly to the side, she stared at us with curiosity, blinking thick lashes over dark eyes. Young, but not young. She was the most beautiful woman I'd ever seen.

"Why do you dance around the cross?" Her lips turned up into a smile.

"We want to see Julia, the nun," Peter said, looking as spellbound by her beauty as I was.

"Why do you want her to show herself?" she asked.

"Protection," Peter said.

"Who do you need protection from?"

"The pipit," we said together.

"A wee pipit?" She held long fingers to her lips to stifle a giggle.

"It touched my head and perched on my arm. It's bad luck, don't you know?" Peter said.

"No, I didn't know. Have you seen the nun before?"

"No, but my ma saw her looking out the window." I pointed to the flame-shaped, ironed-barred window overlooking the courtyard. "Ma said Julia could foretell the future. She even made seven prophesies, and all but one has come true."

"Which one?" The Lady asked.

I scooped a handful of leaves off the ground. "Julia said a terrible blight would come one day, and people wouldn't know the difference between winter and summer. That prophecy is coming true now. Haven't you noticed the blight on the leaves this year? It's like what happened to the potatoes. Some say it might spread to everything, including people."

The Lady frowned. Her eyes suddenly looked older. "The blight comes from a wrong that happened many years ago." She tossed her hair over her shoulder and slid to the ground.

I tried not to stare at her see-through dress, but I couldn't help myself. I expected to see the form of the woman's body but saw straight through her dress to the overgrown graves behind her.

The talisman grew warm against my chest. I cupped the gem in my fingers and slid my thumb over the center, feeling the tiny chip that created the star. It was comforting to hold it.

The Lady placed her hand over mine. It was warmer than I expected. After all, she was a ghost, wasn't she?

"Are you the one?" She asked. I was dumbstruck. Her eyes looked at me and through me at the same time. When I didn't answer, she pulled her hand away, walked around the hole-stone, knelt, and looked at us through the hole in the cross. "Only a knight of the Tuatha De Danann can right the wrong. But you can't be the one. You don't have the sword." She walked into the friary. Despite her beauty, something about the woman made me feel uneasy.

Peter mouthed the words, "Who is she?"

I shrugged, and we followed her into the stairwell, where we found her standing on the seventh stair, where Julia fell to her death. The locals believed that stepping on the seventh stair would bring misfortune.

"I guess she doesn't know she's not supposed to step on it," Peter whispered.

"A knight needs a sword," she said before walking the rest of the way up to the roof.

We followed her up the stairs. I skipped the seventh step. So did Peter, but The Lady had disappeared by the time we reached the roof.

Peter circled the roof. "Where did she go?"

"She's still here, I think. I can't see her, but I can hear her. She says we are in danger."

"What danger?" Peter paled and made the sign of the cross.

The sky darkened. A moth landed on his shoulder. Another moth landed on my arm, and one stuck to the front of Peter's jacket. At first, the moths came one by one out of the chinks in the stone wall. Then a swarm of moths descended from a dark cloud and covered us from head to toe. We pulled them from our lips and eyes and squashed them against our clothes, but they kept coming and coming.

Frantic, Peter stumbled blindly to the stairwell, bolted down the stairs, stepped on the seventh stone, tripped over the next one, and skipped the rest of the steps altogether. He land-ed with a thump at the bottom of the stairs.

"Leave us alone." I held my talisman before me, but when nothing happened, I jumped over the seventh stair, grabbed Peter's arm, and pulled him into the courtyard. "Run," I said.

We ran around the slanted tombstones and along the path that led through the gatehouse. Gradually, the moths lift-ed and flew back toward the friary.

"Holy Mother of God," Peter said in a throaty whisper. "I… I stepped on the seventh stair." He scuffed his shoes in the gravel as if he could wipe away the curse of the seventh step as easily as dog shit. "Bloody pipits, bloody moths. Let's get out of here."

We grabbed our bikes that we had left, leaning against the retaining wall. We mounted them and rode as fast as we could, slowing only when we reached McNeil's farm.

I slammed on my brakes, spewing dirt into the air. Peter did the same, but his bike skidded in the soil and toppled.

Peter pushed the bike off his leg, leaned back on the grass, pulled his knees up, and hugged them to his chest. "I never thought I'd be afraid of moths."

I sat next to him. "Those weren't moths, Peter. I don't know what they were, but they weren't of this world."

"Do you think they're the ghosts of those who die unfor-given and roam the place between heaven and earth?" Peter's voice cracked. It had been changing lately, growing deeper day by day, but this was more than that. It was fear. He cleared his throat and asked, "Do you think that woman was a ghost?

Where did she go? There's only one way up and one way down, and she wasn't on the roof anywhere."

"Nah, that woman was real enough."

"And beautiful too," Peter said. "Besides, Julia would know her own prophesies and why we circled her gravestone for protection. She'd be wearing a nun's robes. Heck, that woman even stepped on the seventh stair."

"True, but did you notice you could see right through her dress?"

Peter gave me a good-natured punch on my arm. "What did you see then?"

"Nothing. That's the weirdest thing. I could see straight through her dress to the graveyard. And you?"

"I could see the shadow of her legs," Peter said.

"No, really?"

"They were as thin as a loon's." Peter looked around suddenly when we heard someone call his name. Mary stood in the barn's doorway and waved to us.

I waved back. "Mary has been in the barn with the kittens all day," I said.

"I know. She loves those kittens."

"She said she was hiding from Declan." I looked across the street at the thatched cottage burned to the ground. I'd heard stories about Declan, people whispering that he and his friends had done it.

Peter stood, walked toward the fence, hoisted himself up, sat on the top rail, and dangled his feet on the other side. "Yeah, he came home last night bragging about a job he got with a rich merchant from Belfast. He made Ma cry. Da told him to get. Poor Mary. The fighting upsets her so."

I yanked fistfuls of long dry grass out of the ground and held it through a slat in the fence, offering it to the black horse I'd seen earlier. The steed sauntered over, blew on my hand, and took the grass between its yellowed teeth.

"It'll be dark soon, and they'll be lighting the bonfires on the hill." Peter jumped to the ground. "I should get Mary out of the barn. She wants to dress up and go door to door."

Scrambling up to the top of the fence, I sat near where I'd etched my mark. I swung my legs over and mounted the stallion. "Let's ride the horses first. C'mon, get the other one."

Peter pulled himself up onto a gray and white gelding. "My horse can outrun any of King Billy's," he boasted as he pulled his sword from his belt and charged toward the barn.

"Not a black horse with eyes of fire and a snort like thunder." I waved my stick in the air and coaxed the stallion to follow at a gallop.

"There's no such horse," Peter said.

"Yes, there is. The pooka. And only one of the Tuatha da Danann dares to ride one."

Peter looped back along the corral perimeter before galloping toward me head-on. As he whizzed by, he cut the air with his sword and brought it down on my hand that held the horse's mane. I yelped and countered with a strike against Peter's shoulder.

Peter teetered and regained his balance. Determined not to be outdone, he circled back.

Out of the corner of my eye, I saw Mary watching.

"Don't be calling the pooka Brannon, or he'll come," she said as I rode by.

She was right. I felt it, a heavy weight pressing against my chest. Voices whispered in my mind, demanding blood. There it was again, that overwhelming urge to hurt Peter. Could Peter hear the voices, too? Is that why he was charging toward me with his cherub face wrinkled with rage?

"Stop," I shouted as I tried to coax the stallion out of the gelding's path, but a pipit, neighing like a horse, swooped down with a cry and spooked it. Even though I had heard pipits making the strange whinnying call, this time, the hair on the back of my neck stood up.

Pipits hated horses, and horses hated pipits and would eat them if they could catch them. The startled horse wheeled around, its ears pressed flat, its teeth snapping at the air.

I tried to reign in the stallion, but both muscular chests collided with a thump. The gelding bucked, sending Peter sliding over its withers and under the stallion, which reared and came down with a sickening thud. I pulled hard on the horse's mane. It reared once more and came to a standstill. With a final cry, the pipit flew to the peak of the barn's roof. There were no more voices, just a terrible scream from Mary.

I slid down the stallion's velvet flanks to Peter's side.

It looked so bad, so hopeless. Peter's body twisted into a knot. His collarbone protruded through his shirt, white like an icicle. His front tooth was embedded in his bottom lip, and the other front tooth was gone somewhere.

The wind blew up another good one, sending dirt and sand swirling about the yard. A quick look at the ground, but no, the tooth was gone, picked up by the wind and carried away.

Run or stay? I didn't know what to do. With a shaky hand, I wiped the blood from Peter's forehead. My tears came like the blood, unstoppable.

Peter's eyes were open, watching me, looking as calm as if he were sitting in a tree. "Darn pipit, eh?" He wheezed as he reached up and grasped the sapphire from around my neck. His startled gaze met mine as his hand released the talisman and fell palm up, revealing a star etched in the center.

Chapter Eight

Brannon

What to do? What to do? Peter was dead. I'd called the pooka on Pooky Night and killed him. A stupid thing to do, but I'd gone and done it, like calling the wind for a few apples. I paced one moment and fell at Peter's side the next. Could I call him back to me, like I'd called the wind? "Wake up. Wake up. Open your eyes. C'mon, Peter."

Mary's screams gave way to sobs. "What's wrong with him? Why won't he wake up?"

I stood and pushed her toward the fence. "He's hurt. Run and get help." Without looking back, she ran across the field toward the road, where I could see a donkey and cart coming. Evan's family and Da were returning home from the dock. The cart stopped. Da would make things right. Da would know what to do.

I gripped the railing and hoisted myself up to the top rung. A splinter pierced the soft web between my thumb and forefinger, but there was no time to squeeze it out. I would have to let it fester. I hollered and waved.

Da, Evan, and four of Evan's kids, three boys and a girl, followed Mary through the long grass spotted with clumps of heather. Shena, his wife, looked on from the wagon with Riley, their youngest boy, in her arms.

Da climbed the fence and knelt on the ground by Peter. I slid onto my knees beside him. "I think he's dead," I sobbed over and over. "He's dead, isn't he?

Da told me to hush, but I couldn't.

"Sweet Jesus," Evan said as he squatted beside me. He hugged me against his chest to muffle my cries. "Gotta get Brannon away. Leave the little one for someone else to find. Nothing can be done here."

Peter's eyes stared up at the overcast sky. Between sobs, I saw Da brush his hand over Peter's eyes once, twice, three times before he could get them to stay closed. He stood and yanked me to my feet. "C'mon. Hurry now."

"No, I won't leave him." I knelt at Peter's side.

Evan brushed a bloodied curl from Peter's eyes. "Poor wee skitter. What happened?" He put a hand on my shoulder.

"I killed him. Me and the pooka." I said between sobs.

"Don't be stupid. You know you didn't," Da said.

"I did. I killed him."

"Shut up!" Da dragged me to my feet again. "You're acting like a gack. Anyone can see that he fell off the horse."

"Granda said he was the wrong color. He said Peter was green, and I was orange, and I ought to make Granda proud for fixing my bike."

"It was an accident, son. That's all. You can't be blaming yourself," Evan said.

"No, I killed him. We were knights, and I trampled him because he's green, and I'm orange."

"Jaysus, I'll do more than just barge you if you don't shut your gob," Da growled.

"Peter?" Mary squeezed through a broken slat in the fence. Evan caught her before she reached Peter's side. She kicked her feet and howled. Her screams drifted across the field. Everyone would hear her. They would come looking to see. Evan had to put her down to silence her. She took Peter's hand, the one etched with the star, and held it to her cheek.

"Aw, Mary," Evan said, looking on helplessly.

"Now, he won't get to see the kitten. The kitten with the six toes," Mary cried.

"I didn't mean to do it," I said.

"You did. I heard you call the pooka. You killed him. You and the pooka. I saw it and the pipit. It made the horse crazy."

"Who did you see?" Evan asked.

"The pooka."

"Don't be saying that, Mary," Evan said. "It was an accident." He placed his arm around her shoulders, but she ducked away, squeezed back through the slats, and fled.

"Christ," Da said. "Now look what you've gone and done by shooting your mouth off with such nonsense. Talk like that will only get us all into a heap of trouble. Some folks will see this as an opportunity to start something. Who knows what Mary will tell her da? Get yourself home. I'll be coming after I take care of this."

I took a few steps, turned, and came back. "I won't leave him. He'll be scared. He needs me. He needs me—"

"Go now before I take a stick to you." Da picked up my makeshift sword.

"Let him be, William. He's hurting," Evan said. "Flynn, bring me a blanket from the wagon. Hurry."

Evan's children turned to watch Flynn. "And the rest of you, get back and stay with your ma." They fled like a litter of frightened kittens toward the waiting wagon.

"What now?" Da turned to face the approaching storm clouds, closing in to suffocate what was left of the afternoon light.

"I'll take him," Evan said. "I'll say I found him on my way home. The poor wee lad must have got trampled. No one's fault. Just happened."

"They'll blame you."

"Nah, how can they?"

"They're gonna look for someone to blame. You know you would if it were your boy. Besides, wee Mary saw."

After walking the barn's length, Evan stopped to speak softly to the frightened horses cowering in the grass: a flea-bitten gray, a blue roan, a piebald, the gelding, and the black stallion. The stallion's nose pressed forward, skin drawn tightly over its face, teeth exposed, nostrils wrinkled up and back.

Ears lay flat, tail thrashed, and its front hooves scratched in the dirt. The horse had a look in its eyes like a bull seeing red. Red. Drops of red mixed with dirt.

Evan had a knack for animals and children. It was his gift, not Da's, though. Da pressed his back against the fence and leaned on it for support. His hand fell on the etching of the horse I had gouged into the weathered wood. A smooth deep sound came then, an old ballad, no words, just a melody. It was an odd time for it, but there it was, a slow melancholy air. Da had always done that, hummed when he was beside himself with worry.

"Da, the blanket." Flynn pushed it through the wooden slats.

"It's Riley's blanket. He's crying from the cold now. Ma says to hurry."

"Beautiful boy. Looks like an angel with them blond curls." Evan picked up Peter's arm to lay it across his chest. "Look at this. A bloodied star on his palm. What on earth could have made that mark?" Evan laid the blanket over Peter.

Tears came in silent streams. Damn talisman, I thought. Why did it do that to Peter? Make a star on his palm? Why didn't it save him?

"I'll take him." Da gathered Peter in his arms.

"We'll go together." Evan matched Da's stride across the field. What could I do but follow?

The children scrambled to one side of the wagon. They sat on top of each other to make room. Shena buried her head in Riley's hair and held him closer while Evan took the reins and drove the cart. Da sat on the wagon's edge with his feet swinging and Peter draped across his lap. I sat beside him.

Da hummed again. Still no words. What were they? Why couldn't I remember them? I wished Da would hum louder and drown out that awful sound of horses thumping together. Like the star on Peter's palm, the day would be etched on my soul forever, and nothing, not even wind, rain, fire, or earth, could ever change that. It would be with me until Manannan came to take me to Tir na nOg. I felt so awful that I hoped that day would come soon, and Peter and I could be together again.

The wind rose higher with the setting sun and rustled the homemade costumes of children dressed for Pooky Night. A ghost's eyes peered through holes ripped out of a tattered bed sheet, a witch raised her broom as if to hex us as she passed by, and goblins howled. I saw envy in Evan's children's eyes. They wouldn't be going door to door for fruit and nuts tonight or celebrating later at the bonfires on the hill. Like me, they didn't dare utter a word. The veil that separated the living and the dead was too close for comfort.

The front door to my house flew open as we passed by. Evan pulled the donkey to an abrupt stop as Ma raced to catch up to us.

"Dear God, dear God," she chanted over and over. "What happened?" She stroked Peter's cheek. Was she hoping he would respond? His hand fell out of the blanket. I took Peter's hand in mine. How fast his body cooled despite the blanket.

"The lad was trampled to death. Nobody's fault, ma'am, just an accident," Evan said.

"You'd better pack your bags, Molly," Shena said as she leaned over the wagon to squeeze Molly's hand. "Accident or no, they'll be looking for someone to blame, and Mary will tell them it's Brannon's fault. Best to go away for a while."

"I'm sorry, Ma. I called the pooka. It's my fault," I whispered.

"Hush now. You're not to blame." She wiped a muddy tear from my cheek.

I glanced at Granda, who was puffing on his pipe in the doorway. The wind carried the smoke toward me. I stifled the urge to vomit from the smell. Before the wagon could continue toward Peter's house, John Kendrick, Peter's da, ran toward us, with Mary trailing behind.

"Mary said Peter was dead. He's only hurt, I told her." Wrinkles crisscrossed John's brow and under his eyes. His face flushed underneath his freckles, and his hand trembled as he reached to touch his son's forehead. One aching sob caught in his throat, and he stopped himself.

"We'll take him home for you," Evan said, telling John with his look that what Mary had said was true.

John looked Da in the eye and held out his arms. "I'll take him," he said.

He might be green, but the sorrow in Kendrick's eyes was the same as any da's. Da placed the child in his father's arms. Evan mumbled something about finding Peter in the field, but I could see that the pain, wedged like a splinter in John's heart, blocked all reason. John staggered with grief. Mary followed behind. Every few steps, she turned back to look at me.

"Nothing good can come from this," Evan said. "Did you see it in his eyes, then?"

"See what?" Da asked.

"Bloody hatred. You need to be ready. When John can think clearly again, he will want answers, and if he doesn't get answers, he'll want revenge."

"Kieran is nearby," Da said. "I saw him today at the pier. He asked about you."

"Strange how I've been thinking about him a lot lately," Ma said. "I've been hoping he would return before Brannon got any older."

"He gave me back Ian's ring. I sold it to pay for repairs. We almost lost the boat and our lives last night."

Ma glanced at me. Ashamed, I hung my head. In my heart, I vowed to get rid of the talisman because I couldn't trust myself to never use it again.

"Is he traveling with the tinkers?" Ma asked.

"I suspect so." Da took a bag of potatoes from the back of the wagon and placed them at my feet.

"Tinkers?" Shena asked.

"Them folks know how to hide." Evan swung the wagon around. "I'll send word to the tinker's camp. Hurry now." The wagon kicked up dust as it rolled away.

Da stooped to pick up the broken gate, torn from its hinges by the wind, and propped it up against the fence. Somehow, I knew Da would never get a chance to fix that gate.

I waited for my ma and da to go into the house before burying the talisman between the apple tree's roots. I packed it down, stomping on it hard and cursing it with the foulest language I could muster. It felt strange leaving it there. Like I had just buried something alive.

My chest felt heavy, and I struggled to breathe. I almost dug it up again when Ma called me into the house. "I don't want you," I said with one final stomp on the grave. "Leave me alone, you stupid stone." I picked up the sack of potatoes, hoisted them onto my shoulder, and ran into the house.

Chapter Nine

Brannon

Flames crackled in the hearth. Floorboards creaked as Da paced up and down the living room. His fist pounded the table. A teacup jiggled against a saucer. "They'll call him a murderer now, you know."

I peered around my bedroom door and listened to Ma, Da, and Granda arguing about me.

"He's just a boy," Ma said. "It wasn't his fault."

"He's almost a man. True or not, it's what they'll all say," Da said.

"What's the matter of it anyway, one less Taig spoiling our fair land?" Granda sat in Ma's rocking chair, squeaking back and forth in front of the fireplace.

"They'll be on our doorstep if we don't get out of here," Da growled. "We have no choice. We have to leave."

"Ah, begone with you. I won't leave without a fight," Granda said. "Any decent man would stay and defend his home."

Da's face grew red. "Any decent man would see his family safe."

A loud noise, like someone banging against the door, shook the house. Ma stiffened, bracing herself for whoever could be outside. Da hesitated before unlatching the door. Slowly, he opened it, but the wind caught the door, ripped it out of his hand, and banged it up against the outside wall. A bitter gust swept through the house, nearly blowing out the fire in the hearth.

"Ah, it's just the wind banging. You're jumping out of your skin for nothing," Granda said.

Ma peered over Da's shoulder, "Look!" She pointed to a strange light flickering in the bog.

I came out of my room to get a better look. "It's the will-o'-the-wisp," I said.

"Oh aye," Granda said without even looking at it. "It's the wicked old Jack O' Lantern, the shoemaker. Barred from heaven and hell for his evil ways. Don't forget to turn your coat inside out so his evil can't lead you astray. I've known many to die out there on the bog."

"Any fool can see it's torchlight. It's the sign Evan told us to watch for. They won't wait long. Brannon, we have to go. Get your things. Hurry now!" Ma took her cloak from the hook by the door and handed me my jacket. I turned it inside out just in case it wasn't the sign Ma hoped for, and the evil

Jack O' Lantern was waiting to steal my soul. I shuddered to think I could end up wandering the bogs with Jack.

I went back into my bedroom for the bag I'd packed. At the last minute, I'd stuffed in my sketchbook, charcoal pencils, and watercolors. Just in case I wouldn't get back home again.

Granda called out from the living room. "Brannon, come see me before you go."

I hurried out of the bedroom and dropped my bag by the front door. "Granda, please come." I choked back tears. I couldn't cry in front of Granda.

"There now. I'll be fine. I'm too old to be leaving me home. One day you'll understand." Granda stoked the fire and sat back down in the chair. "Come. Come here."

I stood by Granda's chair and watched a beetle tap dance across the wooden planks and hide between the floorboards, its shiny brown armor still visible between the cracks.

"Look at you. You've grown into a fine young man, and I'll miss you. I'm damn proud of you, and don't forget it." Granda reached up and pulled me into a hug, squeezing tears to the surface of my eyes. "There now. Off you go."

"Granda, it's not too late to change your mind," Ma said, but Granda waved her away. Her eyes were moist. It surprised me because Granda had never had a kind word for her.

With my bag slung over my shoulder, I stepped outside. Sounds of laughter, music, and song echoed from the hills, where locals celebrated around the bonfires. Silently, I said goodbye to the house, the garden, the surrounding apple trees, and my bike that someone, probably Evan, had propped against the fence. I took a deep breath, inhaling the scent of burning peat and damp grass. We passed Peter's house, silent except for the wind rustling in the trees and our boots shuffling on gravel. Even though it was an hour to midnight, lights shone from every window. I wondered if they were washing Peter's body now. Had the priest come to pray over him? If only I could see Peter one last time. If only I could say sorry.

We veered off the road and took a well-worn trail toward the marshlands. I couldn't shake the nagging feeling that I'd left something behind. I took stock of the items I had packed: a change of clothes, my art supplies, and a warm blanket. I had everything I needed except Granda, which felt terribly wrong.

I stopped to adjust my backpack, so the weight fell squarely on my shoulders. The pack seemed to grow heavier with each step, and worse, the wind had changed direction to blow straight in my face. Hunkering down against the bitter cold, I trudged on, feeling as if I were wading through hip-deep muck.

The oil lantern that Da carried bobbed up and down ahead of me. Trying to keep it in sight, I pressed onward, but something was holding me back, slowing me down. What had I forgotten? In my mind, I saw Granda sitting by the fire, Peter sitting in the apple tree, and the talisman shining through the roots. That was it. It was calling to me, beckoning me back to unearth it. Did it have the power to turn the wind against me? I wasn't sure. I knew that even if I didn't want the talisman, the talisman wanted me. I focused on the lantern light ahead, determined to leave the wretched gem buried. What good was the evil amulet, anyway? It was a bad luck charm. It had let my best friend die.

"What the hell's wrong with you, boy." Da stopped to wait for me.

"Hush, William. Please, don't be so hard on him. He's troubled. Leave him," Ma said. They waited until I had almost caught up, then turned and continued down the path.

"The wind," I tried to say, but a sudden downpour of rain and sleet masked my words. The lantern light and my parents disappeared down one of the many footpaths that crisscrossed the one we traveled. Darkness closed in around me, and with it, fear and anxiety. I had to go back for the gem. I couldn't take the uncomfortable feeling of being without it. Ma and Da would wait for me when they noticed I wasn't behind them, but I hoped I had enough time to turn back without being stopped. I worried that without light to guide me, I would veer off the trail and get lost. I pulled my hood over my head and hunched against the gale. The wind shifted. Instead of slowing me down, it pushed me along the path to my home, where I fell to the ground under the apple tree.

Using my bare hands, I dug in the dirt like a dog after a buried bone. Where was it? It had to be here. I'd just buried it a few hours ago. Could someone else have found it? No, how could they know it was there unless they had been watching me?

I tried to calm down and think—the wrong root. I dug again. Dirt stung the cut on my finger, which throbbed from the splinter still caught beneath the skin. Twice I unearthed a rock about the same size as the talisman before seeing a faint glow beneath the soil. I pried it loose and wiped away the dirt.

"There you are. Damn you. Stop calling me now. You're making me ill." I put the talisman in the crane bag. Gradually my anxiety faded. The wind gentled, and the rain eased to a cold drizzle.

I stood and looked for a moment at my house. A glow from the fire in the hearth filled one of the windows. I imagined Granda asleep in the rocking chair with a book on his lap. More than anything, I wanted to stay with him, drink tea and listen to his stories about the Tuatha De Danann. If only I could turn back time. If only I could forget.

"Please, Granda, I need you," I whispered to the night air. I had lost so much and didn't want to lose Granda too. I stepped to the door and turned the knob, but Granda had locked it.

With a heavy heart, I turned away. What was I thinking? Ma was right. Granda was a stubborn old coot. I'd never be able to change his mind, and he would probably give me a good scolding for coming back.

Something sizzled through the air. For an instant, a ball of fire lit the night sky. Then, the thatched roof erupted in a hiss of sparks, sending columns of black smoke spiraling into the air.

"Granda…" I screamed and leaned my weight against the door. "Fire! Get out, Granda. Get out of the house. The roof is on fire."

Rough hands grabbed me from behind and dragged me down the pathway. Punching and kicking, I fought to break free. Was this the person who had set fire to our house? Had they come to kill me too? I grabbed a handful of hair and heard a yelp. "Jaysus, boy. It's Evan. Stop it. Stop it now."

"Granda," I coughed from the smoke burning my lungs.

"Jaysus, he ain't in there, is he?" Evan said as the roof came crashing into the center of the house. A wave of heat stung my eyes with ash and soot. Blinking back tears, I searched for and found a rock and threw it at the window. The glass should have shattered, but instead, the rock sailed through, leaving only a tiny hole, not big enough to make a difference.

"I'm sorry, lad. It's too late. We can't go in there. I'm so sorry. By the gods, my heart is heavy for you." The apple tree crackled overhead as flames ignited the top branches.

The house didn't fall all at once, but struggled like a wounded animal, succumbing slowly as every joint folded under it.

"Come, we have to get away. Whoever did this will be watching."

"No, we can't leave him," I cried as Evan half-dragged and half-carried me down the road.

Da ran to meet us, with Ma close behind him. She screamed for me, Granda, and her house lost to the fire.

Da pushed past Evan. "Me da. Did he get out? Tell me he did."

Evan ran beside Da. "I don't know. I didn't see him. Maybe he got out through the back door. It's worth checking. I had to get the boy away. Stop now. Stop." He tugged on Da's arm to slow him down. "You can't go in. It's not safe. Think of Molly and Brannon. What would they do without you?"

Da stopped and handed the lantern to Molly. "Go."

"No," she said, "I won't leave you."

"Jaysus, woman, you have to. Wait as long as you can at the meeting place. If I don't come, well, if I can't come, I'll meet up with you later. Brannon, take your ma and run."

Shivering and too dazed to argue, I took Ma's arm and pulled her down the trail to a narrow footpath skirted on both sides by blackberry nettles, down a mossy incline, and into the bog. Fetid odors rose with the mist.

"Which way, Ma? I don't know where to go."

"See that flicker on the other side of the fen? There. We need to go there."

It seemed as if we would never get any closer to it. Twice, the light disappeared, and we stopped and waited in darkness for it to reappear. Then it was beside us.

"Molly." A deep voice made us both jump. A man with a lantern stepped from the shadows. He pulled his hood back, and I saw it was Kieran, the man I'd met at the pier.

Ma fell into his arms. Between sobs, she told him what had happened to Peter, Granda, and our house. When she had finished, she drew me to her side.

"My son," she said.

"We met at the pier." Kieran raised the lantern so that the light shone on my face. I looked away, afraid he would see what I already knew. I was a monster. I'd killed my best friend, my house was on fire, and Granda—I stifled a sob. I wouldn't cry now. There was no time for that. Besides, tears couldn't change what had happened.

"Come." Kieran lowered the light. "We mustn't linger here. Someone may have followed you. Keep close behind me and watch where you step."

Tall reeds swished in the wind on either side of the narrow path. One missed step, and I could find myself knee-deep in water, so I was relieved when Kieran led us to higher ground and into a wooded ravine. It was too dark to see what waited for us in the shadows, but I knew something did. A twig snapped. Kieran dimmed the lantern and motioned for us to duck behind a bush.

I listened. Nothing but the distant roar of waves and my heart thumping. A rustle. Someone was moving toward us. I peered around the bush. Now and then, light streamed through the thick undergrowth. Shouldn't we run and keep ahead of it? It could only be the ones who wanted me dead.

Kieran placed a reassuring hand on my shoulder. *Stay still.*

I thought I heard Kieran's voice in my mind, not in my ears. Whoever followed us had dimmed their lantern and waited on the other side of the path. I could just make out the figure standing under a tree.

The shape looked like a boy. Mist swirled about his feet. He turned his head to one side as if listening for something then stepped out onto the path and brightened his lantern. "Just Connor, sir." He brushed the hair from his eyes and wiped his nose on his sleeve.

Kieran stepped from behind the bush. I followed and squinted to get a better look at the boy. Was this the same Connor I had fought with at the fair? It was.

"They're coming this way—the men who did the burning. 'One life is not enough,' they said. They want the whole family to pay." I noticed a slight tremor in Connor's voice. So, the little thief wasn't as tough as he pretended to be.

I gripped Ma's arm. "We must go back."

"It's not safe," Connor murmured. He shot a glance at me, then at Kieran.

"He's right," Kieran said. "We should split up. I'll take Brannon. Connor, I want you to take Molly to the place we agreed to meet and wait for William."

"No, I'm going back to be with Da." I was thirteen, a man now, and I wanted to make my own decisions.

Kieran raised his hood. "If you go back, you'll put your whole family in danger. There'll come a time to make things right, but now is not that time."

Ma turned me to face her. She looked pale in the lantern light. Dark shadows circled her eyes, lined with worry and fear. "You must go with Kieran."

"But—"

"No questions. Listen and learn. You'll be safe." She kissed me. Her lips were icy against my cheek.

I watched her fall into step behind Connor and disappear into the woods. Kieran motioned for me to follow him. He dimmed the lantern and took a path parallel to the sea. When I didn't follow, he stopped and turned around. "We'll regroup tomorrow at mid-day. Come now."

The moss-covered path was spongy and pitted with water-filled holes, roots, and stones. Slushy one moment and slippery the next, I kept to the edge of the trail so I could grip the overhanging branches to keep my balance. It felt like I slipped two steps backward with every step forward. Shivering in my wet clothes, I wondered how I might sneak away without Kieran noticing me.

I had to go back. I had to know if Granda was still alive. Turning around, I retraced my steps. I hoped it would take Kieran a moment to notice that I no longer followed. And if he did, what then? Surely, he wouldn't force me to go with him.

I licked my lips, cracked and bloody from the bitter wind. Once I thought the wind was my friend. Tonight, the wind was my enemy, making every effort to stop me from going home.

The way back was darker than the way forward. Still, I pressed onwards, tripping over rocks and slipping on moss-covered tree roots. Thorns scraped at my trouser legs and tore holes in my jacket while the rain pelted down. Sheet lightning lit the sky for a few seconds so I could see the way forward. I hoped I wouldn't become lost, one more victim of Jack O' Lantern.

I heard footsteps behind me and felt a bony hand brush against mine. I quickened my pace. A voice whispered, "Murderer. That's what they'll all say. Come with us, and we will give you sanctuary and peace. Take our hands, and we will lead you home." Red eyes peered at me from the bushes. A horse whinnied. Had the pooka come to carry me beyond the veil? Pooky Night wasn't over until dawn.

Thunder rumbled in the distance. Lightning severed the top of a tree and sent it crashing down. I ran for cover, thrashing through the mire until muck plastered me from head to foot. I looked up and saw a light, the will-o'-the-wisp. With a yelp, I dove under a bush.

The wind carried Kieran's voice, speaking in a strange tongue. His words calmed the wind, and the storm faded with a few last cracks of thunder.

When all was quiet, I crawled from beneath the bush. Kieran was standing under the lightning-struck tree with the lantern in hand.

"How did you do that?" I felt foolish. The light I'd seen was not the will-o'-the-wisp after all.

"The same way you do, but I use words as a talisman. Be careful what you think and say, young man. With talent such as yours, you could harm yourself or another."

I thought I'd already done that as I hugged my water-soaked jacket and buried my freezing fingers under my armpits.

Wading through patches of long grass, I followed Kieran across a rock-strewn field to a shelter embedded into the hillside. The soil had eroded to reveal three standing stones and a flat capstone, leaning together to form a single-chambered hideout. A dolmen. Kieran pushed back the tangled wild-grape vines at the entrance before stooping inside.

I hovered in the entranceway. Inside, I saw by lantern light, spirals, zigzags, and concentric circles carved into the limestone walls. A burial tomb. No skeletons, though.

"I've stayed here before. It's not haunted," Kieran teased with a warm smile as he placed the lantern on the ground. "We'll make a fire, put some tea on and turn this hollow into a cozy den."

Cozy would not be a word I would have used to describe spending the night in a burial chamber. But the tomb was dry and warm. It sheltered us from the elements and, hopefully, hid us from the men who wanted me dead.

Chapter Ten

Connor

Manannan's wind brought the storm that beat against the cave, where I seethed with anger. Ebony rocks, looming over the cave's entrance, protected the fire, smoking against the banshee wind. Kieran had chosen the hideout because the jagged rock formations sheltered it.

I listened to the waves crashing against the precipice. I threw a rock at the crag. Molly jerked, lifted her head, and wiped a tear on the edge of her cloak. Her sniffling annoyed me. I envied Brannon, whose ma loved him and would lose herself in sadness at their parting.

Prepared to accept a long night of waiting, I squatted and placed a sod of peat in the center of the fire, then sat on a rock opposite Molly. I took a piece of Ashwood from my pocket and peeled the bark away with a small carving knife.

Broad strokes fueled by my temper sent curls of bark falling around my feet. "He's with Kieran, ma'am. He'll be cared for and safe." I couldn't think of anything else to say to comfort her, and to my relief, she looked up and leaned over the fire to watch me work.

How closely she resembled my da, the high cheekbones and auburn hair. "I've always wondered if I'd ever meet you, Aunt Molly." She stiffened and searched my face for the tell-tale signs of family. "My father is Faolan, your brother." I flicked a wood curl into the fire with the tip of my knife. I didn't intend to upset her, but what did Kieran expect us to talk about? The weather? She frowned. I knew she could see the resemblance.

"I'd heard Faolan had a son, but I haven't seen or spoken to my brother since I was a young girl."

"I see him sometimes when he remembers he has a son."

"I'm sorry. A boy needs a father."

"Not one the likes of him. I have Kieran."

"Faolan carries a heavy burden."

"What burden?"

"You should ask him."

"How can I ask him when I never see him? And if I do, he's usually so blootered he's talking gabshite."

"What about your ma?"

I shrugged. "Heard my ma was a village girl. Her family didn't want no tinker's brat."

"Of course." She warmed her hands over the fire. "What are you carving?"

I brushed the wood shavings off with my thumb. "Truth is, I never know what shape it will take until it comes. I let it be what it must."

Molly nodded. "Brannon has a similar gift with painting and drawing. You must be around his age."

"I'm fifteen." I put the carving in my pocket, took out the piece of oak wood that Kieran had given me, and held it over the fire for Molly to see. "Kieran gave me this wood. He said it's from one of the old trees before they were all cut down and that I must find its beauty. I'm scared to begin. I don't want to ruin it."

"May I see?"

I placed the wood in her hand. She turned it over and over in the light of the fire.

"It's beautiful and so full of energy. It's from a sacred tree, to be sure. I see why you're hesitant to carve it. My adopted father was a stonemason. He used to say that he heard voices in the stone telling him where to cut and shape. I'd watch him run his fingers lightly over it, using his fingers as his eyes to select the perfect place to tap it into pieces that matched. Rarely did he have to strike a stone more than once. I think you need to examine your wood with your eyes, ears, and fingers. If you listen, you will hear the wood's secret."

She handed the oak wood back to me. I closed my eyes and felt the wood pulsate with life. Aunt Molly was right. If I listened, I would know what to do. I opened my eyes.

"I know what it wants to be," I said. I picked up my chisel and made the first stroke, sending wood curling into the fire.

"What did you see?" she asked.

"A seahorse."

"Oh aye, a seahorse. But there's no need to rush. Take your time, Connor."

The wind died suddenly, as it often did in these parts. Intermingled with the measured tapping of the rain and the waves drumming against the cliffs were footsteps moving toward us.

I pocketed the wood but kept the chisel hidden in the palm of my hand. I signaled Molly to be quiet and move back into the cave. Crouching near the entrance, I heard footsteps and heavy breathing. The hollow tap of boots stepping from boulder to boulder, followed by a prolonged scraping, meant that the person had slipped and scrambled for balance. By the hefty sound of his boots against the rock, I knew it was a man, and he was making no effort to hide.

"Jumpin' Jaysus!" The curse ringing through the night air confirmed what my keen ears knew.

"It's William," I said, but Molly already knew who it was. She moved toward the cave's entrance.

William stepped into the light of the peat fire and fell to his knees. His hair, windswept forward over his brow, was dotted with raindrops that dripped a steady stream onto his wind-burned cheeks. He smelled of damp wool, mud, sheep shit, and liquor. If it bothered Molly, she didn't let on as she knelt by his side.

I fled to the back of the cave, where I knew Kieran kept supplies hidden. There was always a blanket, a lantern, dry kindling, smoked fish, salted lamb, and if we were lucky, a bottle of whisky. We were lucky. The bottle had enough for a man to warm his innards. Molly took the blanket and placed it around William's shoulders.

I crouched beside him and offered him the bottle of whisky. He took it and drank. "Who are you?" he asked.

"This is Connor, my nephew," Molly said.

"By the gods, he looks like Peter with them fair curls and all." William pressed the bottle to his lips a second time. "The blasted thing's empty!" He threw it at the cliff, where it smashed against the rocks.

"William, tell me. What happened?" Molly brushed a wet strand from his eye.

"Bloody bastards."

Molly placed her hand on his arm.

"Me da." He wiped the rain from his eyes. "I found him out back. He'd rolled in the grass, but…."

Molly tightened her grip on his arm.

"I shouldn't have left. I should've made him come with us. They burned him in his own home. They would have killed us all."

"Holy Mother," Molly said.

"And don't be saying it. I don't want to hear you calling that woman no more. Bloody Taigs…"

Molly pulled back. By the light of the fire, I saw Molly's eyes, downcast and heavy. She lifted her hood to hide her face. I wondered if I could leave her now, with this man whose grief had turned him against her. The rain had stopped, and the wind too. I wanted to go.

"Where's Brannon?" William barked.

"He's safe, sir, with Kieran," I said. "I'll take you to our camp."

"Jaysus. We won't be going there. Got to go back and bury Da. Evan and Shena have him. We can stay with them until after the wake. Fetch Brannon. We can't be staying here."

"Kieran took him away," I explained.

"Away?"

"I thought it best," Molly said. "Besides, he needs to be with Kieran right now. He's the only one who can teach him. You know, Brannon has a talent for the old ways. You've tried to ignore it, but we can't now. He's a danger to himself and others."

"Jaysus, are you daft? Why did you go and do that? The boy needs to be at his granda's side." William leaned his back against the cave wall, clutched his legs to his chest, and laid his head on his knees. Molly placed her head on his shoulder. If he wept, it was silent.

I couldn't remember the last time I had cried, but I knew I would never weep for my da again, not even if he died in a fire. I packed my belongings in silence. When I was ready, I picked up the spare lantern and said, "I'm going now." They were too absorbed in their grief to look up or say goodbye. It didn't matter. I was relieved to escape.

In an hour, it would be dawn. Two hours west, I would be back at the camp in time for sausages and eggs, but I had to find Kieran and tell him that Brannon's granda had died, and they wanted him back for the wake. I was curious to know what power Brannon possessed that caused two people to die in a single night. The puny kid didn't look capable of causing such trouble. And I was still seething about the talisman. I still wanted it, and if there were a way to get it—not steal it—convince him to give it to me somehow, I would.

I knew Kieran would travel close to the coast, where the paths were easy and food available. If Kieran settled the boy down for the night, I would catch up with them by morning if I could follow the trail. But a mist rose from the marshes and blanketed the footpath in thick fog. I stumbled over rocks slippery with moss and roots zigzagging across the path. The light from the lantern seemed to shine back at me instead of lighting the way. I inched onward, careful to avoid stepping into a quagmire or, worse, over a cliff. But on Pooky night, when dead spirits walked among men, I was more afraid of crossing into the realm of the departed. From the time I was a child, I'd heard the stories of people becoming lost in the fairy mists forever.

I thought I heard voices whispering. Or was it a keening? Yes, a keening for the dead. I walked backward, turned frontward, then backward again, glancing around nervously at every shadow. An icy finger brushed my cheek. Someone or something tugged my hair. I pulled my hood over my head and whipped around, but no one was there. Still, I felt them closing in from all directions and the pressure of their minds bearing down on mine.

"You're not going to make me run like a Ginny Ann," I shouted, but my heart thundered like a bodhran. "I'm not afraid of you, so back off, spirits of Samhain. I'll not be your prize tonight."

But my brave words were short-lived. The stench of death filled the air. To outrun them would be madness. To fight them was foolish. I panicked and ran straight into a patch of stinging nettles. My pant leg ripped as it caught in the brambles. My leg burned, but it wasn't until I pulled a burr from the sleeve of my jacket that I remembered Kieran's words. 'Burdock grows with nettle to tell you it's the remedy.' Crushing the leaves of the burdock plant in my hand, I placed them over the rash to relieve the sting.

Fear, I couldn't let it get to me. If it did, then I would be lost forever. I clenched my fists and shouted into the fog, "Haven't enough people died tonight? You'll not have me. You damn sidhe. I don't care who you are. I'm Connor, and I won't come."

The death-keening banshees shrieked as I raised my voice to call upon Manannan with the words Kieran taught me.

"Fierce Manannan, I summon thee.
High King of the Irish Sea
I am lost between three realms.
Great Mariner, rescue me.

Take me not to Tir na nOg.
But lead me from this murky fog.
Mark my footpath if you please
Great Mariner, rescue me."

I chanted the words, but the fog deepened with each repetition. Why hadn't it worked? Was it because what followed me was greater in evil than these words of protection that Kieran had taught me? No, I had called upon the wrong god.

I dropped my pack on the ground and closed my eyes. If the dark-hearted Manannan didn't answer my request this night, I would call upon Lugh, the sun god. Kieran had assured me that the spirits from the dark realms would never cross into the light of Lugh.

"Blessed Lugh, I call to thee.
Dispel the dark mist from the sea,
Save me from the banshee
As I leave the land of sidhe.

Blessed Lugh, light-bearer be.
Light my steps and help me see.
Light my heart, my mind, my sight.
Enclose me in your shield of light."

As I chanted, a luminous shield surrounded me. The gateway between the living and the dead closed, and the disturbing sense that eyes watched, and hands reached out to grab me and drag me through the gateway before my time faded. A lit path opened before me.

The mist thinned, and I heard a bird chirping. Or was it music drifting through the fog? The sound gave me the courage to continue as I'd heard the melody before. With a grin, I followed the birdsong. Comforted by the smell of brine, I hastened my pace. The mist parted, and I stepped from my shield of light.

Chapter Eleven

Connor

I breathed easier to see dawn's light streaming through a canopy of ash and oak. The light would drive the spirits of Pooky Night back across the veil.

A lark trilled. I looked for the bird among the hazelnut bush. Last night's rain dripped from the branches onto the nuts at the tree's base. I scooped up a handful, cracked one with my teeth, spit out the shell, and ate the nut. I wished I'd had a pocket full of hazelnuts earlier to ward off the evil spirits.

I heard it again—another flourish of bird sounds, not a lark, a flute. I followed the sound to a grove, where I found Kieran leaning against a tree with a flute in hand.

I grinned. "I knew it was you."

"Lost?" Kieran tucked his flute into the interior pocket of his sheepskin jacket.

"A little turned around is all."

"I heard your call but couldn't see you through the fog. I hoped you'd follow the sound of my flute."

"I did. Thank you."

"Why didn't you stay with Molly?"

"Brannon's Granda died in the fire."

Kieran sighed. "Aw, I feared as much. More sad news for the boy."

"They want you to bring him home for the wake." I placed the lantern on a rock and turned down the flame.

"It's dangerous for Brannon to return, but I guess it can't be helped."

"Where is he?"

"Still asleep, I think. Now Connor, don't tell him about his granda, not yet. He's already sick over the death of his friend. Shall we wake him then?"

As we neared the hill cave where Kieran and Brannon had spent the night, I saw Brannon standing in front of the stone entranceway. Clumps of mud and briars clung to the hem of his pants. His hair stood straight up in crusty spikes like a rooster's comb, and his eyes looked strange, darker than usual, unblinking, and lifeless.

"He still looks asleep," I whispered.

Kieran nodded and placed a finger to his lips.

"Duck," Brannon cried and clasped his hands over his head. "It's the pipit. It's come back. Run to the hole-stone cross. Hurry. Julia, the nun, will save us." Kieran caught Brannon in his arms as he ran past, but he punched Kieran in the chest with his fists.

Kieran grabbed his hands and held them.

"Wake up, Brannon," Kieran said softly.

Brannon blinked and pulled away from Kieran. "Where am I? What am I doing here?"

"You were sleepwalking," I said.

Brannon stared at something over my shoulder. I felt a tingle on the back of my neck and glanced around. Nothing. The boy was seeing things. He must be crazier than a coot. Still, it gave me the creeps to see the kid looking over my shoulder like that.

"What?" I asked.

"I thought I saw—"

"What did you see, Brannon?" Kieran brushed a matted strand of hair from Brannon's eyes.

"Me, Granda," Brannon said in a throaty whisper. "He's dead, isn't he?"

"Yes," I said, even though Kieran had asked me not to say so a minute before. Honestly, the words flew from my lips before I could stop myself. What could I do? Brannon had already guessed his granda's fate, perhaps had seen his ghost, so there was no point beating around the bush about it or pretending it didn't happen.

"They found him in the backyard," I said. "He died from the smoke, they think. They want you home for the wake." I didn't mean for my words to sound unfeeling. It would have been worse if Granda's body had burned beyond recognition. At least they had a body to bury.

Tears pooled in Brannon's eyes. Kieran put his arm

around Brannon's shoulder, but he pulled away and ran toward the thicket of hazelnut trees. I chased him and grabbed him by his jacket. He spun and punched me in the gut. Giving Brannon back a bit of his own didn't even occur to me as he punched and kicked me. I knew better than to hit someone who was already down, so I stepped aside.

Brannon fell and buried his head in his arms. His cries were like the groan of the wind coming off the sea during a winter storm.

Kieran knelt beside him and waited. How often had he done the same for me when I was angry at my da? Helpless to offer any comfort, I did the only thing I could. I turned away and gave Brannon his privacy.

Later, Kieran coaxed Brannon to bathe in the hot spring we found bubbling from a fissure in the rocks nearby. While he changed into clean clothes, I gathered kindling. When Brannon returned, he and Kieran were laughing together, sharing a secret I could only guess.

"Now, who would like to make the fire?" Kieran asked.

"Me." Brannon picked up the kindling I had found and heaped it into a pile. "I want to learn how to make fire from nothing."

"You do, do you? I wonder who can teach you that?" Kieran said.

"You. I've seen you do it," Brannon said.

"Me too," I held my breath, not wanting to miss Kieran's explanation.

"To make fire, you must have friction, lightning, or a

crystal to catch the sun's rays. There's nothing magical about that. It's natural. Remember that what appears as magic is often your will in harmony with nature. The secret ingredient is the ability to focus your imagination."

"I have flint," I said. No one at camp could make fire as fast as I could with a flint.

"Let's try without flint or matches. As Brannon says, it is important to be able to make fire from nothing. Let's give it a try. Connor, find a flat piece of cedar for the hearth board, and Brannon, search for a branch to make the spindle. Look for either cattail, horseweed, or goldenrod."

I found the perfect piece of cedar for the hearth board and carved both surfaces so it would lay steady when placed on a flat rock. After Brannon found the right branch for the spindle, he set to carving it with a knife. I used a stone flake to create a divot, an indentation in the hearth board for the spindle.

While Brannon searched for twigs of varying sizes, I scraped the inner bark from a felled cedar and broke it down into hair-like fibers with my hands. I molded the fibers into the shape of a bird's nest and set it aside. I knew that once we had a spark, we would place it into the nest and cover it with a teepee made of twigs. The hard part was getting a spark.

Kieran instructed Brannon to set the spindle into the divot and use his palms to spin it. It was the hard way to make fire, and for all Brannon's grunting and gritting his teeth, he couldn't create a spark. "I can't do it." Brannon threw the sticks down and rubbed his hands. He sucked on the web between his thumb and forefinger. I stifled a laugh.

"Now, this is where a little of the mysterious comes in," Kieran said. "You're an artist, yes? Now picture the fire, feel the warmth, and smell the cinders. Imagine the crackle of the fire on a winter's night and the taste of your ma's mutton stew."

Brannon closed his eyes.

"What do you see?" Kieran said.

"The hearth. My granda has built up the fire with peat and dry twigs. He's rocking in his chair, and I'm seated on the stones close to the fire. It's so warm that I must turn my back to the flames. It's so nice to be home again...." His voice trailed off as if he had disappeared into the comfort of his house. He didn't seem to hear Kieran asking him what else he saw. His face looked more relaxed than I had seen all day, and when his eyes opened, the tinder bundle burst into flame. It wasn't a wee spark from the spindle rubbing against the hearth board but a full-blown fire.

"I did it," he squealed.

The brat shouldn't have been able to do that, and it made my blood boil to see he had made fire from nothing.

If Kieran was surprised, he didn't let on, but I knew by the tone of his voice that he was worried when he said, "Hmm, now that you've made it, can you control it?"

"What do you mean?" Brannon asked.

"Well, for example, can you put the fire out the same way you made it?"

Brannon shrugged.

Kieran looked at me. "What feeds fire?"

"Grass, twigs, branches, peat—"

"Yes, but you're forgetting the most important element."

"Air!" Brannon shouted.

I knew that. I wished I had said it. I wished I, too, could make fire from nothing.

"Yes! Take away the air, and the fire dies. Give it air, and it grows." Kieran waved his hand over the fire and extinguished it.

"But... but how did you do that?" I'd watched every move Kieran had made.

"I took away the air," Kieran said.

"But how?" Brannon poked the ashes with a stick.

"With my will. Have you ever called upon the wind?"

"Yes," Brannon said.

"How did you do it?"

"I spoke to the wind," Brannon said, "and the wind came."

"You used your will to create what you wanted. Creation is the same process as destruction."

"How can that be? They're opposite," I said.

"Yes, but what is destruction but another form of creation? Now, Connor, we'll need a fire to make breakfast. Brannon, come with me, and we'll gather some wild mushrooms and a few herbs to go with the fish I caught this morning."

To my dismay, I had to light the fire with the flint. Using friction instead of magic was humiliating. It wasn't easy to swallow my shame, but I couldn't let Brannon see my resentment. So, I gutted and cleaned the fish, and by the time Kieran and Brannon returned with the herbs and mushrooms, I had almost finished frying it.

"Did your granda teach you how to do that trick with fire?" I still couldn't believe Brannon could learn to do it so quickly.

Brannon slumped over his tea and broke his biscuit into crumbs. "My granda taught me many things, but Ma taught me about the elements."

So, Aunt Molly had gifts too, like my da, I thought. "What did she say about the elements?"

"She said that we are all a part of nature. An artist understands this. She showed me why the earth was brown in some places and black or reddish in others. We used to play a game with the wind. We'd lie on our backs and use the wind to shape the clouds into faces or animals. She said all of nature is my paintbrush. My Granda told me stories about the Tuatha De Danann. He said they were masters of the elements. I miss him. I'll never hear another one of those stories again. Never."

"They will live in your memory, and you will be the storyteller one day. Through you, your Granda will live on." Kieran threw the bones from the fish into the fire.

I thought Brannon would cry as I watched him suck on the web between his fingers. His hand looked swollen, and I wondered if he had hurt it somehow. I wished now that I hadn't asked him about his granda.

"Now, who would like to put out the fire?"

I jumped up at the opportunity to try. As I had seen Kieran do, I imagined the air sucked away as I swept my hand over the fire. It sputtered and fought, but eventually, I drew out enough air that it died down to a few embers. I kicked dirt over the remaining coals and whooped.

"That's the right idea," Kieran smiled. "Now, let's pack up. We have a long way to go today."

I figured that if we hiked at a steady pace, we might reach Ballycastle late in the day. I hoped there would be lots of food at the wake, but Kieran didn't seem to be in a hurry. He tried to distract Brannon from his grief by pointing out landmarks, standing stones etched with spirals, stonewalled ringforts, and the ruins of holy wells. He pointed to the limestone cliffs that rose from the glen.

"Your ancestors used the flint from the rocks to make knives and arrows. See? The stone is marred from their chipping away."

"I have a piece of flint," Brannon said.

"What's the big deal about that? Flint is everywhere." I watched him finger it, put it back in his pocket, and take it out again.

"Peter gave it to me. It has Ogham on it." He passed the flint to Kieran, who rubbed his thumb over the etched strokes.

"Quite right. It is Ogham, the old Irish alphabet."

"Do you know what it says?" Brannon asked.

"It's a musical phrase. You see, the old ones used a form of Ogham to notate music. They used music to heal, bring rain or sun, and seal or open a gateway. Sound used correctly can have double the power of words."

Kieran handed the flint back to Brannon, who opened his crane bag and placed it inside. "Where did Peter find it?"

"At low tide, in a sea cave."

"Mighty dangerous to be playing there."

"We kept an eye on the tide."

"Still, it's easy to become turned around in the passageways and lose your sense of place and time in the dark. Promise me you won't explore those caves without someone who knows how to do it safely."

Brannon nodded.

"Do you think you could find that cave again?" Kieran asked.

"Maybe."

"I'd like you to show it to me. You may have found one of the Tuatha De Danann's secret hideouts."

"Granda said I have the blood of 'em in me." Brannon raised his head proudly.

"Ach, that's gabshite," I scoffed. "You're a tinker like me."

"You never know, Connor. Brannon's Granda could be right. You both could have the blood of the Tuatha De Danann in you. After all, you are cousins."

Brannon stopped in his tracks in a patch of tawny reed spires used for thatching roofs. He pulled one out by the roots and shook the dirt at me. "He's not my cousin."

"Now, Brannon, I know this is a surprise, but Connor is your cousin."

"No, he's not. The sea took Da's brother, and Ma was an only child."

"Molly was adopted, but she was not an only child. She had a brother, and Connor is his son."

"Why didn't she tell me?" He dropped the reed spire at his feet.

"You need to ask her, for that is a sad story. Besides, your da didn't want you to know about your tinker roots, and Molly wanted to forget."

Brannon looked me up and down. "He doesn't look like me."

"Indeed, he is your opposite, but he is your blood." Kieran took a coin and held it between his thumb and forefinger. Sunlight reflected off the metal in a reddish glow. "Have you ever heard the expression two sides of the same coin?"

"Oh aye, Granda always said life and death are two sides of the same coin," Brannon said.

"And I heard Etain say that rewards and punishments are two sides of the same coin. Both are used to make a child mind, but neither works very well," I said.

"True enough, but look at it. Tell me what you see?" Kieran placed it in my palm.

"It's a shilling," I said, looking at it carefully and wondering what I could be missing. "Minted in 1925. A coat of arms. A crowned lion, standing on top of a crown. King George and some words in Latin."

"What do you see, Brannon?" Kieran said.

I passed the coin to Brannon, who turned it over a few times and rolled the edge along his palm. "The same as Connor, two sides and one round edge."

"Exactly, but to understand the two-sided coin, it's important first to consider the similarities. I once knew two boys," Kieran said, slowing his speech to match the rhythm of our steps as we hiked along a cow path. "Like you two, they were cousins. One boy, Aiden, was dark-haired, blue-eyed, and had cheeks rosy with health, and the other, Alex, had sandy-colored hair, green eyes, and pale skin. But he was as robust as the first.

"Aiden loved the water and could outswim any in the village. Alex could run faster than anyone who challenged him.

"They were rivals in everything and constantly competed to see who could catch the most fish, trap the most hares, or hold his breath the longest. They tied in all but running or swimming. Some said they were two sides of the same coin. But, if you looked closely at each side, the differences that marked them were there. For that, they loved and hated each other. One day friends, and the next day enemies. It didn't help that they both fell in love with the same girl."

I thought of Tara and what I would do if I had to fight for her.

"Caitlin was no stranger to them, just the little girl that followed them everywhere. One summer, they saw her singing and dancing in the early morning sun. Her hair, usually braided, hung free, and her dress showed the woman she was to be. The boys were wasp-bitten at the sight of her. The sting of young love clouded their eyes but not their competitive nature. They followed the poor girl day and night, each boy doing his best to get her attention.

"One day, they cornered her and demanded that she choose between them. She said, 'I'll have neither, the way you've been behaving. Go away and don't return until you have learned that I'm not a trophy to be won.'

"Both boys left the town. Alex apprenticed with a banker in the city, and Aiden became a fisherman. Both prospered using their gifts.

"One Christmas, Alex returned to the village and met Aiden in the pub. For a while, they shared stories. Aiden told of Caitlin's marriage to a nearby farmer. Both drank to the red-haired girl and childhood friend.

"Bitter cold nights are often under the full moon, and Aidan offered Alex a ride home. When they neared the village, they heard cries for help. An old man flagged them down."

Kieran stopped to drink water from a flask he had pulled from his pack. He offered the flask to Brannon, who shook his head.

I took a sip and handed it back to Kieran. "What happened next?"

With an amused glint in his eye, Kieran took another long draught. "The man's son and daughter-in-law had taken the boat to visit her brother, who had a fever, but their boat capsized close to the harbor. The men could see the overturned boat bobbing in the water from the road.

"Alex ran to the harbormaster to get torches while Aiden went to bring his fishing boat around. Huffing and puffing, the harbormaster returned with Alex, who still could outrun anyone around.

"Aidan waited for them to board, tacked the sail, and, catching the wind, steered the boat out. Within moments, they came upon the overturned craft where a man clung for his life. Just off the port, they saw a glimmer of white clinging to the broken mast. Aiden dove into the black water without thought for his own well-being while Alex and the harbormaster pulled the man into the boat.

"Aiden's powerful strokes cut through the water. He knew he had only minutes before the chill would take his strength. He reached the woman, pulled her to the side of the craft, and, with Alex's help, lifted her onto the deck."

"Caitlin," I said.

"Yes." Kieran smiled and turned to Brannon, who stood looking down from the hilltop near Evan's home. The smoke from the chimney reached into the clouds, darkening with the setting sun. Someone was walking into the barn. Brannon's da. "What would have happened if these two cousins hadn't worked together?"

"I don't have a cousin," Brannon said, "and if I did, it wouldn't be someone the likes of him."

Brannon raced ahead, slipping in the mud, and sliding to the base of the hill on his bottom. Before we could reach him, Brannon had picked himself up. With his pants drooping with muck, he limped toward the barn.

Chapter Twelve

Brannon

In the barn, two wooden rain barrels and an old door placed on top served as Granda's bier. Flickering light from the oil lanterns cast wraithlike shadows on the cedar walls and rafters. Boughs of evergreen and holly decorated the walls.

I stood silently with Kieran and Connor at the foot of the bier. Shena and some neighboring women had just finished washing Granda's body and shaving off his beard. His face looked younger and barely resembled the man I knew as Granda. It was a blessing that Granda's face had been untouched by the fire that scarred most of his upper body, now covered in a linen shroud. His blackened hands, once strong and fleshy, clutched a crucifix. One of the women set it between his fingers. Da replaced the cross with a clay pipe freshly stuffed with tobacco. He sprinkled snuff over the sheet and sat on the chair vacated by Shena, who had been keeping watch.

Kieran nudged me to go closer. My boots crunching on the dry rushes covering the floor disturbed the blessed silence. The wind sighed, a couple of goats rustled the hay, and the pigeons keened softly in the rafters. It would be my last chance to be alone with my granda before the townsfolk arrived for the wake.

Taking another pipe from his pocket, Da filled and lit it. Sweet tobacco mingled with the musk of goats, rushes, and straw.

"Granda," I began when the barn door opened.

Evan's oldest boy, Flynn, came running through the door with a steaming mug of tea in his hand. "From your missus." He passed the half-full cup of tea to Da. Flynn must have spilled a fair bit of tea as he ran from the house to the barn. A whisky bottle bulged from Flynn's coat pocket.

"I heard the keening coming from Peter's house when I was coming home with Da," Flynn said. "A terrible sound it was. Screaming and crying. Are they coming here, too?"

"Hell, I ain't got money for keening women, Flynn," Da said before sipping the tea. "But there'll be singing tonight. There'll be lots of singing and stories. Now hand me that flask you've got there in your pocket. I'll need it, and your da will do more than just barge you if he catches you drinking up his poteen. Run along now. Folks will be coming soon, and Brannon here needs a few moments with his granda."

As Da filled the cup to the rim, I caught a whiff of the vanilla-scented moonshine whisky. He offered the cup to me.

I grimaced and shook my head, still remembering the burning when I'd snuck a sip of the raw, stiff brew at Christmas.

An icy wind gathered around us as the door opened again. The barn began to fill with people. I wasn't ready to say goodbye, but I had to stand aside so others could pay their respects before taking a seat on the fresh green sods and hay. I wished everyone would go away so I could be alone with Granda.

Ma came to stand beside me, bringing the scent of roses into the dank barn. She took my hand in hers while Da interlaced his fingers in her other hand. Evan stood shoulder to shoulder with Da on his other side. Kieran moved to stand with Connor at the back of the barn.

"Bloody Taigs." The room grew silent as Da's words echoed throughout the barn. Ma stiffened, dropped my hand, and pulled her hand away from Da's. I knew Evan's moonshine fired Da's anger.

"Don't be thinking that now," Evan whispered. "There'll be plenty of time for that later. We'll set things right. You'll see. Right now, it's Molly and Brannon who need you."

Gathering Ma in his arms, Da drew her to his chest. "I didn't mean you, Molly. You know that." He had hurt her, yet she still came to him, warm against his body. This, I knew, was love. She would do the keening for him and cry Da's tears. She would weep for me too.

"C'mon, everyone," Evan said. "Fill your glasses and have some meat and bread. Take a seat. The old scallywag will haunt us if we don't give him a sending-off fit for a king, and wasn't he always reminding us of his royal heritage? Aye, and weren't we all jealous of old Fergus Mac Lir, kin to Manannan, the lord of Tir na nOg himself? Isn't that right, Seamus? Weren't you there with Fergus when he looked upon the sea-god's face?"

"Aye, I was, and it scared the living bejaysus out of me, I tell you. Damn near pissed meself that day, and I haven't set me foot in water since. I became a landlubber and took to farming cows." Seamus shuffled through the rushes and stood by Evan's side. "Now, do you want to hear a tale that will straighten the curls in your hair?"

"Oh, aye," everyone roared.

"It's a mighty fine story and tells of the brave character of our dear Fergus here. May his soul rest for the telling." Seamus stood leaning on his knobstick.

"Tell it right, Seamus. None of that malarkey," Brady said.

"What's the point of a story without some of the good stuff?" Loman asked.

"You both can set me right at any time," Seamus winked.

Da took a seat beside Ma on a bale of hay. I hoped Seamus' story would make her smile. Seamus could spin a yarn like no one else, and by the end, you'd believe it all to be true, even if it wasn't.

After taking a long puff on his pipe, Seamus settled on the chair beside Granda's body. "Now, Fergus here was always boasting that his ancestors, the Mac Lirs, were an old Irish family that hailed back to the old man, Manannan himself. That was why they fished. For many generations, the blood in their veins ran as salty as the Irish Sea. Manannan's gifts saved us when the potatoes turned black, so it was always on Fergus's mind to meet the old god himself and say, 'I'm one of your kin. Remember that on the last day, when I come calling on you in the Land of Youth.' He never thought that day would come so soon. I warn you now to be careful what you ask for because it may be given to you when you least expect it."

How true, I thought. I'd never dreamed Manannan would take Peter so soon to Tir na nOg.

"Well, it was a fine day when Fergus and I set sail to catch the herring. The sky and the sea were the same blue. I swore it felt like we were sailing on the sky.

"Ten boats set sail that day, chasing the herring. There were wagers about and bets on who would catch the most fish. A bunch of braggarts, the lot of us. We meant no harm as we hauled in our nets full of fish. Brady over here boasted that he was a better fisher than Manannan himself. His da cuffed him behind the ear and said, 'Don't be calling or talking about Manannan that way. Are you crazy?' We all laughed. The day was bright, the fishing grand, and the future was ours.

"It was Fergus who smelled the change in the air. Then the wind dropped. We were out further than we had ever sailed before. The clear sky and the fishing made us fearless, so the change took us by surprise. Ah, but the stillness was frightening.

"We had none of them fancy engines in those days, just the power of the sails, so we sat and waited for an hour for the wind, but during that time, there was a change on the horizon where the sky met the sea. The blue sky grayed and turned to an angry black. Some of us started dipping our oars, thinking it was better than waiting for what was coming our way.

"The storm came fast, and with it came a gale so fierce it tore our sails as we raced to trim them."

Evan nudged William with his elbow. "Sounds like us just a few days ago, right, William?"

"Aye, one of the worst we've ever fought," he said.

Ashamed, I looked down and rubbed my aching hand between the thumb and first finger. I wished I hadn't called the wind that caused the storm. It came close to killing Da and Evan.

"Oh, it was even mightier than that one," Seamus said. "Two boats spun before they could hold their sails, and the boom hit Loman on the head and knocked him senseless. His brother grabbed him before he fell overboard, but the monstrous waves struck their boat broadside. The boat tipped, spilling all on board and their catch into the sea.

"By some miracle, we pulled them out of the water, Fergus, and me. We fought to control our boats as the wind and the waves herded us together. We were touching port to starboard when we saw Manannan's horses raise their heads from an enormous wave.

"At that moment, the wind stopped, and the eeriest mist settled around us. We were afraid for Brady, who began to babble that he knew Manannan had come to deal with him for bragging. Brady's da managed to silence him. It was a good thing because those magnificent horses, harnessed with strings of pearls glistening against their sea-foam coats, were moving toward us.

"The large swell proved not to be a wave but Manannan's boat Wave Sweeper. The steeds galloped beside us for a moment, then sped ahead to block any retreat. Those beasts with fiery eyes surrounded our boats. Someone yelled, 'Don't look into their eyes, or they'll steal your soul. Look away! Look away!'

"Wave Sweeper glided toward us, and standing on the prow was the god himself, arms crossed with his thick white hair swept back from his brow. That day, he had his court with him, and their finery glistened in the colors of the sea: turquoise, blue, and green.

"When he came close, he stopped and bellowed, 'Now, who is the greatest fisherman? I've caught all of you and your hard-earned catches, too. Now I'll take back what's mine.'

"He raised his staff, and just as he lowered it, Fergus called out to the great sea-god, 'Why punish us all for the foolishness of one man?'

"Fergus didn't know what made him so fearless. I guess it must have been the injustice that made him bold, like that day he put the run on them, cold-hearted Taig boys, the O'Douls, when they beat me up for my few pounds of Saturday night drinking money. He took them on and got neither a scratch nor a bruise for the effort. One went away with both eyes blackened and the other with a sore head."

"But what about Manannan, the boats, Wave Sweeper, and those white horses?" Flynn jumped up from his perch on the guardrail of the goat's pen.

"Pookas," I said. I felt Ma's cool hand take my hot one. I

wanted to tell her I was sick, and my hand ached to my shoulder, but I didn't dare interrupt the story. It was for Granda.

A deep murmur spread through the barn. Then, when all was silent again, Seamus continued.

"Manannan looked Fergus straight in the eye. He was so close that Fergus could see right up his nostrils. 'Who are you?' The sea-god asked.

"'I am Fergus Mac Lir, a son of the sea, and I have a wife and babes to feed, and I have never wronged you.'

"Manannan looked at him for a moment. 'You speak the truth.' Then Manannan laughed, and his laugh rocked our boats together, but before we could puncture each other's hulls, he said, 'Be off with you, Mac Lir, and give your wife a kiss for me, and tell her that the Fisher King has provided dinner this day.'

"A mighty breaker picked up our boat and carried it to the shore. By the time the others arrived home, Fergus and I had sold our catch for the best price. We had such a celebration that night."

"What happened to the others?" Shena asked.

"Oh, they made it back home. Manannan left the fishers half their catch in honor of Fergus Mac Lir for saving their lives. But Brady and I never sailed again. We didn't want to meet Manannan until it was our time to go to the Land of Youth."

Everyone in the barn cheered, shouted praises, and applauded. After the roar died down, Da stood up, and, with Brady beside him playing the tin whistle and Seamus on the bodhran, he sang,

"I'm a Mac Lir, a son of the sea.
My life is me own, so a fisher I'll be.
The smell of salt brine is a balm for my soul.
Hard work on me boat
Keeps me off of the dole.

Hey ho, I sing to the sea,
To the bearded old god who waits for me.
When the fates turn the tide,
and he offers a ride,
In Tir na nOg, I'll bide.

When the spuds got the blight,
It was a dark night.
Me loved ones got sick, and all died.
So, I took to the sea and offered me life.
But it wasn't me time, so I cried.

Hey ho, I sing to the sea,
To the bearded old god who waits for me.
When the fates turn the tide,
and he offers a ride,
In Tir na nOg, I'll bide."

As the last notes of the tin whistle and the rumble of the bodhran died away, everyone raised a glass of whiskey in a silent toast to Fergus Mac Lir, son of the sea. This time I drank and let the burning whiskey choke my cries.

Chapter Thirteen

Brannon

Someone rattled pots and pans, or was it the wind tossing them around outside? What was that fluttering against the window? The wings of a giant bird? Moths?

"He's burning up," Etain said. Her voice sounded far away.

The damp cloth placed over my forehead felt cool.

"Connor, go tie down the flap," Kieran said.

Someone shook the bed. No, it was me, shivering so hard my teeth chattered, and my legs and arms flayed this way and that. Strong hands held me until the trembling stopped. Sinking back to the softness beneath me, I tried to speak—words formed in my mind but not on my lips.

"Open your eyes, Brannon," Kieran said, but I couldn't open them. Even though my eyes were stuck shut, I could still see. A light shone in the distance. I smelled frankincense and heard chanting. A bell chimed, deep tones, dingdong, dingdong.

The tolling lulled me away from the wind, the voices in the room, and the cool cloth. A stone archway appeared before me. Stepping through, I followed a cobblestone path dusted with a thin layer of snow. The oaken door to a friary was open. The haze of incense lingered in the light cast by burning torches affixed to the stone walls. Chanting droned from deep within the abbey.

I stepped inside. A procession of brown-robed monks chanted evening vespers as they marched past me by candlelight. One monk, the smallest one, peered out from behind his hood and winked.

"Peter? Is that you?"

The novice took a different turn than the rest of the monks and motioned for me to follow him up the winding staircase inside the bell tower.

I counted thirty-three steps leading into the circular room that housed the chapel bell. The hooded figure pulled the rope. The bells clanged, dingdong, dingdong.

When the final clang faded, the young monk's hood fell back to reveal the long snout of a seahorse. Skeletal rings of bone-like armor protected the transparent face where blue eyes fixed on mine. The voice, when it spoke, sounded like Granda. "From the sea, they come, and to the sea, they must return."

My screams ricocheted off the bell. Discordant sounds resonated through the stones, my body, and layers of awakening.

Someone was shaking me and yelling in my ear. "Wake up and quit screaming like a wee baby." Connor's breath reeked of tobacco and fish stew.

After rubbing my eyes, caked with dried tears and grit, I looked up at the bow-topped, wood-and-canvass roof towering above me.

An assortment of cooking utensils hung from the ceiling. Woven tapestries depicting the seacoast, rolling hills dotted with thatched cottages, and a lake cradled in a valley of purple heather hung on the wall. I had never seen such beautiful wall hangings. At the opposite end of the wagon was a door framed by two small windows adorned with ruffled curtains. A wood-burning stove stood in the corner. Except for the smell of kerosene from the lantern and fish stew lingering in the air, the wagon looked clean. Granda's words of warning echoed in my mind as clearly as his words in the bell tower. 'Stay out of them dirty barrel-bodied dens, or you'll end up with a hole in your pocket and a curse on your soul.'

I felt the bandage on my hand. Sadness followed the memory of how the splinter came to be there.

"They thought you might die from a blood infection. Who'd of thought a wee splinter could kill you." Connor sat on a wooden stool by the bed. He leaned into the light of the kerosene lamp, and with a small knife, he carved a piece of wood. His curly locks bobbed up and down with each stroke of his blade. "You've been sleeping for days. Before that, you were puking and shitting your pants. The smell of it was bleeding awful."

"Shut your gob. You're lying." My face flushed.

Connor pointed the tip of his knife at me. "Don't start it."

I wondered, would Connor dare hit me or stab me with the knife? For a moment, we glared at each other. To my relief, Etain came into the wagon, and Connor quickly hid the knife in the palm of his hand. She picked a bowl up off the floor and shook it at Connor. "You ate his stew. You ate all of it. You wee cowbeg."

Connor shrugged. "I had a mouth on me, and I couldn't see the stew going to waste, and I didn't think he was gonna wake up today."

She thrust the bowl at Connor. "Take it and see if Tara's ma has some stew to spare, and you better be hoping she does. Get before I give you a slap."

Connor pocketed his knife. He placed his carving on the table before stomping out of the wagon with the bowl in hand. Etain picked up the carving and rubbed the fine wooden particles from the surface with her thumb before placing it back on the table.

"Hmm. A horse? It's got scales, though." She sat on the bed.

"A seahorse," I said.

"You might be right, part horse, part fish." She placed her warm hand against my brow. "You look as pale as a bled gander. How do you feel?"

"Hungry."

"Good. You gave us a fright. You did. Burning up and delirious. That splinter in your finger festered and gave you the blood fever."

My finger throbbed. I wondered if it would hurt forever.

"Do you remember anything? You were so very ill."

"Not much," I said. Thinking back, I recalled the clip-clop of the horse-drawn wagons and two funerals happening at the same time. One wagon carried Granda and the other Peter. There was keening from one side of Knocklayde Mountain and silence on the other. It was a gray day with a mist that wouldn't burn off, lying low and thick. I remembered dragging my feet behind the wagon, my ma holding me up, almost pulling me along. And I remembered falling and the mist-drenched cobblestones rising toward me. That's it. That's all I could remember. I hoped Etain wouldn't remind me I'd shit my pants.

She bent and gathered the wood shavings from Connor's carving into her hand, opened the door, and threw them outside the wagon. "I'll see what's taking that boy. Get yourself dressed. Your clothes are in that drawer there beneath the bed."

I removed the wool nightshirt that someone had dressed me in and changed back into my clothes, which smelled like lavender and cedarwood. After dressing, I sat at the small table near the stove and examined Connor's carving. I remembered my da's words of warning when I captured the tiny seahorse on my birthday and threw it back into the ocean. Maybe it had died when I threw it back in the water. Maybe such terrible things had happened to me because Manannan was angry.

Etain returned with a bowl of lamb stew spiced with rosemary and sage. And soda bread thick with butter and jam. My stomach growled.

"Polly's stew is the best in the entire land, and her soda bread will melt in your mouth. By the gods, that woman can cook."

While Etain stripped the bed of its linens, I ate in silence.

"Now that you're feeling better, you can share Connor's wagon and help him with the horses."

"He doesn't like me." I scraped the last of the stew from the bowl. I wished I could have a second helping.

"Ah, don't let him scare you. Connor doesn't care much for anyone except himself, Kieran, and maybe Tara. He's sweet on her, but he'll never tell you so."

"Where's Ma and Da?"

"Molly was here until your fever broke, then went with William to find work and a new home. Your Ma and Da want you to stay with us for a while. They worry about your safety and want you to stay hidden. A good idea, considering all that's happened."

Etain folded the blankets and placed them on the feather mattress. "Now run along and find Connor. Ask him to show you the horses. You two have more in common than you know."

I stepped from the wagon and disturbed a flock of ash-gray hoodie crows feeding on a bed of mollusks. The crows' raucous cries echoed off a cliff opposite the edge of the camp. The earthy smell of burning peat hovered over the campsite.

Perched on a step of the neighboring wagon, a girl about my age, with braided reddish-gold hair, embroidered a piece of linen draped over her knees. I drew close enough to see a border of yellow and blue flowers.

"Do you know where Connor is?" I asked.

She looked up, cocked her head to the side, and blinked her pale greenish-brown eyes. "You're the sick boy." She bit the end of a thread.

"I'm better now. Name's Brannon."

"I know." She folded up her linen and placed it in her sewing bag.

I turned to leave, but she fell into step behind me. "I'm Tara. Did you like Ma's stew?"

"Can you cook as good as herself?" I thought about asking her if there was more.

Tara wrinkled her nose. "I hate cooking and sewing too."

"You won't make a good wife then."

"I don't really care. I'm going to be an actress, and I'm going to write stories. If I'm famous, I won't have to cook or clean. I might even go to America. I've earned lots of money dancing and singing at the fairs."

Now that I thought about it, she looked familiar. I'd seen her dancing at the fair the day I met Etain. "What will you write about?"

"Let's see. I guess I'll write about people I know and people I make up. Maybe I'll write a story about you."

"That wouldn't be much of a story."

"Connor said you did something awful."

"Whatever that liar said is not true." I stopped and walked in the opposite direction. She followed me.

"I don't really believe him, silly. Connor always tells lies, and I know he doesn't like you, so of course, he will say nasty things about you. You don't look like you could hurt a flea. Am I right?"

I wished she would buzz off. She was like a fly in my face. "Where are we?"

"Outside Ballycastle, near Ballintoy. Don't you know? You've been sick almost a week, not waking up for days and days."

I dropped my bag and sat on a stump by the remains of the campfire. My legs felt weak, and my head was dizzy.

"You don't look so good," she said.

"Where's Connor's wagon? Etain told me I have to share with him."

"Over there." She pointed to a grove of birch trees, partially hiding Connor's wagon. "Connor won't want to share his wagon with you."

"Why does Connor have his own wagon?"

"It's his da's, but he's been gone a long time. Many years now. It's just as well. No one likes him, not even Connor. C'mon, I'll show you where he goes when he's feeling grumpy."

"What's he mad about?"

"You silly. I told you that already."

She led me into a meadow full of damp, wind-flattened grass. The tinker's herd of horses, stocky and docile, with thick manes and tails, grazed on a nearby hill. Near the ruins of a monastery, overgrown with long grasses, nettles, and heather, Connor groomed a mare, a black and white piebald. Tara called and waved at him. He looked at us as we approached, then went back to work, smoothing the horse's flanks with his hand.

"I know this place." I stumbled on the broken stones that led through an ivy-covered stone archway. Beyond were the steps that led to the top of the bell tower. I felt stupid when Tara reached down to help me up. When I brushed off my trousers, I saw a tiny hole in the knee.

"Have you been here before then?" Tara asked.

"In a dream, but it was different. Now the walls are crumbling. There was a bell tower and a seahorse—"

"A seahorse in the bell tower?" Connor scoffed.

"It was a dream," I said. "Sometimes dreams give me messages and warnings. You were sitting by my bed carving a seahorse."

"Keep your hands off my stuff," Connor dropped a wide-toothed comb into his bag and slung it over his shoulder.

"I didn't touch your seahorse." I wanted to punch him.

"Then why were you dreaming about it?"

"Why were you carving one?" I said as snottily as I could.

"Smartass." Connor threw his bag down and clenched his fists.

I braced myself, even though I knew I was in no shape to fight him and win.

Tara came between us and twisted her finger in the mare's mane. "Etain wants you to show Brannon the horses. She says he's supposed to help you with them."

"I don't need help with the horses." Connor picked a stone out of the ground with his shoe, picked it up, and threw it over my head.

I ducked. "You stupid eejit, you could have hit me."

"If I'd wanted to hit you, I would have."

"Brannon, this is Epona." She patted the mare's neck. "She's Connor's favorite. Right, Connor?"

"Aye, she's special to me," Connor said.

"Will she foal soon?" I asked.

"She's got at least a month to go." The horse whinnied. I stepped back. "Scared of 'em now, are you?" Connor patted Epona on her flanks and sent her trotting off to join the rest of the herd.

I looked out over the field. I wasn't sure if I feared horses, but since Peter's death, I felt uneasy around them, and the black one that strayed into the center of the ruins to graze had a white tuft over its eyes, like the one that had trampled Peter. The scene flashed before me. I heard Peter's scream, the horse's whinny, and the awful thud.

"Well, are you?" Connor said, demanding an answer.

"No, why should I be?"

"Liar."

"I'm not lying."

"Show me," Connor said. "Ride one."

"He doesn't have to prove anything to you, Connor," Tara said.

Connor pursed his lips. "He does if he's gonna help me with the horses. He could get his head kicked in if he doesn't do things right. I ain't gonna work with no Ginny Ann, so you might as well help Tara with her sewing."

Maybe Connor was right? I was scared. The last thing I wanted to do was to ride one. Not now. Not ever. I would have to find another way to impress Connor. "I bet you can't call one of 'em to you."

"Sure, I can. The herd follows me when I call as if I am the lead stallion."

"I mean without making a sound. Focus your mind on one and get only that one to come, with the power of your thoughts."

"You can't do that, can you?" Tara's eyes grew wide.

"No one can do that," Connor said.

"I can, without making a sound."

"Go on outta that," Connor said with a frown.

"Let him try, Connor," Tara said.

"I'll believe it when I see it," Connor said. "Get on with it, then. What are you waiting for? Which one?"

"Epona."

"Good luck. Epona won't come to you. She only comes to me."

Making a horse come couldn't be more difficult than calling the wind, could it? With my eyes closed, I recreated the image of Epona in my mind, but all I could see was the black one with the white tufts. I fingered the talisman hidden in my pocket. Could I use it just one more time? Just to make Connor like me?

No. Not without the sword. The Lady's voice sounded in my mind, not in my ears. I opened my eyes and saw The Lady I'd seen at the Bonamargy Friary standing before me. *No,* she said again.

But it was too late. The horses were stampeding toward

us. Tara screamed, and Connor grabbed my arm and pulled me inside the bell tower until the horses stopped among the ruins.

"Did you see The Lady?" I hoped I had impressed him, but he was angrier than ever and pushed me up against a stone slab. "You stupid eejit. You're not so smart after all. Don't you know you could have killed us by calling the entire herd?"

"What, lady?" Tara asked.

"The one in the white dress," I said as I dodged Connor's fist.

"I ought to pound your head soft as shite," he said. "Don't you know anything? You never treat a horse like that. It's as cruel as the whip to break a horse's trust and friendship."

I felt ashamed. My bragging had almost caused more harm, and somehow The Lady from the friary heard me. That frightened me even more than the stampeding horses or Connor's fist. I pushed past Connor and stepped from the bell tower. The black stallion with the white tuffs over its eyes snorted and pawed the ground. I backed up.

"Malachy won't hurt you. None of our horses are mean," Connor said.

"We've got to get the horses," Tara said. "Looks like a storm is brewing. The horses are spooked now."

"There, boy," Connor said to Malachy as he stroked his nose before mounting him and riding out to bring the rest of the herd home. The horses followed Malachy, and they all came except Epona. "I'll be back for her," Connor said. "Keep an eye on her. She's acting strange now."

Polly's stew felt like a rock in my gut. Had I called the storm along with the horses? Maybe. I couldn't be sure, but

Tara was right. It was going to be nasty. Bitter too, and from the north. The rain fell, a drizzle at first, but I could tell by the wind that the worst was still to come.

A flash of lightning forked overhead. Thunder rumbled in the distance. Epona paced in a circle, switching her tail, groaning, and looking back toward her flank. After pawing the ground, she lay down and rolled onto her side. A moment later, she struggled to stand but lay back on the ground. Her breathing was labored, her mouth open, struggling for air.

"I think she's going to foal," Tara said. "Stay with her. I'll get Connor and some blankets."

I knelt by the mare's side and prayed to Manannan that nothing horrible would happen. Babies came early sometimes. That didn't mean the foal would die. Did it? The rain came down in sheets. I shivered with the cold, and my finger throbbed. I felt in my pocket for the talisman. No, no. I'd made too many mistakes. The mare was sweating, droplets beading on her neck and chest. Hurry Connor. Hurry, I said over and over to myself as I waited. The wait couldn't have been more than five minutes, but it felt like an hour.

"Not yet. It's too soon," Connor shouted and pushed me aside. He took Epona's reins and tried to coax her to stand, but she wouldn't budge.

Then her water broke in a great swoosh. The foal's hooves were visible. There would be no stopping the birth now. Within minutes, the foal appeared, nose first, wedged between the front legs. A few minutes later, the foal's hips came, and Epona pushed it the rest of the way out, still encased in the birth sack.

Connor removed it and checked to ensure the umbilical cord was attached. It was, but there was also a lot of blood.

Thunder cracked overhead. The wind blew stronger. "Jaysus," Connor hissed through his teeth. "She's going to bleed out. I think we'll lose her and the foal too." Connor's eyes shone with fear as he felt the chest behind the foal's elbow for a heartbeat.

"It's slow, too slow." Connor positioned the foal's head downward to drain the fluid and clear its airways. He gently squeezed out more fluid by pressing his thumb and forefinger along the top of the nostrils toward the muzzle. Then, Connor tickled the foal's muzzle with a piece of grass to stimulate the foal's breathing. When that didn't work, he rubbed the foal vigorously with a blanket. Once again, Connor checked the heartbeat. He shook his head. "Nothing."

He closed off one nostril with his hand and blew into the other nostril, but the foal remained limp. He tried again. The rib cage rose and went back down. Up, down. Up, down. I was sure Connor would breathe for it forever if need be. He wasn't going to let the foal die. He blew again and again into the horse's nostril. The foal coughed and after a few weak kicks, it was breathing on its own.

Sighing with relief, I glanced at Tara, who wiped away her tears and placed her hands on the mare's abdomen as if she could stop the bleeding, as if there could be two miracles today.

Nothing I could do but watch as sleet mixed with rain added to the day's misery. The mare would die, and it would be my fault. I prayed, please save her as I rubbed the talisman between my fingers. Out of nowhere, The Lady from the friary appeared before me again. The sapphire felt warm in my palm. I let it fall to the bottom of my pocket.

My people were good with horses, she said. *Horses and sheep.*

Who were your people? I wanted to ask, but The Lady turned and knelt beside Tara. She placed her hands over Tara's and whispered strange words. Tara closed her eyes and whispered the same words as The Lady.

Epona raised her head to rest her muzzle in Connor's hand. He brushed tears from his eyes and leaned his head on hers. Epona's chest no longer labored up and down. It's the end, I thought, as The Lady took her hands away and stood. She placed her hand on Tara's head for a moment, and Tara opened her eyes. She turned to look, but The Lady had already disappeared into the mist rising from the ground.

I moved closer, and just as I was about to say sorry, Epona whinnied, raised her head and tried to stand. Tara and Connor scrambled to stand and back away to give the mare room. The umbilical cord broke. Epona leaned down and nudged her foal until it fought to stand on wobbly legs.

Connor hooted and Tara flung her arms around his neck and hugged him.

"Did you see her?" I asked. I wanted them to know that I had helped, too.

"See who?" Connor asked.

"The Lady. She had her hands over Tara's. If I hadn't called on her, Epona would have died. It's a miracle."

"I didn't think she would live. Not after a bleed like that,"

Connor said before turning toward me and raising his fist. "But just because you can make fire from nothing doesn't mean you can do miracles."

I backed away. "It wasn't me. It was The Lady. Tell him, Tara."

"I don't know what you're talking about," she said.

"He's talking gabshite again." Connor picked up the foal. "Bring Epona. We must get them warm, dry, and out of this blasted storm."

What could I do? I had almost killed their horses. They hated me now. Blood or no, I didn't belong with the tinkers. I would have to leave. Ballycastle wasn't that far away. Anyway, I had a plan. A plan that would make things right again.

Chapter Fourteen

Connor

After tending the horses, I was grateful to come out of the cold and into the warmth of Etain's wagon. I leaned over the stove and rubbed my hands together. The smell of apples and cinnamon filled the room. "The foal is nursing and getting stronger. I think they'll both be all right now, no thanks to Brannon."

"Catch yourself on, Connor." Etain poured me a mug of apple cider. "You know he's still grieving."

"What's with the kid, anyway? The bragging little gack says he can summon the wind." I took my cup of cider and sat beside Tara and Kieran at the table.

"He tried to call Epona and made the entire herd go crazy," Tara added. "No one can do that, can they?"

"No, not usually." Kieran broke a biscuit and dipped it into his cider. "But Brannon is special."

I pounded the table with my fist. "I'd like to deck that special eejit. He almost killed us, Epona and the foal, with his stupid tricks."

"Connor, mind yourself." Etain cuffed me on the back of the head.

"But he kept saying he saw a woman put her hands over Tara's to heal Epona. You know he's lying."

Etain dropped a spoon on the table. She had that look that scared me when I was a child. The look that said something wasn't right.

"And did you see her too, Tara?" Etain asked.

"No." Tara tightened her hands around her mug. "But I felt something."

"No, you didn't." I slammed the mug down on the table. "Why are you sticking up for him?"

"I'm not sticking up for him. I felt something." She glared with all the ferocity of her amber hair.

"By the gods, everyone's going nuts around here. Brannon's seeing ghosts, and you're feeling them." I picked up my mug and downed the rest of the cider in one gulp.

"Let her speak." Etain brushed a curl from Tara's flushed cheek. "Tell me more."

"I didn't see her, but I felt something touch my hands. Cold at first, then very warm." She picked up her mug and placed it back down without a sip.

"Go on," Etain urged her. "You felt her touch and—"

"I heard her speak." She fidgeted with the folds of her sweater, drawing it tightly across her chest.

"Jaysus, you know you didn't," I bristled. Tara had never shown a talent for such gifts or even the slightest bit of interest in it. If there was a voice to be heard, I should have been the one to hear it, not Tara.

"Connor," Kieran said. "None of that now. You, of all people, know how hard this is." He placed a hand on Tara's arm. "Tell me, what did you hear?"

"A voice in my mind said, 'I will show you how to heal.' A halo of light surrounded my hands. It felt like my hands were her hands as I held them over Epona's belly. In my mind, I saw the rupture and the blood gushing out. Then the miracle happened. She sewed the tissue together with a needle and thread made of light. Within moments, the bleeding stopped. Who is she?"

Kieran glanced at Etain before speaking. "I can't say for sure. Perhaps Brannon knows. Where is he?"

"I saw him walking toward the beach." I reached for the ladle to refill my mug with cider. "He'll come home when he's hungry."

"He's not a dog," Tara said.

"I didn't say he was."

"But you made him feel like it was all his fault."

"It was his fault. You were angry with him, too."

Kieran gulped down the rest of his cider and placed the mug on the table. Without another word, he stepped out of the wagon.

"Do you think he's gone to find Brannon?" Tara asked.

"He'll want to hear Brannon's side of things. C'mon.

Let's go. I want to watch Kieran tell the little shit off for making a complete arse of himself."

"Now, Connor, that's none of your business," Etain scolded as we scrambled out of the wagon to follow Kieran.

Chapter Fifteen

Brannon

Some folks were whispering about me, saying that I caused the terrible storms, that I was bad luck. Let them tell their stories. The more fantastic, the better. Then they would have to send me home. Tara was scared of me now, and I couldn't blame Connor for being angry at me. I'd done a stupid thing.

My plan was simple. I would give the sapphire to the sea and sell the pearl. I might even be able to find Faolan, the man who wanted to buy it. Then I could surprise Da with the money.

The path to the shore was steep and slippery with moss. As I stepped between the stones, my boots released the apple-like scent of crushed chamomile. Below the limestone cliffs, sheltered from the wind, I listened to the Atlantic breakers as I watched a steamship in the distance. Maybe it sailed to America. Maybe I could go there one day, where no one knew me or what I'd done.

Someone called my name as I stooped to pick up a fossil, a ribbed spiral-formed ammonite. Squinting against the sun, I saw Kieran walking toward me. I wondered if I would be in trouble with him for calling the horses and using the sapphire. I was sure Connor had given him all the details.

"I love this place. Sometimes I come here to think and clear my head." Kieran picked up a stone and skipped it on the water. "Did you know the Tuatha first set foot in Ireland on this shore?"

I imagined the Tuatha standing on the sand dunes and looking up into the surrounding cliffs, where seabirds lined the ridges. "Granda said they could see the wind and ride the pooka." Suddenly I felt homesick.

"Oh aye, they could," Kieran said.

"Have you ever seen the wind?"

"Can't say as I have. You?"

"Not exactly, but I sometimes feel it and the pooka."

"Are you sure it's the pooka you're feeling?"

"I'm sure." I pulled up my hood to shelter my face from the wind. "The day Peter died, it haunted me as sure as any ghost would on Pooky Night." My throat tightened, choking my words.

"It wasn't your fault, son."

"Yes, it was. I felt it all day. Even Granda felt it because he wanted me to beat up Peter, and I had to stop myself from doing it. That's how the pooka makes you feel, like you want to hurt someone for no reason. When we were racing to the barn, I called the pooka, and Peter's horse suddenly turned and reared. Our horses collided, and he fell under my horse. I didn't think he would die. I killed him and Granda too, all because I called the pooka."

"How do you know it was the pooka?"

"Because I summoned it." I didn't want to talk about it anymore, but Kieran kept asking questions.

"Could it have been an accident? Could something else have spooked the horses?"

"I don't know. I can't remember everything that happened that day or why Peter's horse suddenly reared toward me. Mary was there, but she didn't spook the horse. I know Mary saw something because she said the pooka killed Peter. She said it was my fault."

"What makes you think you could summon the pooka?"

Another question and all I wanted was to run away from Kieran and Connor and all these questions.

I reached into the crane bag and fingered the sapphire, flint, and pearl. I took out the sapphire. "Because of this. Ma said it's magic. I don't want it anymore." I raised my hand to throw it into the ocean.

"Wait." Kieran caught my arm. "Hear what I have to say before you throw it away. Don't fear your gifts. You have touched upon the ways of the old ones, and, like the Tuatha De Danann, you have the power to control the elements, especially the wind. But your talent is raw and unskilled. You must be careful that the elements don't control you."

"How can I do that?" I lowered my arm.

"By becoming one with the elements and not lost within them. Remember, power is intoxicating, and many good men have been led astray by its spell."

Kieran was right. The sapphire had made it possible for me to do things most boys would never think of doing. But I couldn't shake my fear of what it could do or what I could do with it. "I used it and almost killed Epona and her foal."

"It was wrong to call the horses, but Epona's early foaling is a symptom of a sickness in the land. It would have happened anyway. It's the disease that you feel, not the pooka. Haven't you noticed the storms, the leaves rotting before changing color, the sheep's wool spoiled by disease?" Kieran said.

I had seen it. "It's Julia's prophesy."

"Julia?"

"The nun at the Bonamargy Friary."

"Why, yes."

"What can we do to stop it?"

"We can follow the old ways and live in harmony with earth's rhythms. You may be able to call the wind Brannon, but not the pooka. That involves deep magic, which is difficult for even the most experienced person schooled in the old ways. So, I think what happened to Peter was simply an accident."

"I want to believe what you say is true, but—"

"All right then. If you think you have this ability, try summoning the pooka. If you've done it once, you should be able to do it again. Tell me how you did it."

"I don't know exactly. I thought about it, I guess."

Kieran smiled. "A thought only? Do you think the pooka has nothing better to do than come at the thought or mention of its name?"

"You don't believe I can do this, do you?"

"I neither believe nor disbelieve. Go ahead. Summon it. I'd like to see what you are capable of."

I held the talisman before me. "I don't know where to start."

"Think. What did you do before?"

"Well, I didn't call for it like I would call a cat or dog. You see, it happened over time. The night before Peter died, Ma found me drawing in my sleep. She told me to quit drawing them pookas, but I couldn't stop drawing them. There were pictures of horses all over my room. So, I don't know how I did it exactly, only that I know I did."

Kieran knelt, picked up a handful of sand, and let it sift through his fingers. "Then use your talent. Let the seashore be your canvas. But remember, the first law of summoning is to ask first and never force your will on another being."

Kieran sat on a driftwood log to watch while I closed my eyes. I slipped into that place where pictures came, and using my fingers, scored the sand. As easily as drawing with charcoal, I molded the sand to bring the steed to life, its eyes deep, its nostrils flared, and its mane, a cascading crest of waves flowing over its shoulder.

Kieran stood and admired the portrait in the sand, a bas-relief. "Impressive."

"Now, what do I do?"

"Let's see. Can you sculpt its shape with a wave?"

Kieran couldn't be serious. No one could do that. "Water can only hold a form when it is frozen."

"True, but you can shape it like wind shapes clouds," Kieran said. "So, like a potter's wheel is used to mold clay, you can use the wind to spin the water. Now, take the sapphire in hand and visualize the shape of the stallion. See it as it appears in your drawings."

The image of the black horse with fiery eyes came quickly to my mind. How many times had I drawn this same horse prancing among the waves? But how could I make the steed appear in the flesh before me? That stretched my imagination beyond what I believed possible, yet I must have done it the day Peter died. Would the water mold in my hands like clay? I hesitated, afraid that I would fail and yet scared that I would succeed. What if something awful happened again, like when I called the wind for a few apples and almost killed Da and Evan? No, it's too dangerous. I opened my eyes.

"Ask permission," Kieran said.

I'd seen Kieran calm the storm that first night with just a few words, so I closed my eyes and said, "If it be your will, Manannan, let your own come to me."

The wind came from the north as bidden to spin the waves upon earth's wheel. As the water churned, I shaped it with my thoughts. The stallion's muzzle emerged first, spewing a spray of mist from its nostrils. The head came next with ears pressed back and eyes blazing. With each gust, the waves crested, and each trough grew deeper until a white stallion rose fully formed out of one enormous wave. It galloped upon the water with The Lady riding on its back while holding onto its mane.

"It's her," I whispered. "The Lady."

"Is this the horse you've been drawing, Brannon?" Kieran asked.

"No. This horse is white, not black."

"Quite right. That's not the pooka, son. It's Aonbharr." Kieran shook his head in disbelief. He looked as stunned as I felt.

"But… but did I really do this?"

"Indeed, you did, and I have to admit I'm a little more than surprised. Twice I have underestimated your ability. Now, Brannon, I hope you see that it takes more than just a thought or a mention of its name to summon a magical being."

Aonbharr galloped over the breakers until he reached the shore, moving as easily on the sand as on water. He greeted Kieran with a deep bow, lowering his head so Kieran could stroke it. The stallion snorted and blew in his hand.

"Your foster-father sends his greetings," The Lady said. She was as I had seen her at the friary. Her eyes sparkled like the sun skimming across the ocean at sunset.

"Honored one. It's been too long." Kieran held out his hands to lift her down from the horse. As she stepped barefoot onto the sand, I noticed her legs were as skinny as a loon's, just as Peter said.

How The Lady and Kieran knew each other was a mystery. My mind was a whirl of questions.

"Manannan wants you to know that the boy is the answer, but he needs the sword," The Lady said.

"What sword?" I said. "What am I to do with a sword? I'm not a knight."

"Aren't you?" Her voice was like her smile.

"A knight needs a horse." I stroked Aonbharr's muzzle, and he blew into my palm.

"You'll not be having this one," Kieran said.

The sound of pebbles clinking down the cliff face distracted us. We turned and saw Connor watching us from the top of the ridge. Tara was sliding down a gravel path, dislodging rubble, as she hurried toward us.

"The young healer," The Lady said.

"The stallion—it came right out of the water." Tara stopped to catch her breath and curtsied. "My Lady, thank you for helping me heal Epona. Connor would have been heartbroken if she had died."

"You saw her?" I was more than a little miffed with Tara for not sticking up for me. "Why didn't you say so?"

"I'm sorry. I should have told you I felt The Lady and heard her voice. I didn't want to make Connor mad at you." She waved to Connor to join us, but he looked over our heads at a flock of cormorants with wings spread wide, a dark cloud against the setting sun. The Lady gripped the stallion's mane and pulled herself onto its back. The steed whinnied a call of warning.

"Run," The Lady cried.

Throaty honks filled the air as the birds descended to peck at us with their long-hooked beaks. A cormorant pecked at the crane bag hanging from my belt. Swiping at the bird only made it angrier. It flew at my face and landed on my shoulder, digging its sharp claws into my neck. I cried out and felt a thump on my back. Connor knocked the bird off with such force that it lay dead in the sand, its wings spread like a broken fan. After that, the cormorants avoided Connor. They flew around him but didn't light.

Unlike Connor, Kieran drew the birds to him as though he called them. They pecked at his clothes, hair, and face as he mumbled words under his breath. The magic he hoped to conjure against them wasn't working.

One squawking bird entangled itself in Tara's hair. With a sharp tug, it broke free with clumps of hair in its claws.

"To the caves," Connor yelled. "Follow me." He took Tara's hand and ran with her toward the cliffs.

I followed them, but before entering the safety of the sea cave, I searched the ocean for a sign of Aonbharr and The Lady. The cormorants were swarming around them, driving them back into the sea.

"Did you see her this time?" Tara asked Connor, who leaned his back against the cave.

"What? The damn birds?" Connor said.

"No, The Lady riding the horse. It was Aonbharr." I examined my pocket, shredded in ribbons. I rubbed my arm where the cormorants had pecked right through my jacket to my skin.

"Is that true?" Connor asked Kieran, whose cheek dripped blood.

"It is." Kieran dabbed the blood with a linen handkerchief.

"I summoned it," I said proudly.

"And the cormorants too, I bet," Connor scowled at me and turned away.

"Not everything bad is my fault." I clenched my fists. If Connor said just one more thing, I would satisfy my growing fury on his nose. My rage surprised me because it came fast from somewhere deep within me.

"Now, boys. This is not the time to throw blame," Kieran said. "If it's anyone's fault, it's mine for wanting to show Brannon he could not have called a pooka. I've never seen cormorants attack like that before."

"They were scared of Connor," Tara said. "I wonder why?"

Connor pulled his sleeve up to examine the mark, red and swollen around his wrist. "I think it might have something to do with this. It aches straight to the bone."

"What has that got to do with the cormorants?" I had wondered why Connor had the Celtic knot tattooed around his wrist, but was afraid to ask about it until now.

"It happened while exploring the round tower nearby," Connor said proudly. "It's for protection."

So, Connor had more gifts than he recognized.

"Why would cormorants attack us?" Tara asked.

"The birds may have been under some other influence," Kieran explained.

"Like what?" Tara's eyes widened with fear.

"I think the Fomorii came in response to Manannan's horse," Kieran said.

"Manannan banished the Fomorii long ago," Connor said.

I watched Connor pace at the entrance to the cave. I could hear the breakers on the shore, the hiss of pebbles being sucked out to sea, and the occasional cry of a cormorant.

"Banished, not gone," Kieran said. "The truth is, the Fomorii never really left. They were imprisoned."

"Weren't they monsters?" Tara ran her finger through a knot in her hair. "My ma used to say if I didn't behave, I'd end up in the world of the Fomorii, the people of one hand, one foot, or one eye. I used to dream about them when I was little and wake up crying,"

"Not monsters," Kieran said. "They were once a strong and fine-looking race, originally nature gods. They could change their shape at will, most often to a seabird. Sometimes a wolf."

"Moths?" I asked.

Kieran thought for a moment before speaking. "I've never heard of them changing into a moth, but it's possible as they like to choose creatures that fly. Have you seen them in that form?"

"Scores of moths swarmed Peter and me at the Bonamargy Friary when I first saw The Lady," I said.

Kieran was thoughtful for a moment. "The Fomorii were skilled at using nature to their own ends. The plague that affects our crops is an example."

"I've seen moths eating the wool right off the sheep's backs as they graze," I said.

"But the Fomorii were magical, weren't they?" Tara leaned against the cave wall and hugged her knees to her chest for warmth.

"Yes, and no. Some were just farmers. Others had special skills in that they were good at keeping pests away, so grasshoppers would not eat their fields. When they fought, they could use nature as a weapon to make fields of grain rot, animals sick, and pests attack. The Fomorii kept the land in balance, for they understood the earth's cycles. Some years were good. Some were not so good, but they knew the bad times would renew the land. Then the Tuatha came with their fancy tools and worked the land with greater yields even during the rough years."

"Are you saying that the Tuatha were the bad ones, then?" I asked.

"No, this isn't about bad or good. It's about change. Being a master of change doesn't make you bad. When the wind blows hard, the willow survives because it can bend. Rigid trees crack. Does that make the wind bad? No, it's just the wind."

Kieran gathered his wind-tangled hair and twisted it into a knot at the base of his neck. "The Fomorii didn't like change. Their misery was born from that fault. If the old ways were good enough for their ancestors, they were good enough for them. But their lives were harsh, and the elements mastered them at times. If the Fomorii were true students of nature, they would have seen how adaptable to change nature is."

"Why were they banished, then?" I asked.

"Conflict grew when the Tuatha became more successful than the Fomorii. The Fomorii, once the chieftains of Ireland, became servants of the Tuatha to survive. Eventually, they rebelled and attacked. The wars between the two lasted for many years. Even though the Fomorii outnumbered the Tuatha, the Tuatha were wise in the ways of war. With their fields bleeding, their animals driven away, the Fomorii were defeated."

"It doesn't seem right for the Tuatha to have done that to the Fomorii." Tara looked toward the cave's mouth, where the shadow of a bird appeared against the rocks.

"The Fomorii had their faults, too. Some, like their leader Calatin, were magically gifted in the black arts and skilled at mind control. The Tuatha kings, recognizing the Fomorii as the proud and dangerous people they were, knew that nothing short of banishment would stop the further conflict. But even magic decays with time. That's an earth rule: steel rusts, leaves decay, and everything grows old and dies. So, every thousand years, their prison seals must be restored, or the Fomorii will escape their confinement. The Tuatha knew this would happen, and they knew they would need Manannan's sword, wielded by the ones who carried the true blood of the Tuatha, to quash their return. The land's illness is a sign of the breach. You see, the Fomorii never forgave humans for fighting alongside the Tuatha and vowed that people would suffer as they have suffered."

For a moment, I watched the cormorants riding the wind, diving into the water, disappearing under the waves, and resurfacing with fish in their bills. With a quick jerk of the head, they threw the fish up in the air, caught them headfirst, and swallowed them whole. Some birds rested on the rocks with their wings fanned out to dry. Ordinary birds doing what cormorants do. "So, The Lady wants me to find Manannan's sword."

"Not find. Someone must remake the sword, but that's a story for another time. The tide is coming in now. Let's see if we can return to the camp without being attacked. Since the cormorants are afraid of Connor, he should lead the way."

A thin smile formed on Connor's lips as he stepped toward the entrance, peered out, and motioned for us to follow. The sun rippled a pale gold fire on the water's surface, moving closer to the cave with each swell. I shivered. The temperature had dropped with the sun. My breath crystallized before me as I followed Connor up the embankment to the road that led to the camp.

I saw cormorants in every shadow when, in fact, there were none. I looked over my shoulder. Tara was walking so close behind me she kept hitting my heels. I had the urge to push Connor out of the way and run, but I couldn't let him see me acting like a Ginny Ann. I wondered if he, too, felt the evil presence walking beside us, shadowing our steps, without leaving footprints in the sand. It wasn't the pooka. It was something more terrible. If Kieran felt it, he didn't say. He wouldn't want to frighten us since we were already jittering in our wellies. Tara sensed it because when the camp was in view, she ran past Connor and disappeared in the smoke of the glowing campfires. I, too, was relieved to see the camp. It wasn't home, but it would do for temporary refuge.

I felt a touch like fingernails scraping against the back of my neck. My startled cry made Connor turn to look at me, not as if I were a frightened Ginny Ann, but with a troubled expression. So, he felt it too. I saw it in his eyes. Fear. He had the look of someone gaining the sight, and I knew he was asking himself, is that real or imagined? Was he aware of the changes happening to him? I could see them even if Connor couldn't. Changes were happening to me, too. If I hadn't killed Peter, I had to find out who or what did.

Chapter Sixteen

Brannon

After eating Etain's lamb stew, I wound my way through the camp toward Kieran's wagon. Mist rose from the damp ground to mix with smoke from the campfires. I felt uneasy as I walked by a group of men, some smoking pipes, others with whisky flasks in hand, huddled together around a bonfire. Gruff faces, lined by years of living in the elements, watched me in silence.

I jumped when an owl screeched. Shadows took on shapes—wings of a gigantic bird silhouetted against the side of a wagon. The canvas flapping in the wind gave the bird the illusion of flight. Even though wolves were extinct in Ireland, I thought I saw one appear from behind a tree. Its long neck stretched to howl at the waning moon. Was it calling the dark presence I felt at the seashore? Yes, there it was again, like a dagger stuck in my mind.

My heart pumped harder than a hooked fish gasping for air. I ran the rest of the way to Kieran's wagon, darted up the steps, and knocked hard on the door.

"It's open," Tara said from inside.

I kicked off my wellies and stepped into the wagon, relieved to leave my fears outside on the steps with my boots. Candlelight and the faint smell of incense calmed my nerves.

A thick navy carpet woven with white spirals adorned the floor. Where Etain had a side bench in her wagon, Kieran had a bookcase overflowing with books. Beside the bookcase was a small glass cabinet. Inside the cabinet were two silver cups, a small knife with a decorated handle, a pestle and mortar, and a round mirror that fit perfectly inside a glass bowl. On top of the cabinet sat two beeswax candles, a carved wooden box, a jar filled with flax seeds, and a silver flask with a star engraved on its side.

In place of a bedroom nook at the back of the wagon, Kieran had an ash-wood table with two padded benches, one on each side and covered in a dark blue tapestry. Connor sat at the table, carving an apple into the shape of a wolf with the knife he stole from McKinley. I sat opposite him at the table.

Tara tightened her shawl around her shoulders and sat next to Kieran, who was tuning a small Celtic harp. Nicks and scratches in the oak wood marred the carved dolphins running up and down the curved soundboard, but the flaws didn't affect the tone. Its strings sounded with a sweet resonance that made my insides vibrate.

When Kieran had finished tuning the harp, he placed it on the table. He took the bowl, mirror, candle, and jar filled with seeds from the small glass cabinet and put them in the center of the table. He lit the candle and placed it beside the bowl. The light reflecting off the mirror created circular shadows on the walls. "I promised you a story," he said and picked up the harp. "And some music to go with it. Brannon, do you have the flint?"

I placed the flint Peter had given me on the table. "It has music written on it in Ogham," I explained to Tara, who picked it up to look at it.

"I wish I could read it." She placed the flint in front of Kieran.

"Ogham has twenty letters. Each one corresponds to one of the twenty strings on the harp. On this piece of flint, there are only five notes." He plucked each string to demonstrate the sound. "Together, they form this sacred chant."

Kieran played it several times, embellishing the chant in different ways to create a haunting melody. I felt myself growing more relaxed. I'd almost nodded off when the music changed to a lilting tune to accompany Kieran's story.

"Deep in the ocean, a young oyster grew the most beautiful mother-of-pearl inside its shell. Manannan caught its glow as he disembarked from his boat, *Wave Sweeper*. He reached down and plucked the oyster from its bed of sand. In fear, the oyster shut its shell. Manannan said to his warriors, 'The inside of this oyster shell is exquisite, and I require a pearl.' He teased the oyster's shell open and said, 'Oyster, can you make a pearl that is fit for a god?'

"He chipped a small piece from the firestone he wore around his neck and implanted it inside the oyster before returning it to its bed beneath the waves. For an oyster, any grain of sand would be irritating, but grain from the firestone of a god was painful. To soothe the pain, the young oyster grew mother-of-pearl around the fragment, but it took many years before the stone's fire no longer burned.

"Time passed, and Manannan returned one day to the oyster bed. Once again, as he disembarked, he saw an unusual sparkle in the sand. He laughed as he reached down and lifted the oyster from its bed. This time the oyster did not clamp itself shut. With care, Manannan took the pearl from inside the oyster shell. The pearl was like no other in the world. The sea-god was pleased, so he respectfully returned the oyster to its home. 'You've done well. There will be no more burdens for you.'

"Many years passed, and the oyster became a great old oyster. Manannan passed this way one more time. He watched as the pearl fishermen took their harvest, finding pearls in all the oysters except the great old one, so they tossed him to a seagull. Manannan called to the seagull. The young bird landed on his wrist and dropped the old oyster onto his palm. Manannan showed the oyster his sword's hilt, carved into the shape of a seahorse. The eye of the seahorse was the magnificent pearl created by the old oyster. 'Oyster, none will mock you anymore, for you have made a pearl fit for a god. For this, you will live forever.'"

The music stopped, and the room suddenly felt cold and empty.

"What does it mean?" Connor searched Kieran's face for an answer.

"What do you think it means?" Kieran put the harp down on the bench beside him.

"The pearl, the eye. It can't be worth much. Who would want a seahorse's eye, anyway?" Connor said.

"Connor, this is not about the pearl's value but how the oyster made it. The oyster had a gift, the making of a pearl. When the god's firestone tested its gift, the result was a unique creation—a pearl with a heart of fire. All three of you are gifted. What will you do with your gifts? Will one of you find the pearl that could adorn the hilt of a god's sword? Will either of you put fire in the eye of a seahorse?"

When Kieran looked at me, I knew he was asking me to show Tara and Connor that I had both the sapphire and the pearl. I had been gifted with the two most important elements to create the sword. I couldn't tell them. Not yet. I still didn't trust them.

"Where is the sword?" Tara asked.

"Lost in a battle a long time ago," Kieran said. "The pieces were spread across our land. But objects that are a part of a magical weapon have an affinity for each other. When separated, they have an urge that brings them back together, to be whole again."

"But what is my gift?" Connor asked impatiently.

"You have many skills, Connor, but a skill becomes a gift when the craftsman is put to his greatest test."

"What did The Lady mean when she said I was the answer?" I asked.

"She said that?" Connor pressed his lips into a grimace. "Why him?"

"Because his mother failed. Molly was given the sapphire when she was a little girl but was too young to do what was asked of her. I thought it would be Faolan—"

"Faolan?" I interrupted, suddenly remembering the man at the pier who wanted to buy my pearl.

"Yes, Connor's father. I had begun to train him as I thought he would be the one. I was wrong, and an unfortunate accident occurred. I hope it doesn't repeat itself. Your great-grandmother, Etain, kept the sapphire safe, and that day at the fair, the sapphire chose you, Brannon. Molly knew this, and that is why she wanted you to stay with me."

Everything Ma had said was beginning to make sense. I now understood why she was scared of the gem and didn't want me calling the elements. But why didn't she tell me?

"And Connor," Kieran said, placing his hand over Connor's wrist. "This time, it will take three to restore the one. That is the meaning of the triquetra, tattooed on your wrist, a pictorial symbol of the union of three. So not just Brannon, all three of you are being called. Two generations were given the same power. The first failed, and now their children have the legacy."

"What are we being asked to do?" Tara said.

"You have seen the beginning of it. There has been a turn in our world, a pulling away from the land and the natural laws. The land is out of balance. Now is the time for the old ways to reassert themselves."

"Why?" Connor asked. "What is the purpose of bringing the old magic back to the land?"

"To change what I have seen in the future."

"You can see the future?" Tara's eyes grew wide with awe.

"Sometimes."

"How far into the future can you see?" Connor said.

"The farther we look into the future, the more difficult it is to see, as the smallest thing can change an outcome. That's why divination isn't an exact science. So beware, what you see may not be the full truth."

Kieran stood, took the kettle off the top of the stove, and filled the bowl with water. "The future is like a river. The beginning of the river is the source of the stream we are following. When fed by a powerful source, the stream can become a mighty river with tributaries before it merges into the great ocean."

"Rivers? Powerful sources? I don't get it." Connor sat up straight, taking a keen interest in the discussion.

"What is the source of all?" Kieran looked around at each of us. "You three are tributaries of a mighty river. Remember, the best magic takes the least amount of bother. It is simply to look, feel, or hear."

"Or taste and smell," Tara added.

"Quite right. There's alchemy in cooking. When you add the intent to make the best cookies ever, with love, then the results are delicious."

Kieran took one seed and placed it into the water. "Tara, what do you see?"

"A seed sinking to the bottom of a bowl." She giggled and placed her hand over her mouth.

"Connor?"

He frowned and thought for a moment. I wanted to tell him he was trying too hard, but I knew when to keep my gob shut. He wouldn't want advice from his younger cousin.

"What do you see?" Kieran asked again.

"The seed," Connor grumbled. "I wish I could see something else, but I never do."

"You will," Kieran assured him. "Now Brannon."

I didn't want to see anything that would make Connor angrier than he already was, but I was curious to know if I had the gift. Kieran spun another seed on the surface of the water, creating ripples that spiraled toward the edges of the bowl. It's odd how such a tiny seed could make me dizzy and cross-eyed. I blinked, and my vision cleared. The seed had dropped to the bottom of the bowl, and looking up at me from the smooth surface was Connor's face superimposed over my own. Not what I expected. How was that possible? Connor wasn't even looking over my shoulder. He was on the other side of the table.

I looked up. Connor met my gaze with the same intensity as the bowl's face. When I looked down again, the faces were gone. Instead, I saw a black shape floating on the water's surface. It grew until it touched the sides of the bowl. Out of the blackness, a pinpoint of light appeared to be moving toward me until I could determine what it was. Fire. I smelled smoke and heard wood crackling and children crying. Even worse, I sensed the terrible presence that had followed us from the seashore.

I coughed and wiped my stinging eyes. The smoke was choking me, and I couldn't catch my breath. So, this was how Granda died. I pushed the bowl away. The water rippled up to the rim and onto the table.

"Easy, Brannon," Kieran said softly.

"What did you see?" Connor demanded in a voice edged with jealousy.

I wiped my sweaty hands on my pants. "I… I saw fire."

"Where?" Tara stood, found a towel, and mopped up the water.

"I think it was here at the camp, but I can't be sure. Did I see the future?"

"Maybe, maybe not." Kieran dropped another seed into the water. "Look again. Tell us what you see."

I prepared myself for the worst as I looked into the mirrored surface. Nothing. Nothing but a seed at the bottom of the bowl. Good. I didn't want to see any more than that.

"Relax. Don't be afraid to see," Kieran said. "This is your gift. Breathe easy. Exhale slowly."

I'd been holding my breath, bracing myself for some horror that might play out on the water's surface. I wanted to tell Kieran I'd had enough, but the water drew me in. At the bottom of the bowl, the three seeds were joined end to end, like spokes on a wheel. The seeds spun clockwise, and I saw myself standing in a round tower. Light streamed through a window, and suspended in the light was a sword.

"What do you see?" Tara's voice sounded like it was coming from another place.

"I see a sword like the one in the story. Manannán's sword caught in a stream of light."

"Where is it?" Kieran asked.

"The tower."

"The round tower?" Connor blurted out suddenly, his leg hitting the table and shattering the scene.

A wave of dizziness washed over me. I leaned my head into my hands and waited for it to fade away. I hoped I wouldn't vomit Etain's stew all over Kieran's wagon.

"I didn't mean to break Brannon's concentration," Connor said. He looked at Kieran sheepishly. "It's just that things are starting to come together and finally make sense. The round tower near here is where I got this." He rolled up his cuff and traced Manannán's mark with his finger. "Do you think the sword is in the tower somewhere?"

"No, we must remake the sword," Kieran said. "But the tower may be essential to its making."

"I've always wondered why a god would need a sword," Connor said, "yet he always seems to have one in the legends. I mean, if he's all-powerful—"

"Usually, a god gifts a hero with a sword so that it can become a means to draw down the power of a god and focus that power. If you look at the shape of a sword, it lends itself to being an instrument of focus. A sword is a tool of war and death, capable of taking or preserving peace and life— that which cuts can also heal, like a doctor's scalpel. In the days of old, heroes confronted by monsters and superhuman beings needed the power of a god to defeat them. Why do you think we need an ancient sword in this modern time of weaponry?"

"What we must fight is not of this world." I sat up in the chair, thankful that the nausea had gone.

Kieran nodded. "Yes, and the sword-bearer must be a master who can focus the earth's elements through the keen-edged blade."

"Like the Tuatha De Danann," I said.

"Yes! It is the time for the return of the Tuatha, the greatest artists, healers, and magic wielders of all. You three will become masters of the elements. But remember, to be a master of the elements takes self-mastery, which means being at peace and in harmony with oneself and each other. So long as you wrangle with your thoughts, focusing is difficult. If you are angry or sad or even hysterically happy, you cannot achieve the state whereby you can create a spark of fire, cause a seed to sprout, squeeze water from a cloud, or call the wind to fill your sails."

"What about me?" Tara asked.

"You are the third. The fulcrum, or balance point between these two. Like the crosspoint in a sword. You are the dawn, the point between daybreak and nightfall."

"But I don't have any special gifts," She said.

"You have many, and they have just begun to reveal themselves to you. Take the harp."

Tara's eyes grew wide as she placed the harp in her lap. "Oh, I've always wanted to play a musical instrument." She strummed the strings and made a face. "It's out of tune."

"One string is out of tune. Can you find it?" Kieran asked.

She played each string. "It's this one," she said.

Kieran took the harp and showed her how to tune the strings and play the five-note chant. The harp sounded different under her fingers. Her touch was softer yet still had the power to transport me to a deep place where I felt comforted and safe. I could tell by Connor's drooping eyelids that he felt it, too.

Kieran smiled. "Just as I thought. Music is your gift."

Tara stopped playing and leaned the edge of the harp against her cheek. "But how can I help with the music?"

"Music is one of the most potent instruments of magic. It can summon or control emotion, place the listener in a dream state, or invoke a vision. It can bring forgetfulness, and it can heal. Tara, the harp is yours. When someone needs healing, play the chant you have learned, the one from Brannon's flint. Now, it is late—time for bed. We can talk more about this in the morning.

Chapter Seventeen

Brannon

The storm raged through the camp, rattling tin cups, cracking tree branches, rustling leaves, and flapping the canvas folds on the roof and windows. The wagon rocked with each gust. More than once, I heard people talking in whispers as they walked by the wagon. I couldn't hear their words, but when I looked out the window, I saw fear in their eyes. A child's screams sent an icy chill through me. Shadows like winged creatures riding each gust of wind flickered on the walls. Was it my imagination, or were these wraiths the beings that had followed us back from the sea?

I settled into Connor's spare bed at the back of the wagon. The mattress, stuffed with horsehair, was hard and the blankets musty, unlike the lavender-scented ones in Etain's wagon. I tossed and turned, hoping to find a comfortable spot on the mattress.

Thankfully, the room was warm, as Connor had left peat and coal burning in the stove. It was well past midnight, and Connor hadn't come to bed yet. He had given me the upper bunk in favor of the lower one, a dark cave-like alcove. His bed probably had a softer mattress.

So much had happened since I awakened from my fever that morning. The events of the day played over and over in my mind. Whenever I closed my eyes, I saw the white-maned Aonbharr rising out of the waves to greet Kieran. The Lady's strange salutation to Kieran confused me. *Your foster father sends his greetings and wants you to know that the boy is the answer.*

Did she mean Manannan? Manannan was a foster father to Lugh. Kieran couldn't be Lugh, could he? Impossible. That would make him thousands of years old. I dared not ask. If Kieran wanted to tell me, he would, and it wasn't my place to be so bold.

I mulled the day's events over and over in my mind. The Lady had to be mistaken about me. I couldn't be the answer to anything. How could I, a mere boy, be expected to fight these beings? I shivered. All I wanted was to be an artist, not a warrior.

I'd almost nodded off when a sound jerked me wide awake. I sat up. The coals still burning in the stove cast a dim light around the wagon. Nothing there. You're just being silly, I told myself.

A rustle at the door made me dive under the blankets. The door opened. I saw, through half-closed eyes, Connor hunched over the stove. He took a burning coal from the oven and lit the oil lamp using metal tongs. The room brightened for an instant before he turned it down to a soft flicker.

When I thought it safe, I turned on my side to watch Connor rummage in the chest of drawers. He sat on the side bench, yawned, and took out his carving. He pulled the collapsible table down over the chest and ran his finger over the place he had hollowed out for the eye. I watched with awe as he put the finishing touches on the scales with delicate strokes. He carved the tail into a Celtic knot, similar to the one on his wrist. The seahorse was, without question, the most beautiful carving I had ever seen. I couldn't help but wonder how Connor, with his large, weather-worn hands, could create such fine work.

There was also something uncanny about the look on Connor's face as he worked at his craft. Did I look that strange when my gift overcame me? It wasn't just the odd expression that caught my attention. It was Connor's weird atonal humming. I wanted to laugh but knew he would give me a bleeding nose if I uttered even the faintest snicker. I clamped my hand over my mouth and buried my head in the pillow. He must have heard me because I felt his hand pressing down on my head, smothering me. I kicked and pushed the pillow aside.

Connor stood over me. "You sound like a crazy eejit laughing like that in your sleep." He sat back down and resumed his work on his carving.

I lay back, relieved Connor hadn't guessed that I'd been laughing at his singing. I swung my legs over the bed. "Fine time to be doing that in the middle of the night."

"I have to."

"I know that feeling. Sometimes I have to draw at night, and there's no stopping it."

"No, there's no stopping it."

"What will it be?"

"A hilt."

"Of course, the seahorse hilt. Like in the story, Kieran told us about Manannán's sword." Now I understood why Connor was compelled to carve Manannán's hilt. Did he know he was being used as an instrument for the sea-god?

"There." Connor blew fine particles of dust from the seahorse's scales. "It just needs a few coats of polish and an eye." He pulled his boots on and grabbed his jacket off the hook by the door.

"Where are you going?" I jumped from the bunk to the floor.

"Out."

I heard feet scuffing on the stairs outside. Connor opened the door, and Tara rushed into the wagon. She pulled her scarf from her head and let it drape around her neck. Her cheeks were flushed, her lips blue. Frost sparkled on her coat and mittens.

"What's wrong? What are you doing up at this hour?" Connor pulled a twig from her hair.

"It's crazy out there. Everyone's up. I heard one of the girls miscarried tonight. They say there's a fever running through the camp. Many of the children are sick. Etain has been going from wagon to wagon. It's a bad omen when so many are sick at once. Some say that a curse has come upon us."

"They think I'm the curse, don't they?" I mumbled. "I see the way they look at me."

Tara pulled off her mittens and warmed her hands over the stove. "They don't know you. We're a tight-knit clan, and you're—"

"An outsider," Connor interjected.

"He's your blood, Connor. He's one of us whether you like it or not."

A powerful gust rocked the wagon. Connor caught Tara before she fell against the woodstove. When they pulled away from each other's arms, I saw something between them, more than friendship. I looked away.

"Da needs your help. Hurry," she said. When she opened the door, another gust buffeted the wagon and yanked the door out of her hand. It banged against the outside wall. Tara pulled her scarf over her head and tied it under her chin. "Best to stay inside, Brannon. Tonight, the wind is as terrible as a witch's curse." Connor followed her outside and closed the door behind them.

I looked out the window and saw a branch crashing down on one of the wagons. Children were screaming and crying. I couldn't stay in the wagon while terrible things were happening outside. It wasn't right. I had to help.

I scrambled to put my only sweater over the shirt I had worn to bed. I was sure it wouldn't keep me warm enough, so I took Connor's sweater off his bed. It was big and fit over my clothes. I hoped Connor wouldn't mind me borrowing it and an extra pair of wool socks, too. I attached the crane bag to my belt before putting on my jacket and stepping outside.

Fire sprang up everywhere. Sparks lit the night, crackling the bracken and dry vegetation under the trees. Specks of ash floated in the air as women thrashed at the edge of the flames with fire-besoms, feathery birch twigs bound on straight wooden branches. I stopped to help them, but the fire rose higher with every whip of my broom. Sea-green shapes flickered in the center of the flames, reaching out to touch me. The women noticed my effect on the fire and shooed me away. One woman muttered something about me being the cause of it. I thought she might hit me with her flaming branch.

The same happened when I tried to help the children, who ran back and forth from the stream to collect buckets of water to douse the fires. As soon as I extinguished one fire, another flared in its place. Flashes of heat burned my face. The smell was like nothing I had experienced before. These were no ordinary fires, but some wicked acts of nature. The stench of rotten eggs and manure filled the air. I gagged and held my hand in front of my nose.

Horses whinnied as Connor shouted orders to hitch them up to the wagons. They were breaking camp in hopes of leaving the cursed fires behind them. I decided to go too and lead the evil away from these kind folks.

More than anything, I wanted to find my ma. So many questions were swirling in my mind, and I needed answers. Why didn't she tell me she once owned the talisman? Why didn't she tell me about Etain, Connor, and Kieran? Why so many secrets? If she had failed, why did Kieran think I could succeed?

I climbed partway up the hill where I could look down on the camp. I saw Kieran standing on top of a dolmen. In his hand, he had a flask from which he poured water into a cup. I noticed that the flask never ran dry, and the cup never overflowed. Gradually the figures in the flames disappeared, leaving small patches of glowing red to flicker in the valley like will-o'-the-wisp, there one moment, gone the next.

Then the blessed rain came in solid sheets to smother the fires. I ducked beneath a rock outcropping for shelter and watched the wagons move away, one at a time. Before driving the horses forward, Connor didn't check the wagon to see if I was still in it. Once organized into a convoy, they continued west toward Ballintoy.

Dawn's light streaked crimson and gold on the horizon. I waited until the fires had burned out before I left the smoldering black wounds that marked where the camp had been. The wagons had long since disappeared into the distance. Perhaps now, the tinkers would be safe from the terrible sickness that had come to the camp. Some had blamed me, and I was beginning to think they were right. I was sure the evil had followed me back from the seashore just as surely as the sand stuck to my boots. If what The Lady had said was true, that I was the answer, my life and anyone around me would be at risk.

Chapter Eighteen

Brannon

With the sun warming my back, I climbed down the hillside to the road. I hoped my parents would still be in Ballycastle. At the side of the road, I stopped to pick some blackberries. Frost had browned and curled the leaves, but a few berries still clung to the brambles. Did I dare eat them? Everyone knew that after November 1st, the blackberries belonged to the pooka, and it was bad luck to eat them. And it did look like the berries had gone pooka. Some were rotten, some shriveled and hard, while others were marked with white slug tracks, the pooka's spit. Nah, I'd better not tempt the fates. Instead, I looked and found a few hazelnuts, enough to tame my growling stomach. I'd have to keep my eye out for wild turnips, for it could be a long time before I'd get another meal.

It would take about four hours to get to Ballycastle if I could keep a fast-walking pace, but when a farmer on his way to the market stopped and offered me a ride, I was only too happy to accept. I threw my bag in the back of the wagon with the chickens. After climbing in, I sat on top of one of the cages. The chickens clucked, flapped their wings, and pecked at my bottom through the cage slats. Their awful ruckus made the farmer stop the donkey and invite me to sit with him in the wagon.

"Never seen 'em act like that before." The farmer slapped the reins, and the wagon rolled forward. "You got the smell of fox or coon on you, boy?"

"Don't think so, sir." I hoped I didn't stink, or the chickens could smell the evil that had taken over the tinker's camp.

"You smell like you've been sitting too close to the fire, though."

I sniffed my sleeve. The horrible smell of shit and eggs had penetrated right through the fibers of my jacket. "Sorry about that, sir."

"I hope you weren't involved in them fires I saw back there. Patches of ground burned in odd shapes. It looked to me like some kind of devil worship. Them tinkers are famous for that sort of thing, you know."

"No, I didn't know." I didn't know much about the tinkers, but I thought they were kind-hearted, except for Connor.

"Well, I know it to be true firsthand. I had my fortune told by one of them witches once. I didn't like her lies, so I refused to pay her. She cursed me, and damn it all. I lost one chicken every night for thirteen nights."

"How did you know it was a curse, and not a fox, in the henhouse?" I asked.

The farmer looked at me as if I were thick in the head. "I didn't hear a sound in the coop, for one thing. Think about it. Thirteen nights. You go to church, don't you?"

I thought it best to nod my head ever so slightly—not quite a yes, not quite a no.

"Then you know there were thirteen men at the last supper."

"And the thirteenth man—" I began.

"Yes! He betrayed our Lord. Now you understand."

I tried not to look him in the eye. The farmer was loopier than a chicken with no head, but I didn't want to anger him and get thrown off the wagon.

"I like you, boy. I'd always wished for a son but got only girls, so if you're looking for work, I could use some help around the farm. I can't pay much, but my wife's a good cook, and I could give you a room in the barn."

The farmer looked like a kind person. His offer was tempting—to hide somewhere, be a normal kid, forget about the pooka and the Fomorii and all that had happened. But, no, I couldn't take the chance. If I stayed with this man and his family, the Fomorii might come and bring them the blight. "Thank you, but I'm on my way home."

"Good that you have a home. I wondered about that after seeing you digging in the dirt for a wild turnip. Hungry, are you?"

"A little."

He took a crinkled bag from his pocket and opened it. "Not exactly breakfast."

I put my hand in and took out a piece of candy. Yellowman. "Oh, thank you, sir. I'd have Yellowman for breakfast every day if Ma let me."

"Not too good for the teeth, son, but we never think about our teeth when we're young. Now I won't be asking you what you've been up to. I can imagine." He laughed as if recalling something from his youth. "A boy your age has secrets. I know. I made my ma worry more than once and had my arse kicked for it too. It served me right. Yup, I did some stupid things when I was young. All boys do. I can't say as I regret a single one, though."

The farmer dropped me off at a fork in the road. One way led to the center of town, the other to Evan's home. I thanked the farmer, but as I went to get my bag out of the back of the wagon, the chickens started fussing again, clucking and flapping their wings. It had to be more than the smell of smoke on my clothes. Maybe I carried the evil with me. Still feeling uneasy, I jogged down the road toward Evan's house. I hoped my ma and da would still be there.

Chapter Nineteen

Connor

I didn't notice that Brannon had run off until morning. The night before had been chaotic, with fever running through the camp, fires springing up everywhere, and having to pack up and move everyone in the middle of the night.

Kieran was combing the shore, and Tara went from wagon to wagon, asking if anyone had seen Brannon. It had been such a wild night it would have been a miracle if anyone had seen him leave. If Brannon wanted to hide, there were many nooks, crannies, and caves in the hills. I only wanted a few hours of sleep, but Kieran had sent me to find him. Besides, the kid had stolen my favorite sweater knitted by Etain, and I wanted it back.

I set out on Malachy, taking the main road to Ballycastle. Jagged bursts of sunlight fought to shine from behind black storm clouds. If I had been in Brannon's shoes, I would have hitched a ride on the steam train, but Brannon would never have the guts to try something like that. What a sissy. With some luck, I'd find him hanging his head and dragging his feet on the road. But how on earth was I supposed to convince him to return to the camp? It wouldn't be easy to haul him up on the back of Malachy if he didn't want to come. We'd get into another fight for sure.

The hunt for my cousin felt like a useless waste of time. I wanted to be at home, sleeping, eating breakfast, or playing with Epona's foal. I wondered what I should call the filly. To keep from nodding off, I went through the alphabet. Adeen meant little fire, Birgitta, strong, Brenna, little raven. She was black like Malachy but not a raven. Dyana was a dark beauty. That was nice— so was Ethna, meaning graceful. She would most certainly be graceful like her mother. Gweneth meant blessed, and Lavena meant joy, but those names still weren't right. Lola-Jo, meaning inner beauty, had a nice rhythm, but it was too cute. I thought of Rosina, the little rose, Seanna, gracious, and Shayla, a gift. Yes, she was a gift. Shayla would be her name.

I arrived on the outskirts of Ballycastle without seeing Brannon anywhere on the road. Where would the little brat go? To his house that had burned to the ground? What would be the point of that? He might have gone to Evan's place to look for his parents. If I didn't find Brannon, I would check Evan's place on my way back, just in case, but right now, my stomach growled. I'd missed breakfast, and it was almost lunchtime. I pressed Malachy into a gallop, steering him toward the center of town. After dismounting, I left Malachy to wait for me in front of the general store.

I had enough money to buy a halfpenny of candy and a jar of beeswax to polish my carving. I was eyeing the penny candy: malted milk balls, root-beer barrels, candy corn, lemon drops, red and black licorice straps, white sugar balls with a hazelnut in the middle, and rock candy in every color imaginable, when I felt a gentle pressure on my shoulder. Out of the corner of my eye, I saw a gloved hand resting on my shoulder. Startled, I pulled away. "Faolan?" I'd never called my father da. Faolan had never been around long enough to call him that.

"It's been so long you don't recognize your da?" he said.

I wanted to say it's been so long that I'd forgotten I had a da, but I didn't. The change in Faolan left me at a loss for words. He wore a fashionable suit, tailored, not home-made, and smelled like sweet tobacco and oriental spices instead of piss and booze. His hair, still longer than was stylish, was thinning but trimmed recently, and his face was cleanly shaved. I'd never seen my father without gloves and today was no exception, but these were not his usual dirty work gloves made of rough cowhide but finely cured lambskin, and over the gloved middle finger was a gold ring. "You surprised me, is all."

"Are you camped close by?"

"A few hours away."

We stepped out of the store together. I put my hand on Malachy's neck, more for my comfort than the horse's.

Faolan stroked the mane, his ring catching in the horse's hair. "How is everyone?"

"Good enough."

"I'm just about to get some lunch. The hotel across the street has a fine dining room. Come and have something to eat. We could talk and catch up. I'd like to hear what's been going on in your life."

"I don't know. I'm supposed to be looking for—" I began, but Faolan cut me off.

"Surely you can spare an hour for your da, can't you?"

I wished Faolan wouldn't call himself Da. Yet, I had to admit I was more than a little curious to know what had caused this change in him. Besides, I was so hungry I could eat my trousers, smelling of horse shit. Perhaps an hour wouldn't hurt, and I could be on my way again. They most likely found Brannon, and he was resting back at the camp, anyway.

Chapter Twenty

Brannon

Flynn rode a bicycle in front of his house. My bike. The one my granda fixed for me. I hoped I wouldn't have to fight Flynn to get it back.

His sister Moira waved at me from the veranda steps. She held Riley in her arms. He was screaming so hard his face wrinkled like an old troll.

"Your ma and da aren't here," she said, placing Riley on his feet. He stopped bawling and gripped her skirt for balance.

"Aw, I was hoping they'd still be here. Will they be back soon?" My stomach ached with disappointment.

"Hey, Flynn," Moira shouted to her brother on the street, "When will Brannon's ma and da be coming back?"

Flynn skidded to a stop in front of the house. "How should I know?"

"Did they say where they were going?" I asked.

"There was talk about them going to Portrush, but I don't know." Flynn spun one of the pedals with his foot.

Portrush was hours away on the other side of Ballintoy. I wondered if I should try to follow. "Did they take the boat?"

"Oh no, didn't you hear?" Moira said. "Someone burned your da's boat. My da has had to leave town to find work too, and Ma's at the gutting factory. I'm sorry, I thought you knew."

I scuffed my boots through the gravel. I felt sick. The boat had been in my family since before Granda. To be sure, he'd be stomping in heaven to have seen it go up in flames.

"Where you to now?" Moira asked.

"I don't know. I don't have anywhere to go."

"You could stay with us."

"No, he can't," Flynn said.

"Why not?" Moira took Riley's hand as he started to fuss.

"There's hardly enough food for the rest of us."

I knew Evan struggled to keep food on the table, and now he had another child to feed. "Don't worry, Flynn, I can't stay. I'll need my bike, though."

"Take it." Flynn climbed off the bike and held it by the seat so I could grip the handlebars. "I found it at the house. The only thing left from the fire."

"Shut up about that." Moira punched Flynn in the arm, so Riley imitated her and punched Flynn in the leg. Flynn slapped Riley on the head and made him scream.

"You eejit. Now you've set him to howling again." Moira picked up Riley and took him into the house.

I put my bag into the basket and punched it down a little longer and harder than I needed to. If I looked up now, Flynn might see my tears.

"You know there was someone here yesterday asking for you?" Flynn said.

"Who?" I swung my leg over the bar.

"Never seen the man before. He said he was your uncle."

"I don't have an uncle."

"Can't help what he said."

"I mean, I have an uncle, but…." I remembered what Kieran had said about my mother having a brother, Faolan. Could it have been him? If so, why would he be looking for me? "What did he want?"

"How am I supposed to know?"

"Did he say where he was staying?"

"Nope."

"Did you tell him where I was?"

Flynn picked up a stone and threw it at a boulder. It hit the rock, bounced, and flew across the road. "I wasn't supposed to tell, but since he said he was family, I thought it would be all right. I told him you had gone off to live with the tinkers. Oh, and he came in a hackney carriage. It looks like your uncle has more than a few coins to rub together."

Without saying goodbye, I pedaled down the road toward my house. The blackened limestone walls were still standing, but the roof was gone, leaving the house open to the elements. A bird perched on the windowsill, now a dark empty socket. The skeleton of the apple tree was still standing, all the leaves and bark scorched away by the fire. At the top, one lone apple still clung to the ash-covered branches.

I rode by Peter's house. It looked the same as always, yellow curtains in the kitchen window and blue ones in the boys' room where Peter slept with his brothers. I dared not stop riding until I was in front of McNeil's farm. The black stallion was not in the corral, and there were no horses in the meadow.

I left my bike leaning against the fence, climbed over it, and dropped into the corral. The frozen grass crunched under my boots as I walked toward the spot where Peter had fallen, now marked by two crisscrossed swords. The two swords of the Tuatha De Danann. Had someone placed the sticks like that, or had they fallen by chance?

I picked up a stick and snapped it in two and then into three and four, snapping it until the pieces were too small to break. "I'll never wield another sword," I said aloud and threw the broken pieces into the air. "Not even Manannan's magical sword. Find someone else to be your answer."

The barn door opened with a squeak and shut with a bang. Mary stood in the doorway, looking at me as if I were a ghost. Why wouldn't she? She probably thought she'd never see me again. In her mind, I must have died with Peter. I should have. We had been like brothers.

"Mary." I stepped toward her. She hurried back into the barn. I had to talk to her and find out what she remembered about that day. What had she seen? I opened the barn door and heard a rustle.

"Mary, please don't be afraid of me." She peered at me from behind a bale of hay. "I'd like to see the kittens if they're still here?"

"They're gone," she said. "Their mamma took them away."

"Did you look for them? She couldn't have taken them too far, could she?"

"I looked. The kittens are gone. I really wanted the one with the six toes." She came out from her hiding place and stood in the light from the loft window. Blond as Peter, like an angel.

"Let's look again." I squeezed between the bales of hay. Mary watched me as I poked and prodded, looking in every corner. Spider webs, mouse droppings, and a dead bird. A pipit. Not a wound anywhere, but the neck looked broken. Did the wing move? I touched it with my boot, and the bird flew up into my face. Gobsmacked and nearly wetting my cacks, I ducked. Mary's scream almost broke my eardrums.

"Jaysus, Mary, quit that now. We'll have the neighbors coming around. 'Tis a bird, is all."

"It's the pipit that killed Peter." She covered her face with her hands.

"Nah, no bird can do that," I said. Or could it? Suddenly I remembered the pipit swooping down at Peter at the Bonamargy Friary. It had come again later that day and spooked the piebald and stallion. "Where are the horses?"

"Don't know. Sold, I think."

That made sense. McNeil wouldn't want the neighbors to remember that horrible day when one of his horses killed a boy. Mary followed as I searched in each of the stalls for the kittens. It was strange to see the stalls empty of horses.

In one stall, I saw the corner of a wooden crate beneath a bale of hay. I pushed the bale off the container and tried to lift the lid. Someone had nailed it shut.

"Do you think she's in there?" Mary asked. "Wouldn't she smother?"

"I don't think she could get in here," I said, "but let's look just in case." I looked around and found a crowbar leaning up against the wall. I pried open the lid and looked inside. Mary rose on tiptoes so I slammed the lid shut before she could see.

"What's in there?"

"Nothing much." I struggled to lift the heavy bale back on top of the crate.

"She's in there, isn't she? You don't want me to see she's dead."

"Oh no, she's not in there. Honest."

"Let me see," Mary demanded with a pout.

"No, and Mary, don't play here anymore."

"Why?"

"Because it's not safe. Mr. McNeil is using the barn to store guns."

"I know that. I see men bring the guns in here and then take them out again."

I thought of Granda's story about his Catholic friend running guns. Of course, Mary didn't understand that gunrunning was illegal. "Still, it's better that you stay away from here?"

"Because Peter died here?"

Did she still blame me? I searched her face for a sign she did.

"That's why I come," she whispered. "To see Peter."

"Aw, Mary," My heart broke to hear her say it, but then I remembered that I too could see things other people couldn't, like The Lady.

"I don't care if you don't believe me, Brannon Mac Lir," she said, stomping her foot. "I know what I saw. Like I saw the evil pipit. It wasn't a pipit, though. It changed shape."

"What kind of shape?"

"A moth, all tattered and wispy."

"Oh, God," I sat down on the bale. So, it was true. The Fomorii were after me, not Peter.

Mary sat beside me and picked pieces of hay from her dress, faded blue with pink smocking around the neck. "I know it wasn't your fault, Brannon. You were just playing around. The pipit did it. Peter knows too. He's not mad at you. Cross my heart. You're still his best friend."

I couldn't breathe. How could I live with such pain? Would it ever go away? Would I ever feel the joy of the wind whispering in my ears as I rode my bike, be happy when I drew something beautiful, or enjoy the taste of Yellowman? Yellowman. I'd enjoyed it just this morning and could still taste the sweetness stuck to my teeth. In memory of Peter, I vowed I would never eat Yellowman again.

I couldn't stop making a dreadful sound, a sob, but I caught the next one and the one after. I wished Mary would go away and leave me. If I tried to speak, my grief would escape, and there would be no stopping it. She looked at me with sad eyes. Then, I felt her arms wrapped tightly around my neck as if I were her favorite teddy bear, and she would never let it go. Mary comforted me when I should have been comforting her. Her forgiveness took me by surprise and I cried like never before. Mary squeezed me harder with each sob until I had to laugh.

"Can't breathe." I gasped for air and pulled away from her. I knew I would never forget Mary and the feel of her chubby arms warm around my neck. "Mary, I want you to promise me that you'll never come into this barn again. This stuff about guns is dangerous. When you're older, you'll understand. Promise me?"

"Declan said that too."

"Declan knows about this?"

Mary nodded. "He said it was a secret, and he'd whip me good if I told anyone."

I stood and paced the length of the barn. In the last stall at the farthest end, I heard soft mews, and found two furry bundles nestled together in the corner. They looked about five or six weeks old. "Here they are."

Mary knelt and picked up the orange kitten and spread its paw to show me its toes. "See?'

"Japers, he does have six toes." I took off my jacket and pulled Connor's sweater over my head.

Mary took the two kittens and bundled them in the sweater, tying the arms to make a cradle. "It's all right. I'll take care of you," she said.

"Will your da let you have two?"

"Da will let me have whatever I want now."

I heard the sound of an engine idling. A truck. When I opened the barn door, I saw McNeil climbing out of a pickup truck. Declan rode up behind him in a horse and wagon. I closed the door.

"Come, Mary. Let's get out of here." But we couldn't escape without being seen.

Chapter Twenty-One

Connor

Sitting with Faolan in the dining room of the best hotel in town, with its linen tablecloths and sterling silver, made me cringe. The place was too fancy for my liking, and most folks around these parts must have felt the same by the look of all the empty tables. I kicked a chunk of dirt from my boot under the table. Smoke from the night before lingered on my clothes. It's a wonder someone didn't ask me to leave, but they weren't running off their feet with business.

Faolan unfolded the linen napkin, placed it on his lap, and ordered a glass of wine. He sipped it like a gentleman, unlike the man I knew who used to guzzle his whisky or stout and wipe his mouth with the back of his hand. Was this an act or the new him? It made me more than a little uneasy. I brushed my napkin aside because I thought there was no point pretending to be what I wasn't. The menu was a leather-bound book written in French, so there was no use in trying to read it, so I pushed that aside too. I only wanted to eat something simple, like biscuits smothered in pork coddle or a bowl of potato leek soup.

The waiter returned with the wine and a pot of tea for me.

"Have whatever you want." Faolan closed the menu and placed it beside his plate.

"We have a delicious Salmon Soufflé," the waiter suggested. He had a French accent, and he eyed me with pursed lips.

"Chips and fish, please." I picked some dirt from under my thumbnail and wiped it on my pants.

He looked down his nose at me, and I looked up his extra-wide nostrils at him.

"And you, sir?" The waiter glanced at Faolan.

Faolan ordered something with a French name. But when our meals came, I was happy I'd ordered the fish. Faolan's lunch, covered in a white sauce, made my stomach turn, and it didn't look as if there was enough of it to feed a mouse.

I ate quickly, avoiding my father's eyes. I wondered why Faolan was being so nice to me and how he could afford the fancy meal.

"You've grown in the past five years. I hardly recognized you." Faolan leaned back against the plush chair and sipped his wine. He'd barely touched his food.

"You've changed too." I picked up a chip and stuffed it into my mouth. "What do you do now?"

"I guess you could say I'm an entrepreneur. I've learned to use my unique talents, and Connor, that can be very lucrative."

Did Faolan mean magical gifts or his knack for business? Kieran had never told me about Faolan's magical skills, only that Kieran had made a mistake, allowing them to develop too fast.

"I have an interest in many projects. Right now, I buy and sell rare antiquities for wealthy customers looking for the more unusual pieces from history."

"What kind of things?"

"Well, let's see now. I think jewelry is one of the best sellers, especially inlaid with gemstones, rubies, emeralds, sapphires, and pearls. Old swords, Roman-made, are also desirable items. The older, the better. I've found some that date back to the Tuatha De Danann. Even a hilt or piece of a blade that can be dated back to those times can fetch a hefty price.

I travel often, search through ruins, and talk to the locals. So far, I've been fortunate to get my hands on some valuable and unique pieces. Keep an eye out for me. I will pay you very well if you find something of value. I'll be here for a few weeks, as I have some other business in the area. If you like Connor, you could come and work for me. Money's good, and I have some items in my collection that would make Kieran envious if he saw them."

"Like what?"

"Talismans. Speaking of which, did Etain give you the sapphire? I thought she was saving it for you, and I know you're old enough to receive one. I'd love to see it again."

"I'd always thought it would be mine, but she gave it to Brannon. I fought him for it, though." I smiled with pride.

"You have it?" He seemed excited, and I quickly swallowed my pride with a sip of tea.

"No." I sputtered. The tea caught in my throat. "I didn't win the fight, and he still has it."

"I see." Faolan emptied the rest of his wine in one gulp. "Molly's boy. Yes, that makes sense." He motioned for the waiter to bring him another glass of wine. "I have recently come into the possession of an old manuscript written in Latin by a priest who recorded some of the druids' magic. I had it translated. It speaks about the magic of talismans and how to use them. There is one talisman described in that fragment that matches the sapphire perfectly. I'd love to try it out and see if it is the same stone. I believe the sapphire is a keystone."

"What's a keystone?"

"What do keys do, Connor?"

"Open doors."

"Or close them, and there are many kinds of doors between heaven and earth. Keys are also used for tuning."

"Like a harp?"

"Yes, but also for tuning energies to one's will. I'd pay you well if the sapphire ever comes into your possession."

"Are you asking me to steal it from him?"

"No, of course not, but Brannon might part with it one day or be parted from it."

"He would never willingly sell it. I'm sure of that," I said. "And if he lost it and I found it, I would have to give it back."

"But would you?"

"Maybe. Maybe not." I thought about what Kieran had said about McKinley's knife. I'd found it and could have given it back to him, but I didn't. It was wrong, yet I'd wanted it like I wanted the talisman. If the sapphire did come into my possession for some reason, I knew I would never be able to give it back or sell it, for that matter.

The waiter came with the wine and the dessert menu. Even though I was full, I couldn't pass up a free dessert, so I ordered a piece of chocolate cake.

Faolan pulled off his left glove. His deformed fingers curled toward his palm, ridged with scar tissue in the shape of a star. I'd never seen the scar before. I couldn't even remember seeing Faolan without gloves on his hands. The scar looked angry and red, like a sore that had never healed properly.

"How did it happen?" I could barely get the words out. My voice sounded raspy.

"Kieran didn't tell you?" He looked surprised.

"He said I should ask you."

"When Molly was nine years old, I found her with the talisman. She was a little girl, not of the age to receive a talisman, and she had not yet shown her gifts as they usually manifest in adolescence. She kept saying that a lady had given the gem to her. A beautiful lady in a white dress, but she was always a dreamy child living in her fantasy worlds, so I didn't believe her."

"The Lady?"

His eyes narrowed. "You've seen The Lady?"

"No, but both Brannon and Tara have."

"I have never seen her, but it makes sense. I will need her. We will need her."

"For what?"

"Let me finish my story. One day I found Molly sitting on the wagon steps talking to a moth. It was perched on her wrist. She had the sapphire in her other hand. I asked her what she was doing. She said that she was talking to a beautiful fairy. 'It's a moth,' I said, trying to swipe it away. That's when it changed shape, and I saw it for the evil wraith it was.

"Then I noticed moths coming from the cave near where we camped. A few at a time, then more and more. They'd come out of the cave as moths, then change to wraiths. I was scared for Molly and myself. I told her to give me the sapphire, but she wouldn't, and I had to wrestle it from her. The moths swarmed us. I had learned enough from Kieran to use the talisman. I was a boy, not much older than you, and, like most young men, I thought I knew it all. I'd always had a talent with fire, and since the sapphire was a firestone, I thought I could use it to set the moths aflame. Instead, our wagon burst into flames, and my parents were killed while they slept.

"Everyone said I was a bad seed. Maybe they were right because that's what I became. Molly ran away. As far as I know, Molly never used her gifts again. I was angry with her and Kieran, who took the sapphire from me and gave it to Etain for safekeeping."

"What were the moths?"

"I know now they were the Fomorii."

"The scar is from where I held the talisman." He hissed through his teeth as he flexed his fingers and pulled the lambskin glove back on.

Everything Kieran had told me was beginning to make sense. Now I understood why Kieran said Faolan lived under a terrible burden. "Kieran told us about the Fomorii. I think Kieran hopes Brannon is the one to drive the Fomorii back, but I think Brannon is scared because he ran away. I'm supposed to be looking for him right now."

"Brannon is just a boy. He'll fail, for he's as unprepared as I was. Kieran will make the same mistake again. My mistake was great, but Kieran's was greater. While he waits for a boy to become a man, every year, on the anniversary of my parent's death, when the veil between worlds is thin, I have returned to try to restore the broken seals. Every year I have failed, and the land becomes sicker because Kieran refuses to help me. Know this, Connor, with every failure to banish these beings, they grow stronger. I have only one more chance to banish the ones who have escaped and to reseal the Fomorii prison. The seals will vanish completely in three days, and all the Fomorii will be set free." He clasped his gloved hands in front of him and fell silent when the waiter came with my chocolate cake.

I stuck my finger in the icing and licked it. As good as it tasted, I didn't feel like eating it now. When no one was looking, I took my linen napkin and wrapped the cake in it and the silver fork, too. I thought it would make a lovely bracelet when melted down.

Faolan didn't try to stop me from taking the fork. Instead, he said, "Still carving?"

I took the seahorse carving out of my pocket and placed it on the table. Faolan picked it up and ran the tip of his gloved fingers over the finely carved ridges and scales. "A seahorse. Fine, very fine. I'm impressed."

"It needs one more sanding before I polish it with beeswax."

"A hilt?"

"I didn't plan for it to be a hilt, but that's what it's become. Tara's da will help me forge a blade for it."

"Seanán. There never was a better smith. I'd like to see the sword when it's finished. You know, Connor, I could use your talents one day to create copies of some of the pieces my clients are looking for."

So, Faolan hadn't changed much if he hoped to use my talent to create forgeries. "Not sure I'll ever be good enough for that," I said.

"Then you don't know how gifted you are. This carving is an excellent piece of work. Now, what do you plan to use for the eye?"

"I don't know yet. A stone, I guess."

"A gem would give it power—a ruby or a pearl, perhaps. A pearl comes from the sea, so I would say that's your best choice. You have told me about Brannon's gifts, but what about your own?"

"Kieran said my gifts will come when I'm ready."

Faolan sat back in the chair and crossed his arms, obviously disappointed in me. "When I was your age, my gifts had fully manifested, but I was a stubborn child and didn't listen well. I have since learned many things about my birthright, things Kieran was unable, or should I say, unwilling, to teach me. Nothing special yet?"

I wanted to be special, like Brannon. I wanted Kieran to look at me like he looked at Tara when she said she heard voices. In some strange way, I also wanted Faolan to be proud of me, as if that would make him love me more. I pulled my sleeve up to expose my wrist so Faolan could see the knot-shaped tattoo.

Faolan put his wineglass on the table, extended his gloved hand, and drew my wrist as close as the table that divided us would allow.

"Interesting pattern for a tattoo. How did this happen? Did you do this yourself with fire?"

I bit my lip to squelch my sudden burst of anger. Of course, it would only be natural for Faolan to think I had done this to myself. I pulled my hand away. "Fire made the mark, but I didn't do it. It was Manannan's doing," I said proudly. "It's for protection."

"By the gods. How did it come to be there?"

"It happened in the round tower near here." I told him how the lightning that struck the tower had scared the bejaysus out of me. "When it circled my wrist, I thought I'd be heading for the Land of Youth before my time. When it stopped, it left this mark."

"What did Kieran say about it?"

"That ready-or-not, my training must begin."

"Rightly so."

"He's been teaching me some things."

"Like what?"

Faolan seemed interested in what I'd learned. In truth, Kieran hadn't taught me much. I would have to lie. "You know, about the elements and such." If he suspected a lie, he didn't let on. I knew to keep a level gaze on him. It was hard, but I did it.

"You know Manannan marked you for a reason, don't you?"

I looked down at my wrist and fingered the knot.

"Well, you'll know in time." He wiped his mouth with the linen napkin. "So, what about Brannon?"

"What about him?" I said through clenched teeth. "The brat is an eejit. Why should you care about him?"

"He's got something I need."

"What does he have?"

"The eye of the seahorse. I alone have the power and knowledge to use the gems, but I must have both of them. One will not work without the other, for they will complete the sword together. Manannan's sword. That is what I need to banish these monsters from the land forever."

I gasped. So, the damn kid had both gems and didn't tell us. "How do you know he has Manannan's pearl?"

"I saw him with it at the pier. I'd almost convinced him to let me buy it when Kieran interfered. Brannon hasn't shown it to you?"

"I doubt he ever will. We don't like each other. He almost killed Epona yesterday. The little show-off tried to make

Epona come to him and ended up summoning a terrible storm and spooking the horses. It caused Epona to foal early, and we almost lost them both."

"How did he do that?"

"I think he used the sapphire. He also used it to call The Lady who saved Fiona with Tara's help?"

"The Lady?"

"I wonder if it's the same lady Molly saw," I said.

"By the gods, you might be right." His gloved hand hit the table so hard that tea splashed from my cup into the saucer. "Connor, my boy, I could use your help with this, and in exchange, I will teach you things that Kieran would never show you. You'd be helping me to right a wrong."

"How?"

"Bring me Brannon and make sure he has the gems with him. He might be interested to hear what I know about his talisman. His role in this is unclear to me, but I may need his talents and yours too." Faolan took out his wallet and handed me two one-pound notes. It was the most money I'd ever had. "Get yourself something special now."

I folded the bills and stuffed them into my pocket. I stood and put the cake and fork under my shirt.

Faolan laughed. It surprised me, as I'd never heard him laugh before. When I turned to leave, I felt his gloved hand on my arm. "When you find Brannon, bring him to my boat, *Breath of Cerridwen*. I promise you. You won't regret it."

I didn't say I would, and I didn't say I wouldn't, but I managed to thank him for lunch. I felt more confused than ever before. It was like McKinley's knife. One moment, it felt right to keep it, and in the next, it felt wrong. It wasn't until I'd cleared the restaurant doors that I could breathe easier. The story Faolan told me about the talisman explained so much, and maybe, just maybe, there was some good in Faolan after all.

Chapter Twenty-Two

Brannon

I crouched behind a bale of hay beside Mary, who leaned against me for comfort. "If your brother sees me, he'll kill me." I felt her shaking as she held the kittens against her chest. For now, their mews had stopped.

As the barn door opened, slanted sunlight traveled across the stalls. Mary buried her head in Connor's sweater when the light brushed her cheek.

"If you didn't come today, I was going to pitch the guns in the ocean," McNeil said.

"Ach and get us both killed for sure. If Faolan doesn't get this load to Belfast in time, we're as good as dead anyway. I can't understand the holdup, and he's not saying. But he's as good a cover as we can get, and you know there're not many people willing to help us."

I recognized Declan's voice, husky from too much liquor and cigarettes. I wondered if Connor knew his father was a gunrunner. "The constabulary has been checking every Catholic home in the county since you burned Mac Lir's house. It was a damn stupid thing to do, Declan. Yesterday, they arrested O'Doul's son just for knowing you. It's only a matter of time before they begin poking their noses around here. We're known to do business, you and I."

Mary cowered and hung her head, her hair making a tent for the kittens in her lap. Poor wee one would feel terrible hearing that her brother was a murderer. I wanted to tell her I didn't blame her for her brother's evil, but I dared not move or whisper one word.

If only I had one of those rifles, I might—no, I couldn't—an eye for an eye was not right. Somehow, I'd have to bury the rage, filling my mind with thoughts of murder. It was all I could do to stay hidden and not smash my fists into Declan's face. I had to keep calm. My life depended on it, and so did Mary's.

"I didn't know the old man was still in the house. I thought he had run away with the rest of 'em." Declan said. "He was a tough old scrapper, though."

"That he was, but in business, he was fair."

"Ach, the cussing old piss was mean to Peter, so I think he got what he deserved. Damn right, he did."

"But did you have to burn the boat, too?"

"I wanted to make sure they would leave, and they did," Declan spat.

"Let's load the wagon. After you deliver the guns, you'd better lie low for a while. And Declan, don't ever come back."

They grunted from the crate's weight as they carried it past the stall where we were hiding. I heard the crate thump into the back of the wagon and the men's boots crunching on the hay-strewn ground when they returned to the barn for the rest of the guns.

"Look," McNeil said. "My crowbar has been moved. Someone's been poking around in here and whoever it was, pried this crate open."

I heard the sound of the lid sliding off the crate.

"Anything missing?" Declan asked.

"Don't know. I'd have to count the guns, but there's no time for that. I just want them out of here," McNeil snapped. "God knows when the constabulary will find a reason to search my place."

The kittens mewed. Mary placed her hands over them to quiet them, but it made them wiggle, and they cried even more.

"Did you hear that?" McNeil spun around.

"Hear what?"

"Kittens. I wondered what the mother cat did with them," McNeil said. "She took 'em away because she knew I was going to drown them."

Out of the corner of my eye, I saw a pipit perched in the rafters above us. The bird cocked its head to one side as if watching us. Something about that bird felt evil. It dropped and circled over the stall where we were hiding. Mary screamed as it swooped directly at her face.

"Mary," Declan barked as he opened the stall door. "I told you not to play in here."

Mary stood to conceal me as I squeezed between the wall and bales of hay. I watched through a crack in the mound of bales.

McNeil, a heavyset man with large, bulging eyes, pushed past Declan. "What are you doing in there?"

"You said I could have the kittens." Mary tightened her arms around her mewing bundle.

"Was it you who opened that crate in the next stall?"

"She's not strong enough for that," Declan said.

"But she's heard everything we've said."

"She knows to keep her gob shut, don't you, Mary? If you don't, I'll take them kittens and drown them. Now get and don't ever come back in here again."

Mary waited for the men to clear the stall and, without looking back, ran from the barn. Through the slats in the wood, I saw her blue dress rustle by. She stopped to peer through a knothole from the other side, but I waved her away.

The sound of nails pounding into the crate reminded me of the sealing of Granda's coffin. I shivered at the thought and tried not to think about it. Would they find me if I stayed hidden behind the bales of hay? Maybe. Maybe not. One thing I knew for sure, if they saw me, they'd kill me as quickly as they killed Granda. If I were going to get away, I'd have to go now while they were busy sealing the crate. I stood, but before I could escape, the pipit cried out and lunged down to peck at my face. When I tried to shoo it away, it landed on the back of my hand and nipped me. I yelped and ran from the stall right into McNeil, who grabbed me and flung me against the wall. The pipit rose to roost in the rafters.

"Well, I'll be jiggered. Aren't you the boy who was riding my horses the day Peter was trampled? Declan, look who I found poking around the barn."

Doing the only thing I could think of to save myself, I kicked McNeil between the legs. As McNeil doubled over, I bolted out of the stall and almost reached the barn door when Declan caught me and wrestled me to the ground.

"What's this," Declan tore the crane bag from the loop in my belt. With his knee pinning me to the ground, he opened the bag and emptied the gems into his palm. He threw the pouch into the corner and pocketed the gems before McNeil could see them. "Blood money," Declan whispered as he grabbed me by the arm and pulled me to my feet. "Keep your gob shut," Declan warned as MacNeil came around the corner of the stall.

His face was redder than a blootered sailor's, and his cussing nastier than any I'd heard.

"I ought to beat you 'til you're tattie bread. What'll we do with him now? He's heard everything, and so has your sister."

"Mary will keep quiet. I'll make sure of that," Declan said, "but the only way to keep this boy's cakehole shut is to nail it shut."

"I'll not have another death on my farm," McNeil said.

"There's an empty crate. Put him in there, and I'll dispose of it," Declan said.

"Get rid of him. I don't care how or where. Just do it." McNeil took some rope and tied my hands behind my back while Declan held me. There was no point in struggling.

Declan gagged me with a dirty handkerchief that smelled of whisky and sweat and pushed me out of the stall. He led me to the front of the barn, where Declan took the lid off an empty crate. "Get in," he said.

If they were going to kill me, I wouldn't make it easy for them. There was no way I was getting into that crate without a fight. When I kicked Declan in the shins, McNeil swung me around and punched me in the nose. My blood spattered over McNeil's face. He wiped it on his sleeve and shoved me over the crate's edge. I felt the wood thump against my tailbone—pain shot through my back. The lid came down with a bang. I counted the nails, thirteen in all. Then nothing but darkness.

Chapter Twenty-Three

Connor

I was thinking about the strange meeting with Faolan when I saw a little girl running along the road with something bundled up in a sweater, not just any sweater, but my sweater. The one Brannon had stolen from the wagon. I knew it was mine because Etain had let me choose the colors before she knitted it for me. She never knitted the same sweater twice. It was an original and I knew without a doubt it was mine. How on earth did the little girl get it? Did Brannon give it to her? If so, then she might know where he was.

I trotted alongside her. "Nice sweater you got there."

She kept her head down and walked faster.

"Is it yours?"

She shook her head and kept walking. I noticed that her wool bundle was moving in strange ways.

"What do you have there?"

"Kittens. One with six toes," she said without slowing down.

"Get away with you. Is it true, then?"

"Oh, yes."

"May I see?"

She looked at me then and at my horse. "I'm not allowed to talk to you and your kind," she said.

"And tell me, what kind is that?"

"You know what you are."

"I'm Brannon Mac Lir's cousin."

"You're not."

"Honest. Ask him if you don't believe me. I know you've seen him because that sweater is mine, and he was wearing it when he left. If you look inside, you'll see my name, Connor, embroidered on the inside around the neck. My great-grandma made it for me. Who are you?"

"Mary." She stopped and unrolled the sweater as I slipped off Malachy and knelt to catch one of the kittens from running away. The orange one with the six toes. I examined its paws.

"Ooh, a mitten kitten," I said. "He's so soft, and he'll make a good hunter with them boxing mitts. A good luck cat, too."

"You can't have him. He's mine." Mary checked the sweater and ran her finger over my name embroidered on the inside. She looked up at me with her large brown eyes. "I can't see how you could be Brannon's cousin, though."

"Me either. But he is. Brannon's my blood on my da's side."

"You don't look like Brannon."

"No, but that's the way of it. He's gone missing, and I must find him." Connor followed her gaze across the meadow toward the barn. Two men were loading a crate onto a wagon.

"He's hiding in the barn," she said. "My brother will kill him if he finds him there."

"Who is your brother?"

"Declan."

"Why would he hurt Brannon?"

"Because he killed Brannon's granda. He thinks Brannon killed Peter, but he didn't. It was the pipit."

"Bloody hell." I handed Mary the wiggling kitten and mounted the horse. I urged Malachy to hop the stone fence and gallop across the field toward the barn. When we traveled to Ballycastle for the wake, I remembered Kieran pointing the farm out. It would make sense that Brannon would go back there.

By the time I had arrived at the barn, the younger man, whom I had guessed was Declan, had driven away in a horse and wagon loaded with crates, moving north, while the older man had gone south in a pickup truck. The farmer must be doing well, as few could afford a truck in these parts.

I saw a bike leaning against the barn and recognized Brannon's bag in the basket. After pulling it out and swinging it over my shoulder, I opened the barn door. Pain shot from my tattooed wrist to my shoulder. Fomorii?

Wings flapped—the pipit dove toward me. I ducked and placed my hand over my head for a shield. The bird circled once, then flew up and out through a hole in the rafters.

"Brannon? It's me, Connor." I looked around and saw drops of fresh blood in the hay near the door and Brannon's crane bag lying in the corner. I picked it up. Empty except for the flint. I suspected the men stole the gems from Brannon. Faolan wouldn't be happy to learn that they were gone. I was sure Brannon had been in a fight, and I feared my cousin had seen the worst of it. Who were those people, and what was in those crates?

I rushed out of the barn and mounted Malachy. I wondered if I should follow the wagon or the truck. Wagon or truck, I kept saying over and over in my mind. Kicking Malachy into a gallop, I followed the truck because I could see only one person in the wagon, but I couldn't see if there was anyone else in the truck's cab. Where would they be going? Would I be able to catch up to them now? I had gone as far as the Bonamargy Friary when a woman appeared before me on the road. The Lady. Brannon's Lady. Malachy stopped and reared. Before The Lady disappeared, she pointed in the direction of the wagon. I knew The Lady was telling me I was going the wrong way.

Turning Malachy around, I took a shortcut along a cow path through a meadow of grazing sheep. Within minutes, I saw the wagon kicking up a trail of dust on the dirt road. Staying off the main road and out of sight, I followed the wagon as it turned off and bumped along a narrow dirt track that rose to the top of the sea cliff.

I tethered the horse behind a thicket of blackberry bushes. Crouching from boulder to boulder, I crept toward the wagon. Declan had backed the wagon up to the edge of the crag. He climbed into the back of the wagon and shoved the crate to the edge. With a grunt, he pushed it out of the cart and over the cliff. I heard the crate hit the water. Declan smiled before getting back into the wagon and headed toward the main road.

I had a bad feeling. Mary said Declan would kill Brannon if he found him. Surely, he wouldn't have nailed the boy in the crate. Was the man that evil? Maybe. He had killed Brannon's granda, so he might be nasty enough to drown Brannon as easily as a sack of helpless kittens. I looked over the cliff's edge at the crate bobbing up and down with each swell. I had to know what was in the container, and I didn't have much time.

The crate wouldn't stay afloat for long, and if I didn't hurry, the tide would take it out of reach. I didn't like the idea of taking a dip in the ocean. It would be cold—damn cold. I slid down the embankment and removed my boots and jacket. With no time to brace for the icy water, I plunged in. "Bloody hell," I gasped. The cold took my breath away. "Damn, kid. Why did you go and run away like that?" I gritted my teeth and swam toward the sinking crate.

The riptides were dangerous in this area, and I couldn't go much further without being caught in them. The crate was drifting away from me faster than I could swim. "Dammit, Manannan, blessed sea-god, help me!" I felt the current change, and instead of pulling the crate away from me, the tide sent it back along glassy crests toward the shore. I swam back and, finding footing on the sandbar, waded as fast as possible to reach the crate before the waves pulled it away from me again. Using all my strength, I dragged the crate onto the rocky shore.

"You in there, kid?" I said, trying to catch my breath. "Brannon, I hope you're not in there." Frantically, I tried to pry the lid open with my fingers. "Jaysus, look at all those nails." I picked up a thin flat rock and tried to wedge it between the lid and the crate. It was a hair too thick. I tossed it over my shoulder and searched my pockets for McKinley's knife. "Damn, where did I put it?" I scrambled for my jacket and found it on the rock where I had left it. No knife, though. "So where? Please, Manannan, help me find it. I promise to give the knife back to McKinley if you do."

Then I remembered I'd slipped the knife into the side of my left boot. I pulled it out, ran back to the crate, knelt, and examined it for its weakest spot. One board had a flaw, a knothole that caused a small hole close to the edge of a corner. With the knife, I worked the spot until the board lifted. In the waning light, I saw something inside the crate—wet clothes, maybe a boy. "Brannon, is that you?" I yanked off the first board, stuck my hand inside, and felt a wet lump. An arm. Fingers.

"Manannan, help me. He might be dead already. Jaysus, I'm going to beat the shit out of that man for doing this to you. Hang on. Hang on, kid." Bracing my foot against the box, I yanked the board free. One more board and I could pull him out. But that wood was nailed harder than the first. It splintered. Cursing, I peeled the wood away one strip at a time.

Brannon was curled up at the bottom of the crate. Dead or unconscious, there was no way to tell. With trembling hands, I turned the box on its side and pulled Brannon out.

Without opening his eyes, Brannon spewed water and then lost consciousness again.

It would be difficult to lead Malachy down the embankment to the shore, but I could do it if I could find a path. I took a moment to look for a place where the stallion could maintain a footing. I saw nothing but sheer rock. It would be far too dangerous for the stallion. I couldn't take the chance that Malachy would sprain a leg, or worse. Time was running out for Brannon. Shock and the cold water could kill him soon. I had no choice but to carry him on my back. I hauled Brannon up and clasped his arms around my neck. Taking one step at a time, I climbed the rocks.

Chapter Twenty-Four

Connor

For three days, Brannon lay curled in a fetal position, limp as a sick dog. He refused to eat or speak. He hardly even moved. Being nailed in a crate and thrown into the sea would make any person's mind go away for a while. Maybe Brannon's mind would never come back.

"Hey, Brannon, I didn't risk my life to have you lie in bed like that. The three of us have work to do. We've got to find those gems for one." I sat on the edge of the bed with a bowl of chicken broth in my hands. Every day I tried to coax Brannon to eat, and every day I felt angrier and more frustrated when he didn't eat. I wanted to shake the kid. I didn't agree to be his nursemaid, and he'd better not die in my wagon. I begged Etain to look after him, but she refused. She had warmed his body, but no one could bring back his mind. Now it was up to

Brannon. She said there was nothing more she could do than what I was already doing.

I don't know where Kieran got the stupid idea that the best place for Brannon was with me. Before Kieran left the camp, he told me to keep trying to reach Brannon and not to worry. Kieran said he'd be back in a day or so.

Great. A day or so. It seemed like forever. Why did Kieran think I could help my cousin? Didn't he see that the damage to Brannon's mind was far worse than the bruises on his body? Heck, I'd prefer to nurse a colicky foal. At least a horse responded to my care.

I rolled Brannon onto his back and put a pillow under his head. His eyes were dark pools, looking at nothing. I brought a spoonful of soup to his lips, but it was like feeding one of Tara's dolls. Soup dripped down his chin.

"You're gonna die, you know. It's not right to do this to us, and what about your ma and da? Don't you care about them anymore? Wake up, you eejit. Damn it all, anyway. If you're going to die, I wish you'd hurry and do it. I haven't got time for this nonsense."

Ach, there was no point raging at the deaf. Nothing I said or did could change what would be. Manannan had taken Brannon's mind. It was only a matter of time before his body would follow, and the sooner, the better. I brushed tears from my eyes. Frustrated tears, not sad ones. I didn't care if he lived or died. I opened the door and tossed the bowl across the camp. The bowl almost hit Tara, who was walking toward the wagon. She came every day to offer her help and support. Today she brought her harp.

She picked up the bowl and brought it into the wagon. "Hey, it looks like you need a break."

"I do. God knows I've tried everything to reach him."

"Let me try. I've been practicing and have composed a few songs of my own. Maybe my music will bring him back."

"I don't think he'll hear you, but you can try." I went outside, sat on the wagon step, and breathed a sigh of relief to be free of Brannon for a while. Snow had fallen in the night, and the air was fresh and crisp. Now the sky was clear, and the sun transformed the light dusting of snow into ice crystals.

Tentative strains of music drifted from the wagon as Tara warmed up her harp. She stopped and started, then found her song. Yes, she had a gift. The music soothed my bad temper more than a steaming bowl of mutton stew. The weight of the last few days lifted, and I found myself humming along. Then the music stopped, and the wagon door opened. I groaned at the thought of going back in.

"Connor," Tara whispered. "Come see this."

I stepped back into the wagon and sat on a side bench near the bed. Brannon was sitting up, his eyes still dark and looking far away. Tara sat opposite me and strummed her harp. After a few moments, Brannon moved his right hand in time to the music. What did that mean? When she stopped playing, he put his hand down.

"Are you feeling better now, Brannon?" Tara asked.

His head dropped, and his chin rested on his chest. He was going to curl up again.

"Play some more," I urged. "Do you remember the chant from the piece of flint that Peter gave Brannon?"

"I think so." Plucking the strings, Tara searched for the notes. "I think I've got it."

Brannon's head lifted from his chest. The fingers on his right hand twitched. His arm rose and, with his thumb and index finger, pressed together as if he were holding a pencil. He moved in time to the music.

"Strange," I said. "It looks like he's drawing something in the air."

I rummaged in a drawer for a pencil and a notebook. I put the pencil in Brannon's hand and the notebook on his lap. Catching Brannon's hand in mid-air, I pulled it down to the notebook and held it over the paper until Brannon moved the pencil. Swirls at first, a bunch of scribbles, then Brannon drew a seahorse, exactly like the one I had carved.

I turned the page over, and Brannon drew the body of a man floating in the ocean. The face had a scar running across the length of the man's forehead.

When Tara stopped playing to look at the drawing, Brannon's arm went limp. "Who is it?" she asked.

"It's Declan, Peter's brother, and the man who tried to kill Brannon. Mary, Peter's sister, told me Declan killed Brannon's granda. After what Declan's done, I can't blame Brannon for wanting to see him floating dead in the ocean."

"Brannon's looking a little better. Now, maybe he'll eat something." Tara placed her harp on the table. "I'll go ask Ma for some soup."

I shoved more peat into the stove. Then, I took from my bedroom alcove the sword I had forged. I'd never enjoyed metalwork as much as creating this blade. I liked the feel of the steel as I'd marked its shape and length from the image that appeared in my mind. I tempered the metal by laying it in the fire, hammering and hammering until my shoulders ached and my face, sweaty with exertion, glowed red as the fire in the forge.

I'll never forget the sound of the sword coming to life, hissing as I immersed it in water to cool, its edges ready for polishing and sharpening. Seanán had helped me shape the crosspiece and fasten the hilt to the tang. I melted the silver fork I'd taken from the hotel into strands that I twisted into a Celtic knot where the hilt and crosspiece met, the same knot that adorned my wrist. For three days, the forging had kept me sane.

"Look, Brannon, I made a sword and affixed the seahorse hilt I carved. Do you want to hold it?"

I placed the sword across Brannon's lap. Brannon raised his head, opened his eyes, gripped the hilt, and held the sword before him. Suddenly, he looked older. His hair had a halo of white, and wrinkles creased his brow.

"I am the pearl, the eye of truth," Brannon spoke in a voice deeper than his own. "I see through illusions. The Lady is the sapphire, the keystone that will re-tune the land. Together, we are the sword."

Before I could stop him, Brannon ran the blade across the palm of his hand and bloodied it.

"Jaysus, what are you doing?" I pulled the sword away, grabbed Brannon's hand, and turned it over. The wound faded away, leaving a mark on Brannon's palm. A scar in the shape of a seahorse.

Shaken by what I had seen and heard, I took the sword and put it back into the alcove. "Blood or no, you'll not have this sword, Brannon."

"What sword?" Brannon lay back and pulled the blanket up to his neck.

Holy God, the kid had come back to himself. His eyes were still darker than usual, but other than that, he looked like himself again. "Don't you remember? You ran the blade across your palm and bloodied it. Damn you for doing that." I grabbed Brannon's wrist and turned his hand over to show him the scar on his palm. "If I hadn't seen it happen with my own eyes, I would have thought you were trying to trick me."

Brannon pulled his hand away to look at the scar. "I don't remember. Honest, I don't. I just wish this would stop. I never asked for this."

"Like it or not, you're stuck with it. I didn't save your sorry ass just to hear you whine like a spoiled brat."

Brannon sat up and swung his legs over the bunk. "I guess I owe you now."

"Nah, you don't. I did what I did because I had to."

Tara opened the door and stepped into the wagon with a bowl of potato leek soup, freshly made and smelling yummy. She sat on the edge of the bed.

"Look at you? I guess my harp music brought you back, after all?"

"Music?" Brannon took the bowl and dipped the spoon into the soup.

"He doesn't remember the music," I said. "He doesn't remember anything."

"Oh well, that keeps me humble now, doesn't it? And guess what? Kieran's back, and he brought Brannon a big surprise. He's coming with it right now."

I heard voices approaching the wagon. Brannon sat up a little straighter as the wagon door opened. A cool breeze preceded a woman with a shawl over her head, and behind her was Kieran. I had seen the woman's shawl before, as it was one of Etain's. The woman pulled the shawl down around her neck.

"Ma!" Brannon nearly spilled his soup. Tara took it from him and placed it on the table. She moved away from the bed so Molly could gather Brannon into her arms. She held him for a long time until Brannon squirmed out of her embrace.

"Connor, if you hadn't been there—I shudder to think what would have happened. With all my heart, I thank you."

"Yeah, well, he's blood." I picked up the sketches Brannon had done and gave them to Kieran. "Brannon drew these pictures while Tara was playing her harp. The music helped bring him around."

Kieran smiled. "Tara, your gift is developing." He looked at the drawing of the seahorse first and then at the picture of the man floating face-up in the water. He passed it to Molly.

"He's always done this sort of thing, a kind of sleep drawing," Molly said. "Sometimes his drawings foretell the future."

"Declan stole my talisman and the pearl Manannan gave me on my birthday," Brannon said. "I heard him say that he set fire to our house and boat, too. And Ma, he confessed to McNeil that he killed Granda." Brannon's voice broke. He cleared it and asked, "Where's Da?"

"Safe. He's in Portrush with Evan. They found work there."

"Ma, why didn't you tell me about the sapphire?"

"I was going to, but when Peter and Granda died, everything went crazy. After Etain gave it to you, I sent word to Kieran. I hoped to convince your da to let you study with him. I wanted to take it away from you, but I knew that once you bloodied the stone, there would be no separating you from it. Even now, you must feel it calling you."

"It's strange how I feel lost without it. I look for the talisman and then remember it's gone."

"Is this talisman Manannan's sapphire?" I shared one of the side benches with Tara.

"It is." Kieran sat on a bench across from me. "Brannon's star sapphire was Manannan's firestone. You remember the story I told you of the pearl, how Manannan created it from a chip of his firestone?"

"Yes, my sapphire has a tiny chip in the center, in the shape of a star," Brannon said. "Is it the same chip that created the pearl?"

Kieran nodded. "The sapphire has a long history. When the Tuatha De Danann settled in Ireland, they brought many treasures. Some of them were gemstones from other countries. One was a star sapphire, naturally polished in a stream in Northern India. The man who found it traded it to a Persian traveler, who then sold it to a Tuatha De Danann named Manannan. He knew the stone was special because of its beautiful blue color and the clarity of the star that graced the center. Human hands had never shaped it, yet the stone was a perfect oval and so smooth that a silk scarf would glide across it. The size of the stone, as large as an English sovereign, was also astounding for such a perfect gem. Manannan was a master smith and banded the sapphire in white gold. When he wore it around his neck, he discovered something strange about the stone. It focused his thoughts. When he wondered how to do something he'd never done before, the gem responded with answers. It not only sharpened his magical gifts, but also filled his mind with endless ideas. Manannan realized he could not always wear the stone because it would never let him rest. Wanting to keep it at his side, he forged a sword and set the sapphire into the hilt. That sword became known as The Answerer."

"The Lady," Brannon blurted out.

Kieran paused for a moment. "Yes, she's the spirit of Manannan's sword, The Answerer."

"I need to show you something." I took my sword from the alcove, withdrew it from its sheath, and passed it to Kieran.

Kieran examined the workmanship and tested the balance. "Connor, the sword is exquisite. It is just as I remembered Manannan's sword to be. Now, we need to find the gems to make it whole again and restore it to its original power."

"I don't understand. How could you have seen Manannan's sword?" I said. "Do you mean in a vision?"

Kieran's lips curved ever so slightly as if he was holding back a well-guarded secret. I had never heard Kieran tell stories of his childhood or even where he received his training in the old ways. No one seemed to know anything about him, yet all looked to him for guidance. The man was a mystery.

"Well," Kieran's eyes sparkled. "That's a story for another time. Tell me, Connor, how did you find the seahorse in the oak wood?"

"Aunt Molly told me to listen to the wood with my fingers. It would tell me what shape it wanted to be. Then, the seahorse appeared in my mind."

"Ah, you see? You're coming into your own. Sometimes the sea-god's ways are subtle, but you heard him and allowed yourself to be an instrument of his will. I'm as proud of you as any father could be of his son."

"A tool. That's all I am," I said bitterly.

"I hope you know it's a great honor to be called to do Manannan's work."

"I do, but—"

"There is something else troubling you."

"It's just that when I let Brannon hold the sword, he changed." I tried to keep my voice steady, to hide my fear that Kieran would give the sword I worked so hard to make to my annoying cousin. "I swear I saw someone else looking at me through his eyes. Someone older, with a deeper voice. He said he was the pearl, the eye of truth, and that The Lady was the sapphire. Together, they made up the sword."

"I said that?" Brannon asked.

"And he ran the blade across his palm and bloodied it. Show them the scar."

Brannon turned his hand over to show them the mark on his palm. "I don't remember doing it, and I promise I won't take your sword away."

"What does this mean?" Molly held Brannon's hand in hers and studied the mark.

Kieran was thoughtful for a moment. "I'm not sure, but Brannon's blood is rich with the wisdom and magic of the old ones, the Tuatha de Danann. He, too, is an instrument of the sea-god. I wish I had been here to see his transformation. Only time will tell how this will shape him."

Kieran held the sword before him. "The Fomorii, like this sword, can be both beautiful and deadly. When Manannan fought the Fomorii, he used the sword to drive them into their prison. Years later, when Manannan went to Tir na nOg, the gems dropped from his sword and remained on earth to help others as they once helped the Tuatha De Danann."

"To banish the Fomorii every one thousand years?" I asked.

"And that is what your father has tried to do and has failed," Kieran said. "He is not the one. Whenever he uses his magic and fails, he gives the Fomorii more power. We have seen that in the blight that spoils our land and the sickness taking our young and old. Despite what happened, he wants the sapphire because he thinks it will give him the power he needs for his revenge."

"You can't blame him for that. The Fomorii killed his parents," I said.

"Faolan's misuse of power killed them, and yes, it's true that when the Fomorii escaped, they caused havoc with our land and people. That's because they feel it's their right."

"How can it be their right?" Brannon said. "They killed my best friend, and they almost got me killed. How can you stick up for them? If it weren't for a Fomorii in the form of a pipit, Peter would not be dead. Mary saw the wee bird swoop down and spook the horse."

"Brannon, there are always two sides in a conflict," Molly said.

"That's right," Kieran interjected on her behalf. "The Fomorii lived in Ireland long before the Tuatha. They coexisted from day one, but the Fomorii regarded the Tuatha with suspicion and protected their own. That was their biggest mistake. For every wrong the Fomorii committed, the Tuatha committed worse against the Fomorii. They wanted to show the Fomorii that they were stronger and better, but they forgot that the island belonged to the Fomorii before them. They fought, and with each battle, the war grew worse. At the last battle, the Tuatha ambushed the Fomorii. When their magic failed, Manannan used his sword to banish them. A mist rose from the ground, and they found themselves between worlds. Not living, but not dead."

"What are we to do?" Tara said. "Banish them again? Is that the right thing to do?"

"Even though their plight is compelling, we can't let the Fomorii rage," Kieran said, "and rage they will if they aren't stopped. History tells us that."

Kieran handed the sword back to me. "We must find those gems before Faolan tries again."

"Declan stole them from me. And Ma, he's running guns. I overheard him talking. He was supposed to deliver them to Faolan."

Molly sighed. "I'm not surprised."

Gunrunning. So, Faolan was into more than antiquities. I cleared my throat, feeling that tight sensation that came just before tears. How silly to feel this way about a man who'd never been a father. "I saw him when I went into town to look for Brannon. He seemed changed. Nice clothes, clean-shaven. He has a lot of money and a schooner. I thought he had turned his life around. He offered me a job working with him."

"I'm sorry he's disappointed you again," Molly said.

"Ach, I shouldn't have got my hopes up. Anyway, he told me about the Fomorii and how he messed up everything and started the fire. He's convinced he's the one. He says Brannon will fail as he failed. And you're right. He's planning to try again, with or without the gems. He knows Brannon has the sapphire and the pearl and wants me to bring Brannon to his boat, *Breath of Cerridwen*."

"Perhaps I should visit him. Today is the anniversary of our parents' death, so Faolan will try the banishment before the day is out," Molly said.

"He told me today is the last chance to restore the seals," I said.

"Quite right," Kieran added.

"I want to go with you," Brannon said.

"We all would," I chimed in.

Molly shook her head and placed her hand on his forehead. "No, you need to rest. Besides, I don't want the children in any more danger."

"But I'm the one, not Faolan. The Lady said so herself. I have to go. If the talisman is in town, I may feel it. It may draw me to it," Brannon argued.

"It's too dangerous even for you, Molly," Kieran said. "Declan may still have the gems. I'll ask around. Maybe someone has seen or heard something. With any luck, Declan may have tried to pawn the gems in one of the local shops. Connor, prepare my horse."

Tara followed me out of the wagon. "I'm going into town," I said. "There's still so much I need to ask Faolan. Watch Brannon for me. He's being brave, but he still doesn't look well. I'll take Malachy. Don't worry."

As I crossed the field toward the horses, I attached the sword to my belt. For now, it was mine, and I would hold on to it for as long as possible. After all, the seahorse still needed an eye.

Chapter Twenty-Five

Connor

I found the *Breath of Cerridwen*, a topsail schooner, docked at the end of the pier. Sails on the foremast and mainmast were lowered, exposing the maze of rigging that connected and manipulated the sails. A deckhand, a boy about fourteen, worked to restore the golden color to the teak decks and bulwarks with linseed oil.

"Is Faolan here?" I tried not to breathe deeply. I'd never liked the smell of linseed oil. It sickened me, and I wondered how the boy could stand it.

Without looking up, the boy rubbed the oil into the wood with a rag. "He left orders not to be bothered, and he'll have my head if I disturb him for someone the likes of you."

"I'm his son."

"And I'm the King of England." He spat over the gunnels.

"You'd better ask him. I hate to think what he'd do when he finds you've turned me away."

The boy placed the cloth in his back pocket and wiped his hands on his pants, already stained with oil, dirt, and paint. "You better be who you say you are, or I'll kick your arse from here to Tir na nOg."

Just try it, I thought as I stepped across the gangway and followed the boy toward the bow. The deckhand braced himself before knocking lightly on the door. I heard a shuffle from within the room.

The boy knocked louder. "It's Rory, sir. There's a boy here, and he says he's your son."

Faolan's muffled voice from the other side of the door invited me to come in.

Faolan's quarters smelled like sandalwood oil and snuffed candles. A large round window gave a view of the pier, the ship's wheel, and the ocean beyond. Navigation maps covered the walls, showing routes to France, Spain, and Egypt, down the coast of Africa, and around the Cape to India. Antiquities from all over the world cluttered the cabin. Mahogany wood framed a sitting nook upholstered in tan leather. An old manuscript written in an ancient script lay on the table amid dirty dishes Rory should have cleared days ago. The shelves in the bookcase overflowed with books.

I stooped to read the titles, some in Latin, some in Gaelic, and some in languages I didn't recognize. "Can you read these books?"

"Most of them, not all." Faolan looked up from the journal he was writing in. On the corner of the desk was a bronze statue of a half-woman and half-cat. I picked it up, surprised by the weight. The cat had an emerald jewel hanging from one of its ears and a gold ring in its nose. Winged scarabs decorated its chest and the top of its head.

"The Egyptian god Baste. It dates from around 600 BC. Notice the wedjat amulet, also known as the Eye of Ra."

I placed the statue back on the desk. So, the Eye of Ra was the symbol engraved on the ring Faolan wore.

"The Egyptians carved the Eye of Ra into the bow of a boat to ensure a safe passage," he explained. "It's an Egyptian symbol of protection."

"You've been to Egypt?"

"Many times. The magic I learned there is as old as the Tuatha and equally powerful."

Faolan dipped his pen into the inkwell and wrote a few more words in his journal. After blotting the ink, he stuck the pen in its holder, closed the journal, and placed it beside the statue of Baste.

Faolan ran his fingers, each bound with strips of linen, through his hair, smoothing it back from his brow. It looked like he had slept in his clothes. His shirt billowed beneath his vest, and his sleeves rolled to his elbows. "I've been thinking a lot about you lately. There's so much I'd like to tell you now that you're of an age to understand. But today is my last chance to deal with the Fomorii."

"Why today?"

"Because it's the anniversary of the Tuatha's victory over the Fomorii and the day Manannan banished them from the world. I'd hoped you'd bring Brannon with you and the gems." His voice sounded weary with fatigue.

"He's been sick and almost died."

"With the fever? It's raging through the village. Many have died." Faolan got up from the desk and sat in one of two mahogany chairs upholstered in rich burgundy velvet with winged lion heads carved into the armrests. "In the old tales, the Fomorii caused a blight that attacked the young and the old."

I sat in the other chair. For all its beauty, it was as comfortable as riding a mule. "We've lost some of our own to it too, but it's not that. If you remember, I was supposed to be looking for Brannon the day I met you."

"I do," Faolan said. "What happened?"

"He ran into a man who stole his gemstones, nailed him in a crate, and threw him over a cliff and into the sea. I swam out and rescued him. It's a miracle I was there to see the crate go over the cliff, or he would have drowned."

Faolan had that look that used to make me run for cover. "Does Brannon know this man?"

"Yes. His name is Declan. He blames Brannon for the death of his brother." I thought it best not to mention the gunrunning and that Brannon overheard Declan and McNeil talking about delivering the shipment to Faolan. "Do you know him?"

Faolan gripped the lion-head armrests. "Yes, he works for me."

"Declan admitted to killing Brannon's granda."

"I'd heard about the fire, but—I didn't know Declan had set it. I'll have to—"

A knock on the door interrupted Faolan. "Tea, sir." Rory entered the cabin with a silver tea set and a tray loaded with with fruit, apple squares, boiled eggs, and biscuits topped with kippers and marmalade. He placed it on the table. "Anything else, sir?"

"Find Declan and tell him to come to my quarters."

Rory stooped to clear away the dirty dishes.

"Leave them," Faolan said sharply.

"Yes, sir." Rory glanced at me before rushing out of the room. There was fear in his eyes.

"He might still have the gems," I said while eyeing the plate of goodies.

"Maybe. If not, we might find out what Declan did with them. Now help yourself." Faolan poured a cup of tea and sat back down at his desk to look over a manuscript.

I took a biscuit topped with marmalade and kippers. The lapping of the waves against the boat and a seagull's cry filled the silence as I ate and waited. I was uneasy about seeing Declan again. The man was a murderer and didn't think twice about killing. Things could turn nasty when Faolan confronted him. I hoped Declan didn't have a gun.

I almost choked on my biscuit when I heard a rap on the door. I had a bad feeling that this wouldn't go well. Rory opened the door, and Declan strode in like a cock in a henhouse, his face as red as a rooster's comb. He was an ugly brute with a scar across his forehead, a cockeyed smile, and a pimply com-plexion. Faolan offered him tea, a strange gesture considering what Declan had done. But that was Faolan's way—to do the unexpected. Faolan would broadside Declan with hospitality.

Declan went straight for the dessert tray and popped an olive in his mouth. "So, when will we be leaving? I'm anxious to get to Belfast and deliver the order. You know my clients will be getting a bit nervous by now."

"I come and go as I please, and let me remind you I'm not so enamored of the cause that I'm in any hurry. This is your deal, not mine. Right now, I have more important business to take care of. We'll sail when I decide to."

"So, why were you looking for me?"

"I thought you'd like to meet my son, Connor."

Declan glanced at me, then poured a cup of tea. The delicate china looked ridiculous in his calloused hands as he downed the tea in one gulp. Crass even for my taste. "Hell, I didn't know you had a son." He picked up another biscuit, pulled off the kipper, ate it, then put the biscuit back on the tray. "Then again, I don't know much about you. Your boy's dressed like a tinker." He laughed nervously. "Hey, why not? I've been stunned by some of 'em girls myself."

"Yes, his mother was beautiful, but not one of my people," Faolan said in a quiet, even tone.

It surprised me to hear Faolan talk about my mother like he cared about her, even loved her. Not the one-night fling I had always imagined her to be. I wished Faolan would say more. I didn't even know her name.

"You? A tinker?" Declan snorted loudly. "Well then, you've done mighty well for yourself."

"I think so—and you? I hear you've come into some wealth of your own."

Declan's eyes narrowed. He took a boiled egg and devoured it whole. "Who told you that?"

"My son."

Declan took another egg and ate it whole. His hand hovered over the biscuits and settled on an apple square. He looked down his nose at me. "I've never met you before today. Sure, you got the right man?" He licked his finger and gathered crumbs off the dessert plate.

"It's true, we've never met, but I know someone who knows you," I said.

"Who's that now?" He poured himself another cup of tea.

"Brannon Mac Lir."

Declan paled and swallowed hard. "That little prod killed my brother."

"You know he didn't. You blame him because it furthers the cause. We all know that. And he told me about the gun-running." I hadn't meant to mention the guns. It just slipped out with my hatred for the man. Besides, I wanted to break Declan's nose and maybe a rib or two.

"You'd better watch what you're saying, boy."

"Why? Because you know it's true?"

"You're gonna let your boy shoot his gob off like that?" Declan growled. "Does he know you and I are in business together?"

"You work for me. That is the extent of our business. Anything else you do is your concern," Faolan said.

"Still, he ought to be careful what he says or who he's accusing." Declan wiped his mouth on his sleeve.

"You tried to kill him," I retorted. "I saw the crate you put him in go over the cliff, and I swam out and brought it back to shore."

The vein under Declan's scar throbbed. "The boy saw the guns. McNeil told me to get rid of him. We knew he wouldn't keep his gob shut. Look, we'd better set sail. Lord knows how many people he's blabbed to, and the constabulary will hang you and me if they catch us."

"Not if I get rid of the guns and you too," Faolan said.

Declan's eyes shifted from me to Faolan. Faolan was between Declan and the door. If he planned to run, Faolan would stop him. If he didn't, I would.

"Where are the gemstones you stole from the boy?" Faolan asked.

"I took 'em—blood money. Brannon killed my brother. It's only fair. What was the little sissy doing with gemstones, anyway? I bet he stole 'em from his ma."

"Brannon is my nephew." Faolan slid his lambskin gloves over his bandaged fingers, methodically pressing the leather between each finger.

I tensed. The hairs on the back of my neck rose.

"Do you still have the gemstones?" Faolan tucked his shirt into his pants and buttoned up his vest.

"I sold them. And I have to admit, I couldn't get rid of

those gems fast enough. Crazy how they made me feel. I swear those gems are bewitched or something. It felt like I was carrying a pocketful of boulders instead of two small stones, and, by Jaysus, they gave me one hell of a headache. I felt physically sick handling them. That pork-faced jeweler didn't know his arse from a hole in the ground. He kept asking me where I got them. Then a lady came into the store, a pretty woman. She offered to buy the gems and gave me ten times what the jeweler offered. He wasn't happy, but what could he do but back away from the deal?" A thin layer of sweat beaded on his forehead. "Jaysus, it's hot as hell in here."

"Did she tell you her name?" Faolan asked.

"No, I didn't ask." Declan tore off his jacket and dropped it on the floor. His face flushed red, and sweat streamed down his cheeks. "I took the money and left. I didn't see where she went, but I'm sure she's staying in town somewhere. She wasn't from around here. I could tell that. She was too well dressed for a village girl. It looked like she was off to a fancy party or something." Declan held the teacup to his lips and took a sip when suddenly it began to boil and steam. Burning his lip, he cursed and dropped the cup on the floor. The fine china shattered.

Faolan wore a smug half-smile. "Declan, I think you're becoming quite a liability."

Before I could blink, Declan had a knife pointed at Faolan. Just as quickly, I pulled my sword from its sheath.

Faolan held a hand up to stop me. "No need to bloody such a fine weapon." Undaunted, Faolan kept his eyes on the knife that began to glow red hot.

"Bloody hell!" Declan yelped and dropped the knife. Sweat poured down his reddened face. "I'm burning up."

"You must be catching the fever," Faolan said. "I heard it spread all over town. Many have died from it."

I saw fire in Faolan's eyes and knew this was more than a fever. Where had Faolan learned to do this?

"Bloody witchcraft? I've heard the crew talking. They're scared of you. Some of 'em have seen you do strange things. I didn't believe them till now. What are you, some kind of demon? They burn people like you—"

"It looks to me like you're the one who's burning," Faolan said without taking his eyes from Declan.

Swearing, Declan pushed past Faolan and burst out of the cabin. Through the window, I watched him run the length of the pier, tear off his shirt and jump into the water.

"How did you do that?" My voice jumped an octave.

Faolan turned away from the window. "I've always had an affinity for fire. I think one day your abilities will far exceed mine, though."

That thought both excited and terrified me.

"The sword." It was a demand, not a request. I handed it to him.

Taking his monocle from his vest pocket, Faolan looked closer at the hilt. "How did you fuse the blade and hilt? There are no seams or fixings of any kind."

"I didn't have to. I brought the hilt and blade together, and they fit perfectly. No need for fixings. Tara's da helped me."

"Of course, Seanán would have the magic touch. A gifted smith. I'm glad he has taken you on as his apprentice."

It felt good to have Faolan look at me with admiration.

"Impressive. I'm proud of you, son." Faolan handed me the sword.

I slid it into the sheath. "What about the gems? Are they lost to us now?"

"I suspect that the woman who bought the gems from Declan is one of Manannán's people," Faolan said.

"Why do you think that?"

"The gems made Declan and the jeweler uncomfortable, but the woman could buy them without feeling anything. Magic stones are like that. If not meant for you, they'll make you feel ill, even kill you."

"Could it be The Lady?"

"Perhaps, but—"

"I have seen her and so has Brannon and Tara. I would never have found Brannon in time if it wasn't for her. Kieran says she's The Answerer."

"Why yes, it makes sense. Manannán's sword. Finally, it's all coming together. I hope there's still time." Faolan paced the length of the cabin. He stooped to pull a folder from a drawer. Inside was a document written in Ogham on linen paper. "In a cave close to here, I found this manuscript, which cites The Lady." His hands shook as he looked through the pages. "It says, 'Manannán gave the magical sword, The Answerer, to his foster son, Lugh. When Lugh pulled it from the scabbard, a blue light poured from the gemstone in the center of the crosspiece.

Before his eyes, a beautiful lady appeared. To wield the sword and use its magic, you must befriend The Lady, for if she dislikes the bearer, the sword becomes a curse to the wielder.' If I'm right, then The Lady will give the gems to Brannon before this day is over. I want to speak with the jeweler, though. He may give me some more information about her. Wait here for me. I have much to discuss and share with you. And if we can find the gems, I know we can use your sword. Connor, there's one more thing. The pearl is not for you. Don't even touch it."

"Why?"

"It could weaken someone—someone of your lineage. It might even kill you."

"I don't understand. What do you mean by my lineage?"

Faolan took his coat from the wardrobe. "I'll explain when I come back from the jeweler. I must go now. There's not much time."

I walked Faolan to the gangplank. Then I circled the outside deck, looking over the boat's edge, but I didn't see anyone floating in the waves. Still, I shivered. What kind of magic could make a man feel like he was burning up? Faolan was more dangerous than I had ever imagined him to be. Who was this man who had fathered me? What was this about lineage?

Chapter Twenty-Six

Connor

Back inside Faolan's quarters, I picked up the leather-bound notebook I saw him writing in. I thought it was a ship's log, but the cover was etched with the alchemic symbols Kieran had shown me for air, earth, water, and fire. I turned to the first page. The handwriting was difficult to read, with poorly formed letters half-printed and half-written. Despite the poor script, I could read the first entry.

> When I told Kieran that I wanted to pass through the veil and return, he warned me it would be a mistake to go down that path. He said I'm magically gifted, but my ability to make sound choices is flawed— that arrogant ass. I was furious and did it, anyway. I wanted to show him he was

wrong about me. If I could pass through the veil and return, I would have the gift of prophecy. The ability to visit the spirit world is considered the highest initiation and would be the accomplishment of my grade.

No wonder Kieran was reluctant to teach me. Like Faolan, was impatient to begin my training. I turned the page.

What a fool I was. Just before midnight, I went to the sea cave, when the tide was at its lowest, and performed the ritual. I could feel the power of my intent flow into me like hot lava. I heard voices calling to me and could see shapes shadowing the veil. At first, I didn't know who they were. Later, I discovered they were Fomorii. Why were they here? I hadn't called them to me. You see, I didn't know the rules of the veil. If someone performs a magical ritual between Samhain and the Winter Solstice, when the veil is the thinnest, and they don't use proper protection, they create a rift. Without knowing, I breached a seal and made a gateway through which some of the Fomorii escaped. It opened only for a second, but it was enough to set some of the demons free. At first, they looked like moths. Then, two materialized before me. The man, his robes tattered, his body thin yet with the strength of ten men, grabbed me around the neck and demanded I release the rest of his people. I told him I couldn't. I didn't know how. The other, a young woman, told him to let me go. He threw me against the cave wall, and I hit my head and passed out. I awoke at dawn with a terrible headache. I stumbled home and found Molly sitting on the wagon steps. She told me she had awakened from a dream and saw a lady in a white dress. She gave Molly a sapphire. I remembered Kieran saying that a sapphire would appear before the Fomorii could all escape. Could this be the one? If so, I was sure it was meant to be mine and not my sister's. I took it from her, and knowing a little gem magic, I chanted the words of banishment, but something went wrong, and the wagon burst into flames. Molly escaped, but my parents—Manannan give me strength—they didn't even wake up. Why didn't I listen to Kieran?

Molly was right. Faolan lived with terrible guilt. I wondered if she would ever forgive her brother. I closed the book, intending to put it back, but curiosity got the better of me, and I opened it again and read.

It's been almost a year since the fire killed my parents. I can finally write again, although sometimes the pain is unbearable. I wonder if my hands will ever heal or if they will remain a constant reminder of my foolishness. That is all I can write today as my hands bleed from the effort.

I avoided the dried blood spots on the paper and turned the page.

At first, I thought I had imagined her, but the woman who had come through the veil visited me every night to ease my pain and heal my burns. Her name is Orla. She told me about her people and about Calatin, the man who'd escaped with her. She said he's an evil being on both sides of the veil. The fact that not all Fomorii are bad was something I had never considered, given the legends we heard as children. When I healed and regained my strength, Orla disappeared. I thought my heart would break.

I wanted to know more about this mysterious woman and scanned the pages for her name.

Kieran has refused to teach me, so I have left my people for a job on a merchant ship. I'm looking forward to traveling to different countries. I think of Orla every day.

Faolan was twenty-five when he returned to Ireland. One night, Orla came to him.

I'm in love. Only the ignorant describe the Fomorii as misshapen creatures having one eye or limb. The Fomorii are beautiful supernatural beings skilled in magic. Orla has taught me more in a few months than all my teachers combined, including Kieran.

I fingered a lump of wax stuck to the bottom of the page before turning to the next entry, dated a year later.

My life is over. How could I be so stupid? I'm almost unable to write this, but I must for my son.

My heart skipped a beat when the cabin door clicked open. With no time to return the journal to the chest, I tucked it between the cushion and the arm of the chair. Faolan stood in the doorway with Tara and Brannon. Tara followed Faolan into the room while Brannon held back to stand in the doorway.

Tara placed her harp bag on the floor. "I was worried about you and convinced Brannon to come with me."

"They were arguing with Rory," Faolan added. "He wouldn't let them come on board to see you until I returned."

"And Connor," Tara glanced nervously at Brannon. "We saw some men pulling Declan's body from the water."

I got out of the chair. "Is that true? Declan's dead?"

Faolan closed the door behind him. "Why are you so upset? He tried to kill young Brannon here, and he murdered his granda. I wouldn't shed a single tear for the likes of him. Would you, Brannon? Surely, you wanted him dead."

Brannon's face turned ashen. "It was an unnatural death."

Faolan put his gloved hand on Brannon's shoulder. "Unnatural? What makes you say that?"

Brannon stepped aside and came further into the cabin. "I know, is all," The accusatory look in Brannon's eyes said everything.

Faolan smiled thinly. "Well, then, the gods have acted for your protection. Manannan, be praised. Yes?"

Brannon drew away from Faolan to look out the cabin window. "I don't know if I should praise or curse him." A cormorant landed on the rail outside, drew its wings wide, and squawked before flying out of view.

"Cormorants. They attacked us before." Tara stood beside Brannon at the window.

"He's here," Brannon said. "He's waiting for us."

"Indeed, he is," Faolan said.

"Who?" Tara asked.

"Calatin, the evil Fomorii king Faolan released when he was my age. Faolan has been trying to banish him ever since." I pulled the journal from between the cushions where I had hidden it. I couldn't tell if the heat that rose on my face was Faolan's doing or my fear, which was considerable after seeing what he did to Declan.

"I underestimated you." Faolan looked at me with dark eyes, a mixture of surprise and anger. "I wish you had waited. How far did you get?"

"Orla. Was she my mother?"

Faolan held out his hand and took the journal from me. His gloved fingers lingered over the symbols etched into the leather cover before placing it inside a wooden chest inlaid with mother-of-pearl. He mumbled something in a language I had never heard before—an incantation. The lock clicked inside the chest.

"Was Orla my mother?" I asked again.

"Yes." Faolan studied my face, waiting to see how I would react to the news.

"But she was a Fomorii." I couldn't stop my voice from cracking or my knees from shaking.

"Yes, Orla was Fomorii. You must have read that I breached the veil, and she escaped with Calatin. It was a grave mistake. But she was kind to me, and I fell in love with her."

Brannon turned away from the window on hearing the news that I was Fomorii. Would he think I was the enemy now? Probably. Would Tara? She looked down at her hands and avoided my eyes. When she finally looked up at me, I saw fear in her eyes.

"Are you saying that Connor is part Fomorii?" Brannon asked.

"Yes, that is what I'm saying." Faolan moved to stand beside Brannon at the window. "And he favors her more than me, and you, Brannon, favor me more than your mother or father."

"That's gobshite," Brannon said, turning away. "I'm not like you at all."

Faolan half-smiled. "Well, we shall see about that, my young nephew."

I put my hand out to take Tara's. I needed to feel her close to me but she shook her head and backed away.

"You're not human," she said.

"Neither was the Tuatha De Danann. Both were of the human form, though," Faolan said.

"But they were supernatural beings," I blurted out, still not believing I was half Fomorii. "What is there about me that is Fomorii?"

"Time will tell, Connor. The Fomorii gifts are slower to manifest but just as powerful. You may or may not develop them. We shall see. But know this. You are Orla's child. You look so much like her, your eyes, your hair—"

"No, you're lying. Where is Orla? What happened to her?"

It surprised me to see pain flicker for a moment across Faolan's face. "She died a few days after you were born. I didn't know what to do with you, so I gave you to Etain and told her that your mother was a village girl." He cleared his throat and turned to stare out the window.

"It was Samhain, and I made the traditional Barmbrack, yeast bread with fruit and raisins. Inside, I hid a ring set with the pearl I found when I was a boy. As you know, hiding a ring in Barmbrack is common for a young man to propose. I wanted to surprise Orla, as she had given me a son, and I wanted to make our union official. We sat down with a cup of tea, and she broke off a small piece. Somehow, the pearl had come away from the setting. I saw it hidden in the dough as she placed it to her lips. Oh, what a terrible moment. Tears came to her eyes as she held the pearl in her fingers. 'Oh Faolan, what have you done? Poisoned me with Manannan's eye of the seahorse.' She died in my arms."

"The eye of the seahorse," Brannon said. He looked as stunned as I felt.

I felt my knees weaken and held onto the back of the chair for balance.

"Yes, the eye, Manannan's pearl." Faolan turned away from the window to look at Brannon. "I didn't know what it was. I found it one day while I was walking on the seashore. It had washed up at my feet."

"And you recognized it that day you saw me at the pier," Brannon said.

"I suspected it was the same one," Faolan said.

"It's lost now." Brannon shoved his hand into his pocket as if he might still find it there by some miracle.

"Connor told me what happened." Faolan looked at me with more compassion than I had ever seen him give me. I didn't want his compassion or love. I wanted to show him I didn't need him, so I pulled my shirt sleeve up to display the tattoo. "No wonder Manannan marked my wrist with this knot when I entered the tower. But why now?"

"Because you have come of age and because the seals are dissolving. Now is the time when the Fomorii will escape," Faolan explained. "But Connor, you are only part Fomorii."

"This can't be true." Tara's eyes shone with tears. "Is it even possible? I mean, a human and a Fomorii? I know it's in the legends, but—"

"Legends are born from truths," Faolan said. "I didn't know then that Molly was to receive the sapphire and I the pearl, and together we would forge the sword. Actually, three of us were supposed to work together."

"Who was the third one?" Tara asked.

"Seanán."

Tara placed a shaky hand to her mouth. "Da?"

"So that's why he knew what to do when we forged the sword together." I rested my hand on the hilt.

"Seanán and I were childhood friends, but we grew apart when I left our people. I haven't seen him since I last visited Connor.

"That was five years ago," I said.

"It was difficult to see you, as you reminded me of my mistake and subsequent loss. Now that this task has fallen to the three of you, I'd like to help."

"We must return to the camp," Brannon said. "Kieran will be looking for us, and Ma will worry."

"Where are you camped?" Faolan asked.

I hesitated to tell him when Tara said, "Near Ballintoy harbor."

"I can bring the boat around to the harbor. You could be home before anyone misses you."

"What about the horses?" I said. "They're my responsibility. I can't leave them."

"I'll have someone bring them aboard. Please sit down. We must make plans. Believe it or not, Connor, my cause is the same as yours, to banish Calatin."

"But we don't have the gems," Brannon said. "They were stolen."

"I suspect The Lady bought them from Declan and that she'll return them to you before sunrise tomorrow.

"But if she doesn't?" I said.

Faolan sat in one of the mahogany chairs as if the guilt of what he had done weighed him down. "If she doesn't, we are all lost. Calatin and his people will reclaim this land."

Chapter Twenty-Seven

Brannon

I stood on the deck of the *Breath of Cerridwen* and leaned my face into the wind. Manannan's breath cleared my mind of the anxiety I felt in Faolan's presence. The wind, perfect for steady, even sailing, roared in my ears, muffling the gull's cries and the waves beating against the hull. With taut sails, the boat rose and fell in an easy rhythm, keeping as close to the shore as the rocks would allow.

I missed Peter. I missed him desperately, Peter, my anam cara, my soul friend. Connor and Tara had each other, but I was alone, friendless. I thought about the two cousins in Kieran's story, the boys who competed for everything yet were still friends. Blood or not, Connor would never be my friend. He was Fomorii, the Tuatha's greatest enemy. Whose side would he choose to defend when the moment came to banish his people?

By all the gods of war, I wondered how I, a mere boy, was supposed to defeat Calatin, a shape-shifting magical god-man. Tara was right. It all sounded like a fairytale, the stuff of legends and bedtime stories. Damn the gods. Damn them all to hell for casting me in the role of hero. I spit into the surf. As if to answer my sudden irreverent act, the next gust sent spray over the gunnels to splash me in the face. I didn't try to duck or move away. Without the help of the sea-god, I might as well go home and admit to everyone that I was a Ginny Ann. I whispered an apology and asked for the courage to carry out the task. I had to do it. I had to do it for Peter.

"We are alike, you know," Faolan said.

I turned my back to the wind and saw Faolan leaning against the gunnels. He raised his collar against the sea-borne chill.

"I'm not at all like you." I wiped the sea spray from my face with my jacket sleeve. "You wanted to be the one, but I never did. I'd give anything to make it all go away."

"If I were you, I'd try summoning The Lady."

"You're not me. Do it yourself if you're that anxious to talk with her." I didn't want to call upon The Lady without Kieran by my side. Something had always gone wrong when I tried to use my gifts. Torrential storms had come when I wanted a few apples, a herd of horses came when I had called only one, and Aonbharr when I had wished for a pooka.

"I could help you." Faolan stepped next to me and leaned over the rail to look at the two-foot chop slapping against the hull.

I forced myself not to step back. Instead, I half-turned my face to the wind, a shield against my uncle's scrutiny.

"You've called her before, haven't you?"

"Not on purpose. I was trying to summon the pooka."

A playful smile spread across Faolan's face. "What fun? I'd never thought to do that. What made you call the pooka?"

"The day Peter died, I thought it was because I had summoned the pooka—it being Pooky Night and all. I felt responsible. Kieran wanted me to try calling it, to show me it wasn't possible for someone of my ability to do that. Instead, The Lady came riding Aonbharr."

Faolan's eyes narrowed. Silently, he regarded me for a moment before speaking. "Sounds like Kieran was wrong about you. Perhaps I, too, have misjudged your gifts. What happened next?"

"The cormorants attacked us. Kieran said they were Fomorii."

"Yes, they often take the form of cormorants."

"Pipits too?"

"Oh yes. The pipit is Calatin's favorite form. An unassuming bird, but a dangerous one. I take it you saw a pipit."

I nodded, gripped the railing, and looked into the waves churning against the side of the boat. "Mary, Peter's sister, told me the pipit had spooked the horse that trampled Peter. She called it a pooka bird, but she's just a wee girl. Who knows what she saw that day?"

"I don't think it was the pooka. Most likely, it was Calatin. Mary must be a special little girl to have sensed that the pipit was more than it appeared. Did you have the talisman with you?"

I nodded.

"Calatin wanted you, not your friend." Faolan rested a gloved hand on my arm. I felt the urge to move away, not because Faolan's touch was malicious but because it was warm and sympathetic, and I didn't want to start bawling. "You still blame yourself, don't you?"

"If Peter wasn't with me that day, if I hadn't suggested we ride the horses, if—"

"So many ifs. I know. I blamed myself for many years after our wagon caught fire and killed my parents. Orla told me it was Calatin who had followed me to the wagon. He wanted to destroy the sapphire because Manannan's firestone, combined with the pearl, was the only thing on earth that would defeat him. When he set fire to the wagon, I held the sapphire in my hands."

I glanced at Faolan's gloved hand gripping the gunwale. For the first time, I could get a good look at the ring. I'd seen the Egyptian symbol for protection, the Eye of Ra, in a book at school.

"You see, fire can destroy a talisman or, at the very least, alter it." Faolan turned me to face him. "We can fight this together, but you have to trust me. Let me be your friend. Together we can summon The Lady."

Faolan sounded sincere. Perhaps we shared the same pain after all. But be friends? I didn't think so. I faced back into the sea breeze and wiped the wind-flung saltwater from my eyes.

"Don't grieve, Brannon," Faolan said gently. "Peter lives with Manannan on his blessed isle now." He pointed to where the sky rested on the water. "One summer, I saw it almost every night, glistening on the horizon in the west. I'll never forget the sight of it shimmering in the light of the moon. Have you ever had a yearning, Brannon? I'd swear that isle called to me."

"Really? Tir na nOg?"

"Summer 1908. So many people saw it, you couldn't put it down to an illusion." Faolan took a pipe from his pocket and stuffed it. With a match, he sparked the tobacco and puffed to get it going. The aroma drifted on the breeze, a pleasant apple and cherry wood scent, unlike Granda's pipe. His pipe smelled like whisky with a hint of burning peat. "I can't force you to call The Lady, but the sooner she gives you those gems, the sooner we can plan our attack. There's not much time." He blew smoke rings into the wind like Granda used to do.

"How do you know she has the gems?"

"By how the jeweler described her, 'so beautiful she couldn't be of this world.' And it makes sense that she would keep her eye on them. They are a part of her."

I shoved my hands into my pockets. I couldn't stop checking for the sapphire, even though I knew it wasn't there. "How can I get her to come to me without the talisman? I'm nothing without it."

"You are the chosen one. The Lady will come to you with or without the talisman. Use your art to summon her, just as Kieran taught you. Your art is as potent as the talisman if you know how to use it, and I think you do. Magic works by attracting like-to-like. Paint her picture in your mind just as you would on canvas. Visualization is a key to your magical gifts."

Closing my eyes, I traced Aonbharr's outline in my mind, then filled in the details: the silver mane and tail flowing into the ocean crests, the sleek coat speckled with sea-foam, and the nostrils moist with ocean spray. I didn't draw in the eyes, though. Not yet. My instincts told me that the eyes would bring the steed to life, and I didn't want that to happen until I had finished drawing The Lady. The wind blew her hair into soft curls that streamed to her waist. Like ocean waves, her white gossamer dress washed over the stallion's back. When I'd finished sketching in The Lady's sea-green eyes, I drew Aonbharr's fiery ones. With the last stroke, the stallion reared, and The Lady came alive before us. She was not as solid as before but clearly herself, composed of wisps of cloud and beads of surf.

"My young knight," she smiled softly. "Believe in your abilities. It's time. Go to the round tower. Manannan's sacred place."

"But I've lost the gems," I said.

The Lady opened her hand to reveal the sapphire and pearl in her palm.

Faolan whispered strange words under his breath, and she answered him in the same language. Faolan acknowledged her with a slight nod.

"Faolan, your journey has taken you far, but it has also taken you away from us," she said. "Yield to the boy. His success depends on it." She took my hands, placed the gems in my cupped palms, and closed my fingers over them. After she released my hand, I put the gems in my pocket.

"You put all our hopes in an untrained boy," Faolan said bitterly. "It's a lot to expect from him. I knew more at his age and failed. Since then, I have spent a lifetime of study and practice, and with Orla's guidance, I learned Fomorii magic. I have abilities—"

"We know what you can and cannot do." The Lady sounded like a mother reprimanding a child.

Faolan's face hardened.

"At one time, we thought you, your sister, and Seanán would be the ones," she said. "We were wrong."

How could Manannan do anything wrong? He was perfect, wasn't he? Such thoughts terrified me.

"You're making another mistake," Faolan said. Outwardly, he looked composed, but I could feel him seething inside. Faolan didn't want to be my friend. He only wanted me to call The Lady so that he could have the gems.

"We hope you are wrong, Faolan. Still, we have placed our faith in Brannon."

I wanted to ask her why me, but before I could utter a word, a sudden gust rose from the sea and carried her away. The wind also brought a flock of cormorants. Their cries rang out over the boat as they descended on the masts, rigging, and deck. A pipit landed on the gunwale within arm's reach of me. I tried to shout a warning, but a sharp pain brought me to my knees. I clutched my head and moaned. Waves of nausea gripped my stomach. There wasn't much in my gut, but what was there came spewing out onto the deck.

Soft lambskin covered my temples. My mind felt stretched like a rope in a tug of war between Calatin and Faolan, who battled to take control—Calatin wanting to kill me, Faolan killing me with his efforts to release the Fomorii king from my mind.

"Fight him, Brannon. Send him away. You have the power to do it. Use your mind, your body, and your will. Make a picture."

I grasped hold of Faolan's words as if they were a lifeline. With a deep breath, I summoned a hailstorm that would harass the birds and blow them from the vessel and far out to sea. Hail responded out of a clear sky, pounding the deck with a Bodhran's rat-ta-ta-tat. Then the wind whipped the water into ten-foot waves. I felt Calatin release me as the boat listed, sending Faolan and me sliding down the slippery deck, made treacherous with hailstones and sea spray. I stretched to reach for a handhold, but all my fingers could grasp was the smooth water-slick deck.

With one hand gripping the rigging, Faolan caught my ankle with the other hand to prevent me from slipping overboard. I reached back and grabbed Faolan's arm as the boat righted itself. Faolan stood and shouted orders to his crew. Harassed by the cormorants, the crew members tried to lower the sails. Weakened by the birds' razor beaks and the ferocious wind, the mainsail tore from the mast. The schooner spun, rose on a crest where it rested for a frightening moment, and plummeted into a trough. Flung against the reef, it grazed the edge of a rock. The boat groaned as water poured over the deck with each successive wave. Clinging to a handrail, I thought I might arrive at Tir na nOg sooner than I expected.

"Let the storm go, Brannon," Faolan shouted over the wind. "Calatin and his people have been driven back."

I didn't realize how hard I was hanging onto the storm. With a sigh, I breathed out and imagined a calm sea. A final wave dropped the ship's bow upon the sand south of the rocks that had almost destroyed the vessel. The stern, still partially floating in the surf, was taking on water.

Tara and Connor stumbled onto the deck from the cabins below. Dazed, I stood beside Faolan, who looked as shaken as the rest of us. I peered over the hull, where crew members lowered the gangplank, creating a steep ramp to the beach.

Chapter Twenty-Eight

Brannon

I watched one of the crewmembers climb down to inspect the hull.

"Sir, the tear. It ain't so bad," he said. "We can fix it and push the boat back out to sea. We can do it with all hands, sir."

"I know this beach. The tide comes in here quite high," Faolan said as he leaned over the railing. "That may be all we need to push her back out."

The taste of evil lingered, chilling me to the bone. Tara found a blanket and wrapped it around my shoulders. Still, I couldn't stop shaking beneath it.

"You stupid eejit. You did this, didn't you?" Connor looked as green as I felt. "Just like the time you almost killed Epona." Connor balled his fist and raised it.

"Connor," Faolan said sharply. "Brannon summoned

The Lady and the storm because I asked him to. She gave the gems back to Brannon."

"You damned near killed all of us," Connor murmured and held his stomach.

"He did what he had to do to save us, Connor," Faolan said. "If he hadn't, we'd all be feeding the fish."

Tara rummaged in her harp case for a little pouch of herbs. She handed us each a dried mint leaf. "It'll help ease the seasickness."

I chewed the leaf. It soothed the ache in my stomach. "The Lady said to go to the round tower."

"I think we should disembark and do as The Lady advised." Faolan waved away Tara's offer of a mint leaf. "The round tower is sacred to Manannan. You'll be safe there. Connor, get the horses."

"They'll be hell to pay if they're hurt, and it's going to be difficult getting frightened horses down that gangplank," Connor said before rushing below deck.

"Rory," Faolan called to the boy hanging over the rail, watching the crew inspect the breach. "Take Brannon and find him some dry clothes."

I followed Rory below deck to his dark, cramped quarters. There were three upper and three lower berths attached to the hull. Wet towels hung from a fishing line that someone had strung across the room and attached to a nail. Rory searched through the drawer beneath his bunk for a sweater and a pair of trousers. They smelled like they had never been washed, but they were warm and dry.

"Bloody strange having them cormorants attack like that." Rory handed me a pair of socks. "And that uncanny storm. Have you ever seen one like that before?"

What could I say? That some mythical evil being had tried to take over my mind and that I had summoned the storm to save myself?

Rory stepped outside the cabin to allow me to change. Shaking, I removed my wet clothes and put on the dry ones. I wished I had my crane bag for the gems, but my jacket pocket would have to do. It was damp, but it was all I had, and I was thankful that Etain had repaired the rip in the pocket while I lay sick in her cabin.

After changing, I made my way back up the companionway to the main deck. I glanced over the gunwale and saw Tara waiting on the shore with Anya, her chestnut mare. She was watching Connor struggle to coax Malachy down the gangplank. Even though Connor spoke softly, the stallion neighed, pulled on the reins, and kicked all the way to the shore.

The sky lightened, and the sun warmed the deck, yet I felt a storm brewing. Shielding my eyes from the sun's glare, I glanced at the rigging for a sign of the pipit. Calatin and his people may have backed away, but they hadn't gone far. I was sure of that. Something brushed my arm. I saw a flash of black and white, and then a man stood before me. Calatin.

Behind him, a flock of cormorants dove to keep the crew in check by pecking at their heads and faces, forcing them to retreat below deck. Faolan fought off two cormorants pecking at his head. He picked up a casting net and flung it at them.

Both birds were caught and dragged through the air and over the side of the boat.

Three strides and Faolan stood between Calatin and me.

"You could save yourself, your ship, and your crew by handing over the boy," Calatin said. "Or, if the young knight would like to come willingly—"

"Your fight is with me, not the boy," Faolan said.

"True. Except the boy carries the means of my destruction."

He looked at me for a long time as if sizing me up. I didn't allow myself to back away from the demigod's scrutiny. Instead, I stood my ground and took the opportunity to get a better look at him. He wore over a white shirt, a black cloak that fluttered like wings behind him, and dark trousers tucked into knee-length leather boots. Blond curls like Connor's framed Calatin's rugged yet pleasant face, not the hideous creature I had expected him to be. The only flaw I could see was that the Fomorii had six fingers on each hand. Just like Mary's kitten. His eyes were deep blue with tiny flecks of gold. I wondered if Connor would look like this man when he was older and if the power of the Fomorii would be his to wield. It didn't look like he had a sword or weapon of any kind, but then I doubted that such a being would need weapons.

"I have a grudge against you." My voice sounded braver than I felt. "You killed my best friend."

"And what do you intend to do about that?" Calatin smiled.

I fingered the sapphire and pearl in the fold of my pocket. I had the means to defeat him but not the knowledge of how to do it.

Calatin raised an eyebrow. "Well?"

"You will pay for what you did."

"Brave words." Calatin's laugh angered me. "Revenge, it makes us crazy. I also seek revenge and freedom for my people for the wrongs committed against us. The people of Manannan will suffer as we have, and you, Faolan, will pay for the murder of Orla, my granddaughter."

Faolan's impeccable composure wavered for an instant, then snapped back with all the fierceness of the man he was.

"Why she would choose you is beyond me," Calatin said with disgust. "But that misguided woman was always taken with humans. You weren't the first to catch her eye."

The punch came out of nowhere. Not magic, just a good old-fashioned blow to the jaw, like you'd see in any barroom brawl. It happened so fast that all I heard was the smack of metal against Calatin's jawbone, which left the imprint from Faolan's ring, the Eye of Ra blistering on Calatin's cheek. So, the demigod could bleed, just as any mortal man could. Calatin roared and, with the back of his hand, hit Faolan in the face. Faolan staggered against the gunnels. He bent and picked up a length of rope used to anchor supplies. A single flick sent fire running down its length to scorch the corner of Calatin's cloak. With a flourish as elegant as a bullfighter, Calatin slipped it off and tossed the burning cloak over Faolan.

Remembering what Kieran had taught me about fire, I clutched the talisman, and with only half a second to create an image in my mind, I willed the air around the fire to vanish and starve the flame. It worked. The cloak looked as it did before, untouched by fire as it fell over Faolan. Calatin glanced at me and snatched up his cloak. Both Faolan and the burning rope were gone. It appeared as if Faolan had vanished into midair. I wondered if he had slipped off the boat's edge and into the water.

Out of the corner of my eye, I saw Connor galloping up the gangplank toward us. Malachy whinnied as Connor charged forward to grab my hand and swing me up to sit behind him on the stallion. I felt Connor shaking through his coat as I hugged him around the waist to keep myself from falling off. Had Connor heard that Calatin was his great-grandfather? Did Calatin know Connor was his blood?

Calatin stood in Malachy's path, blocking the way back to the gangplank. Connor urged the stallion forward. If the demigod did not move, Connor would plow right into him.

"Stop," I yelled. The memory of hooves crushing flesh and bone made me cringe, but Connor would not stop. Neither would Calatin, who pulled his cloak tightly around his body and transformed back into the pipit. Malachy screamed and reared as the bird flew up into his face. I felt Connor shift his weight to keep us from falling. The crazed horse backed away from the gangplank and wheeled in a circle, whinnying, kicking, and snapping at the pipit, flitting back and forth, making neighing sounds.

Connor pulled on the reigns and uttered soft words, harsh curses, and kicks, but nothing changed Malachy's behavior. In the last attempt, Connor gave Malachy the reigns. Suddenly, the horse lurched forward and ran the length of the deck. He was going to jump ship on the rocky side of the boat, not the ocean side. It was suicide for the horse and probably death for both of us.

The plaintive cry of a crane rang out overhead. It swooped down in a flash of white across the horse's path as it sailed through the air. I braced myself for the end.

Strange how time slows down when it is your last few moments. Seabreeze cooled my face and ruffled my hair. On the horizon, to the west, I saw the glint of something reflecting off the afternoon sun. Tir na nOg? The tip of the rocks, some lumpy with barnacles, some slippery with seaweed, rose beneath us.

The landing nearly knocked me off the stallion. Malachy stumbled once, then resumed at an even pace until he stopped. The horse had cleared the rocks to land on the smooth sand on the other side of the rocky shore—an impossible distance for any horse to jump.

Thanking all the gods and goddesses I could think of, I looked up at the sky and saw the crane pursuing the pipit over the sea. Connor reined in the horse and turned him around. We dismounted and guided Malachy over the rocks toward the beached schooner. It was slow going, as one wrong step could injure the horse.

Some of the crew had come back onto the deck. I had no idea what the crew members saw, but they looked like frightened sheep, dazed by the strange events.

Tara, straddling her mare, met us at the spot where Faolan had disappeared over the edge of the schooner.

Faolan's right glove floated in the water with the gold ring etched with the Eye of Ra still attached to the third finger. Waves lapped up to touch Connor's boots as he stooped to pick up the glove. After placing the ring in his pocket, he dropped the charred glove onto the sand.

"Don't think the worst," Tara said. "He must have got away."

"Are you crazy?" Connor snapped. "Do you know what we're dealing with here? It's beyond us. If Faolan couldn't stop him…." Connor kicked the glove, which stuck to the toe of his boot. He scraped it off on a rock.

"Faolan will meet us at the tower if he can. We'd better get going," I said.

Connor frowned. "Don't be an eejit. You know he's dead."

"And it's all my fault," I shouted.

"Yes, it is." Connor grabbed the front of my jacket.

"Stop it." Tara gripped Connor's arm. "Let him go. We're wasting time. We've got to get out of here before Calatin comes back."

With a shove, Connor released my jacket. He took Malachy's reigns and swung up onto the horse's back.

"I'll ride with Connor." Tara handed Anya's reins to me and whispered, "Please don't fight with him."

"I'll try," I said. Connor was worried about his father and grieving for a mother he never knew. He didn't even know who he was. No wonder he wanted to kick someone's ass.

Connor offered Tara a hand and pulled her up behind him. He nudged Malachy into a gallop without looking or saying anything to me.

I hesitated before mounting Anya. I hadn't ridden alone since Peter had died. I braced myself and pulled up onto the mare. The mare's back rippled with my weight. Did she sense my fear? Gently, I urged her forward into a slow walk and then eased her to a trot and finally a cantor. Sweat beaded on my lip, and my legs trembled. In my heart, I loved horses, but after what happened to Peter, I was also afraid of them. "Damn, pooka, I won't let you do this to me," I said aloud.

I leaned forward and stroked Anya's neck. "Alright, girl, we can do this." Without having to kick or slap the reins, Anya responded by springing into a gallop. Through the trees, I saw the tip of the round tower. In the sky above the belfry, a lone crane circled.

Chapter Twenty-Nine

Brannon

The round tower stood directly ahead, bordered by a hawthorn, ash, and elm grove. Taking the lead, Connor guided Malachy along a bumpy path rippled with roots. "Be careful through here. These roots can trip a horse as easy as it can you or me."

"Look. A crane." Tara's voice carried across the small space between us as the horses trotted side by side through a meadow of bracken, gorse, and black-faced sheep munching on long grass. The sheep bleated and shuffled to get out of the horses' way. "Is it the same crane that chased Calatin away?"

"If it is, it's no ordinary crane," I said, remembering Granda telling me that the crane was Manannan's sacred bird. I swallowed hard. I couldn't think about Granda.

The clouds had parted, and the afternoon sun streamed

through the branches, highlighting the amber in Connor's blond curls. From behind, Connor was strikingly similar to Calatin.

Perhaps a bit too short for a Fomorii—more like his da's people—but Fomorii, nonetheless. I felt sorry for Connor. Who would ever want to be related to one of them? They were monsters, and Calatin was proof of that. But what could Connor do? Lineage was fate, not a person's fault. Blood was blood, after all. Could I trust Connor now? Maybe. He risked his life to save mine even though he didn't like me very much. Besides, Declan wasn't Fomorii and was just as evil as Calatin.

I was itching to ask Connor what he thought about being Calatin's great-grandson, but I didn't dare mention it. I might get my front teeth knocked out for the asking.

As we cleared the trees, I felt more and more anxious. I guided my horse abreast of Connor's once more. The tower stood before us like a rocket pointing to the sky. As we drew closer, I looked over my shoulder to my right and left but saw nothing out of the ordinary. We passed the witch's stone and the two shallow, water-filled hollows. Still, something was different about the tower. It looked like it was crumbling. I squinted and recognized what it was. Moths.

As we drew closer, one landed on Tara's head and another on her back. She ruffled her hair, and the moth flew down the front of her coat. She screamed, "Get them off of me!"

"What's wrong?" Connor said, glancing behind.

"Moths," I explained, brushing them out of the mare's mane. "Didn't Kieran say that the Fomorii could control nature? Look, they're clinging to the tower's walls."

The closer we got to the tower, the more the moths swarmed us. They drove the horses mad, landing on their faces and crawling into their ears. The steeds shook their heads, wheeled in panic, snorted, and snapped their teeth. Squirming to keep my balance, I held on with one hand and swiped at the moths with the other. Anya whinnied and bucked. She stopped and refused to move forward. With a stubborn neigh, she turned and galloped back to the grove. Malachy kicked and pulled against the reins, but this time, Connor's touch and soothing words calmed the stallion. When Malachy had settled down, Connor rode back toward the grove where Anya and I had taken cover. The moths returned to the tower in great swarms.

Connor helped Tara slide from Malachy's back. She shook her sweater, riding skirt, and hair, and with each shake, she uttered a cry of disgust. "I hate moths. It's not normal for them to attack like this. Is it?"

"They swarmed Peter and me at the Bonamargy Friary," I said. "I didn't know, but Calatin must have been watching me even then."

"Did you notice the moths burned when they landed on your skin?" Tara said.

"Strange." I inspected a welt on the back of my hand. "I didn't think that moths could bite. They don't even have a mouth, do they?"

"Some do have mouths, and some don't but these moths ooze something disgusting," Tara said. "Can't that talisman get rid of them?"

"It doesn't work like that. It wouldn't repel the cormorants, but it can bring the wind or a storm or The Lady because she is connected to it somehow. And the talisman couldn't save Peter."

"What did you do last time they attacked you?" Tara ran her fingers through her hair one more time.

"Run. The moths seem to have a limited range. The further we got from the friary, the less they bothered us. They're attracted to the tower as if they are protecting something there."

"Is this goop poisonous?" Tara pulled the sleeves of her sweater to her elbows and rubbed the red welts left by the moths.

"I think it might be if you get enough of it on you," I said.

"Once we are in the tower, we should be safe. Faolan said they couldn't enter a place sacred to Manannan," Connor said. "Do you think you could stand the moths if we made a run for it? Malachy's back is just the right height for me to stand on. Brannon, you go first. Then I'll lift Tara, and you can pull her in."

Tara shook her head no. "Even if I could stand the moths, I don't think the horses could. They're spooked."

"Malachy will listen to me. All three of us can ride him. We'll leave Anya here."

Once we had mounted, Connor pressed Malachy into a gallop toward the tower. The moths swarmed as they did before. Tara buried her face in Connor's back. I closed my eyes and willed my mind away from the creepy feeling of insects climbing up my pant legs and down my shirt, leaving a trail of itchy welts.

Connor steadied the stallion while I pulled myself through the door. "Now, your turn, Tara. Let me stand first. Then I'll guide you up." With ease, Connor balanced on Malachy's back. Even though the moths blanketed the horse, Malachy held still while Connor lifted Tara to the ledge. I took her hands and pulled her through. Once Tara had cleared the sill, Connor hoisted himself through the door. Malachy, covered from head to foot, bolted with a cloud of moths lifting from his body.

"How are we going to get out?" Tara shifted her harp case on her shoulder.

"I'll call Malachy to come and get us," Connor said.

A breeze flowed through the open windows and stirred the musty scent of moss and damp stone through the chamber. Under the eastern window and opposite the western one, two pillars supported a flat stone, an altar. The place felt sacred.

"What do we do now?" Connor paced in a circle.

"Call The Lady," Tara whispered.

"The Lady is here," I said. "I can feel her."

Sunlight streamed through the window onto the altar. Dust motes swirling in the slanted rays gathered together until The Lady appeared before us. Her hair fell loosely to her waist over the soft folds of her white dress. It looked modern enough, like one my ma would have worn, only nicer with a soft sheen where the light fell on it. In some ways, she looked as young as Tara, but The Lady's eyes were deep with wisdom.

"The sword," The Lady said.

Connor opened his jacket and pulled the sword from the scabbard. The Lady extended her hand to receive it.

When Connor hesitated, Tara rested her hand on his arm. "You must do this."

Out of the corner of my eye, I saw the crane perch on the sill of the open doorway. Connor looked at the crane for a moment before extending the sword hilt with the blade resting on his other arm. The Lady's long fingers curled around the hilt. She tested its balance as she sliced the air. She looked at every detail: the carved seahorse, the crosspiece, and the double-sided blade.

"Connor, I have never handled a finer sword. Every detail of the seahorse hilt is exquisite. You've made the hand's place smooth without losing the carving's beauty. The forging is of the old style, with the metal folded, heated, and hammered to a thin edge, and the crosspiece fits as if you made the sword from one piece. Manannan himself would be proud to own this sword."

She extended the hilt to me, but Connor stepped forward to receive the sword. I couldn't blame him. If I had made the sword, I wouldn't want to give it up.

"Connor, do you give the sword freely?" She neither commanded nor insisted but looked at him with kind eyes.

"If it has to be." Connor took the sword from The Lady and turned to me.

I hesitated to take it. "What do I need to do?"

Connor half-smiled. "Take the damn sword before I change my mind."

I knew it was hard for Connor to give up the sword, but I didn't know how hard it was until I held it in my own hands. Even without the gemstones, the sword felt as much a part of me as an arm or leg.

"Affix the pearl in the seahorse's eye and the sapphire where the crosspiece joins the sword," The Lady said.

"How do I do that?"

"As you place the stones, Tara will play the harp. Do you still have the flint with the music notated in Ogham?"

"No. Declan stole the flint with the gems." I felt a knot in my stomach. I wished I hadn't lost the crane bag Kieran had given me. Had we come this far to fail because I had also lost the flint?

"I think I can remember it. Kieran taught it to me." Tara pulled her harp from its bag.

"Are you sure? You must play the notes as written on the flint, or we will shatter the making," The Lady said.

Connor shuffled his feet angrily in the dirt. "Tell me— why him? Why should Brannon be the one? I made the sword." Connor lunged for it.

The Lady reached out and grabbed Connor's wrist, covering the tattoo. He looked down, avoiding her eyes. "I'm sorry," he said. "It's so hard."

"Connor, remember you have Fomorii blood. Manannan's mark around your wrist may protect you from death, but once the pearl is attached to the sword, the eye of the seahorse will steal your strength and weaken you. Yes, you are the maker, Connor, but Brannon is the wielder, and Tara binds the maker and the wielder together. By giving Brannon the sword, you have not lost but gained, as you soon will realize."

"I found the crane bag in the McNeil's barn," Connor said, taking it from his pocket. "I guess Declan thought the flint was useless and tossed it away." He took the flint from the bag and handed it to Tara.

"Hurry, there's not much time," The Lady said. "Brannon, place the sword on the altar so you can fix the jewels. Connor, stand opposite Brannon. Tara, bring your harp and stand opposite me. Play the chant slowly nine times. The first three times to place the stones, the second three times for the binding, and on the last three, well, you will see if it has worked."

As Tara strummed the first note, I placed the pearl into the hollow made for the eye, and before the chant ended, I set the sapphire at the center point in the crosspiece. As Tara played the chant a second time, the sunlight ignited the sapphire. Blue fire expanded from the gem to the pommel and from the stone to the blade's tip.

On the first chord of the last chant, The Lady picked up the sword and smiled, "I am The Answerer. Call on me, and I will guide you." Together they rose into the light, spinning so fast that The Lady's form blurred into the sword. Each musical phrase pulled the sword higher and higher until the blade was suspended above us. As the last note echoed through the tower, the sword fell point down into the altar. The Lady and the sword were now one.

Connor stepped toward the altar and leaned forward to take the sword.

I placed my hand on his arm to stop him. Connor brushed me off with a look as fierce as any demigod.

"Remember what The Lady said. You're part Fomorii Connor."

Connor stepped away and allowed me to come forward. "The Lady's in there now," I said. "It isn't just a sword made of wood and metal. It's alive with her spirit. Look how the eye of the seahorse glows."

The crane cried out. Together we turned toward the doorsill, where the crane cocked its head and looked at us with one eye. It cried again and launched itself from the tower. The host of moths perched all over the outside walls followed it.

"It's leading the moths away," Tara whispered.

I wondered if it was the same bird that had chased Calatin away. It might even be the same crane that gave me the pearl on my birthday. From the beginning, the sea-god knew what he was doing. Now all I had to do was to pick up the sword and accept my fate. Connor and Tara were waiting. So was The Lady. The sword was the key to fixing what they had set into place thousands of years ago. The sword would change my life forever.

Tara put her harp back into its bag and slung it across her shoulder. "Aren't you going to take it?"

When I placed my hand on the hilt, I saw The Lady's face flash before my mind. I pulled my hand away and stepped back.

"What's wrong?" Tara asked.

"You must choose to accept it or not," Connor said. "I know what I would do if I were in your shoes."

A horse neighed. Connor looked out the doorway, and his face brightened as he waved to someone outside. "Kieran has come with a wagon. He has Malachy and Anya tied to the back of it."

Tara looked over Connor's shoulder. "How did you know we were here?" she asked.

"I was looking for you and found the horses," Kieran's voice drifted through the doorway. "And that unexpected windstorm had Brannon's magical signature."

"Signature?" I had never heard of such a thing.

"Yes, as you develop your gift, you'll get to recognize a person's magical style, just like you can recognize the art of famous painters. They all have their unique brush strokes. For example, Faolan's style is fiery. When he uses magic, and I turn my attention to him, I sense the flavor of strong eastern spices, but your style, Brannon, is like a cool breeze."

Connor hung out of the doorway and dropped into the back of the wagon. Tara swung her legs over the ledge so Connor could help her down. She sat next to Kieran. Talking faster than usual, Tara filled Kieran in. She told him about the fight between Faolan and Calatin, that Faolan was missing, and how music helped The Lady merge with the sword. "But Brannon is afraid to take the sword out of the stone altar," she added.

Kieran stood up in the wagon and pulled himself into the tower. It felt right to have him stand by my side. It took all my willpower to keep my knees from buckling beneath me. "The Lady, somehow she and the sword—"

"Are one. I know." Kieran knelt by the sword and bowed his head. "My Lady."

Feeling out of place, I knelt beside him.

"In all the years I have walked this earth and held this sword, I have never forgotten the first time I met her. There is not a lady on earth like the spirit of this sword. You will love her like no other. What a gift. What a joy to see her whole again." Kieran stood and placed his hand on my shoulder. "She has come to be your companion on this journey. To guide you and offer counsel. It's time. Take the sword."

I stood and gripped the seahorse hilt in my palm. My fear turned to a deep sense of peace as I pulled it out of the altar. It came quickly, singing the same five notes as the chant Tara had played.

"I don't know what she wants me to do," I said.

"Ask her. She is The Answerer."

Silently, I asked The Lady for guidance. The answer came. "We must go to the same cave where Peter found the flint. There, we will reset the seals."

Chapter Thirty

Brannon

The Answerer brushed against my leg as I climbed a boulder and looked over the cliff. The surf thundered against the crag, spewing a fine spray into the air. "The cave is below us," I said. "It's difficult to see because a rock ridge hides it."

From the back of the wagon, Kieran unloaded supplies. "Come and have some food and drink. We need to plan." He handed two oil lanterns to Connor, a length of rope, and a flask of cider to Tara. I climbed down the cliff to sit on the rocks by the wagon.

Kieran opened the food sack and took out a round of goat's cheese, soda bread, dried herring, and an apple for each of us. The thought of eating made me sick. I pocketed the apple.

"Brannon, how did you find the cave?" Kieran asked.

"By accident. When a button popped off Peter's sweater, it flew through the air and landed in front of the entrance."

"Go on outta that." Connor stuffed a chunk of cheese into his mouth. "You don't really think that Manannan pulled Peter's button off and tossed it toward the cave just so you could find the flint, do you?"

"Stranger things have happened," Kieran said. "How far into the cave did you go?" Kieran broke off a piece of soda bread and offered it to me. I waved it away. My stomach grew tighter with every passing moment.

"We didn't go very far, just beyond the first chamber. It didn't feel safe to go any further, and I was worried about the tide."

"We're in luck as the tide is just going out," Kieran said, "but it will begin its return at sunrise."

"I hope they can fix Faolan's schooner before high tide. Do you think Faolan is still alive? I found his glove in the water and…" Connor swallowed hard.

"Faolan's name means wolf," Kieran said, "and like the wolf, he has more tricks up his sleeve than anyone I know. Even as a child, I swear that lad could disappear into thin air whenever he was in trouble. Besides, I would know if he had died. And Connor, don't you think you would know, too?"

Connor twisted the stem of his apple. "We weren't close, but I used to sense when he was going to visit me, which wasn't very often. But something strange happened when I picked up his glove that had washed onto the shore. The glove's fingers gripped mine."

"Japers," Tara shivered and pulled her hands into the cuff of her sweater.

Connor placed his hand in his pocket and held up a gold ring. "Faolan wore this ring over his gloved third finger on his right hand. When I removed the ring, I felt that he was watching me. I even looked over my shoulder to see if he was there. I pushed the thought away because I knew he must be dead. After all, no one can defeat a god."

"Can't they?" Kieran asked as he took the ring from Connor and looked closely at it. "Ah, so it was the Eye of Ra that brought about the changes in Faolan. He will want this amulet back."

"I found it," Connor said as he took the ring from Kieran. "It's mine now."

"No, Connor, this is not yours to keep," Kieran said, but before he could stop him, Connor placed it on his finger.

"It fits." Connor held his hand up for us to admire. His smile quickly turned to a grimace. "Damn thing," Connor cried in pain. He cursed the ring, his father, and Manannan. "I can't get it off. It's tight, and it's burning my finger." Blood pooled around the gold rim.

"Let me try." Tara took his hand and tried to free the ring, but the pain was too much for Connor, and he pushed her away. I caught her before she could fall onto the stones.

Connor looked at Kieran for help.

"Don't panic. Close your eyes," Kieran said. "What is the ring telling you?"

Connor did what Kieran asked, and after a moment, he opened his eyes, breathed a sigh of relief, and removed the ring.

"I saw one of the crew members pulling Faolan out of the water. He's alive."

Kieran patted Connor on the back. "See? All you had to do was listen."

"Look," Tara said. "The bleeding has stopped, and there isn't even a faint mark where the ring was."

"You know," Connor said while placing the ring back in his pocket, "I didn't think Faolan cared about anyone but himself, but I know he loved my ma. Did you know she was Fomorii?"

"He told you?" Kieran put the remains of our meal into the sack.

"No, I read about her in Faolan's journal. Her name was Orla. Is that why you were holding me back? You didn't trust me?" The muscles in Connor's jaw tensed.

"I suspected there was something different about you," Kieran began slowly, "such as your fascination with the darker aspects of magic. Like your father, you looked for ways to impose your will on others. So, I made sure that no harm should come to you or anyone else. I stressed the development in you of those gifts that create instead of destroy. Harder for you but more potent in the end. Gradually, you grew out of your destructive tendencies. The Fomorii were gifted at metalworking, as was their bond with nature. Hence, your natural gift with horses and metals."

"But did you know about Calatin?" Connor pressed his lips together. "That he was my great-grandfather—my blood."

"Not at first. Faolan told me when you were seven. It explained many things about you."

"Did Faolan know Calatin killed his parents?"

"When your father found out about Calatin, it was too late. Orla and Faolan had already fallen in love."

"Then, what am I doing on this quest to banish my people?" Connor absent-mindedly crushed a clam's shell beneath his boot.

"You'd ask that question after meeting Calatin? Look what he and a few of his followers have done. If they're released, they'll take revenge on all of us. They aim to rule and enslave all the people of Ireland. Are they your people? Blood ties can be strong, but friendships built over many years can even be stronger."

Conner gave his apple core to Malachy and leaned his forehead against the horse's neck. "I'm confused. I don't know who to trust or where to turn."

"Are you with us or not?" I stood on the cliff's edge and looked down at the narrow path that would take us to the cave. The setting sun's blood-tipped rays floating on the water's surface pointed to the entrance.

Connor spun to face me. "How can you ask me that? Didn't I save your life?" He glared at the blade at my side. "Didn't I give you my sword?"

"You had no choice."

Connor spat at my boot. "I should have left your sorry arse floating in the sea, you ungrateful—"

I put my hand on the sword. I could kill Connor if I had to, but what was I thinking? These weren't my thoughts—the blight. I'd felt it before when Peter died. "It's the Fomorii," I cried. "Can't you feel them? They want us to fight each other."

Connor pulled up his sleeve. The tattoo around his wrist was red.

"Pack up," Kieran said. "We must go. Now stay close and follow my lead. The tide is low enough for us to enter the cave, but the first two chambers will still be slippery. Don't go down the side passages. There is only one way to the seals. If you get lost, we won't have time to find you. I'll go first, followed by Brannon, Tara, and Connor." Stay alert. Calatin will try to stop us."

We followed Kieran to the base of the cliff, where a fissure in the rocks was big enough for a man to squeeze through.

Before entering, I noticed Connor light the lanterns without flint or a match. So, he'd been practicing.

The cave opened into a vast cathedral-like cavern, where the roof extended at least forty feet above our heads. Rows of stalactites hung from the ceiling like sword clusters.

The tide was low, but a few rebel waves roared up to the entrance to block the fading light and spew thick foam into the cave. We ran from the mist to a pebbly mound at the back of the cavern. From deep within the dark recesses, a draft blew.

"This cave goes on for miles underneath the ground," Kieran said.

I heard the faint subterranean rumbling of the sea crashing through corridors deep within the rock. Only once had I explored beyond the first chamber, and then only for a short distance down the tunnel where Peter found the flint. Peter wanted to explore further, but I convinced him it wasn't safe. The tide was coming in, and we didn't have a lantern. That was only part of my fear. The real reason was that I felt something ancient and malicious. Like I felt now, only stronger. I hoped we wouldn't need to travel too far inside the cave to find the seals.

Our footsteps echoed through the passageway, but there was another sound, a scuffling. Was something or someone following us?

Kieran stooped and entered a narrow tunnel. Tara peered in and stopped.

"What's wrong?" Connor tried to push her forward, but she dug in her heels and wouldn't budge.

"It looks pretty cramped in there," she said.

"Get going." Connor nudged her forward.

"Don't push me," she snapped.

"What's wrong?" Kieran called through the tunnel.

"She's a sissy when it comes to small spaces," Connor said.

"Shut your gob." Tara stooped and stepped into the tunnel. "It's stuffy in here, that's all. And what's that pukey smell?" She turned and tried to push Connor out of the way. "I feel sick." She covered her mouth and gagged.

"Not on me, you don't." Connor pushed her, and she fell against me.

"Close your eyes," I said. "Think of something else. A picture, a song, anything that makes you happy. Trust me. It'll work." Sweet Jaysus, I didn't want her to puke on me.

"The tunnel opens up shortly," Kieran reassured her. "You can do this."

I felt her breath on my neck and her boots brushing against my heels. When the passageway widened, she pushed by me, but Kieran caught her as she tried to squeeze between him and the wall.

"Slow down, Tara," he said. "Don't run. You could slip or step over the ledge and into the abyss. Lantern light cast shadows on Tara's face. Her lips were white, her eyes enormous. She clung to him as we stepped into another chamber.

The air turned colder. Spray from a nearby waterfall that tumbled into an underground stream made the stones slick. Mist swirled about our feet, shadowing the ground in a gray cloak.

"There are stone steps here. We will go down fifteen steps, turn right, and take twenty-five more into a lower chamber."

"You've been here before?" Tara asked.

"A long time ago. Now be careful. The steps are narrow. To your right is a wall. To your left is—nothing."

I counted the steps aloud. My voice echoed through the cave.

"Shut up," Connor growled behind me. "I can't focus."

I hugged the wall, running my hand over the wet stones. "Fifteen," I said aloud and slid my foot to the right, groping for the turn. Something flew over me and touched the top of my head. Connor grabbed me around the waist and held me until I could get my balance. "Japers, what was that?"

"A bat, I think." Connor sounded shaken.

"I can't see a darn thing," I said.

"Keep to the wall." Kieran's voice came from somewhere below us.

My foot felt open space as I searched for the turning stone. I pulled my foot back and ran it closer to the wall, found my footing, and made the turn. I waited on the second step for Connor, who scraped his foot along the stone, groping for the same spot.

"Good God, where is it?" he said under his breath, then stepped behind me.

"Be careful. The stones are slippery." Kieran's voice rose from below us. "Take your time. Test each stone before you put your foot down."

"How will we get back?" Tara's voice trembled.

"Going back is easier because you know what to expect. Now, just five more steps."

Five more steps for Tara, ten more for me. Then what? Would we even make it out of this descent into hell? And what waited for us at the end of all of this? I was sure that whatever had swiped at my head was larger than a bat. There it was again—a swoosh of wings overhead. I looked up and saw something swooping down upon us from the shadows.

"Bloody hell." Connor slipped and banged into me. I stumbled down two more steps before I could stop. Connor's lantern clanged against the precipice and disappeared into the abyss.

"Connor? Brannon?" Diffused light from Kieran's lantern seeped through the fog.

"I'm all right, but Connor—I heard his lantern go over the edge," I said. I wanted to lend my voice to Tara's scream filling the chamber with a shrill echo. Then I heard a faint cry.

"I hear something. Tara, be quiet. Be very quiet. A hush fell over the cave.

"Help," Connor cried out. "Hurry, I'm falling."

Crawling on my hands and knees, I felt the stone above me and the one above that. Nothing. My heart pounded in the long moments that followed. I couldn't see anything through the thick fog that floated up from the nether regions below. I patted the edge of the upper step and felt Connor's fingers barely holding on by the tips.

"Hurry, damn you," Connor said in a strained whisper.

I gripped Connor's wrist while he dug his boots into the rocks to help me haul him up and over the edge of the staircase and onto the stone slab. We leaned against the rock face, breathing heavily and rubbing our arms.

"Thanks," Connor said.

"Well, I owed you one," I said. "I guess we're even."

"Two," Connor said. "You owed me two."

Lantern light bobbed toward us as Kieran climbed the steps. He knelt and shone the light on Connor, whose face was pale as goat's milk. "Can you go on?" Kieran asked. His voice sounded as shaky as I felt.

Connor nodded and hugged the wall as we followed Kieran the rest of the way down the steps. With the one lantern, we could see only a few feet in front of us, where stalagmites stood like soldiers before us. The wind hissed between the crevices, the ghostly voices of banished gods.

"Watch your step," Kieran warned in a calm voice. "The ground is covered in ice." Kieran discovered a torch on the wall beside him and pulled it from its sconce. Faster than Connor and I could ever do, he lit it. "Connor, take the lantern and wait for me here. I want to check the seals in the antechamber. If broken, I'll warn you. I'll try to hold the Fomorii off while you escape." He left us clinging to the wall beside the staircase and disappeared around the corner.

We waited and listened for his return but heard only our breathing. Without warning, a whoosh of beating wings filled the air. Something bumped me and sent me flying onto the ice. It skimmed the back of my neck as I skated across the ice on my belly. I didn't stop until I hit a stalagmite. I heard Tara scream and Connor curse as they were both pushed onto the frozen surface. Connor slid by me and stopped near an archway. I couldn't see what had happened to Tara. Before I could warn them, the stalagmites began to move and transform into Fomorii warriors.

I scrambled to my feet, struggled to keep my balance on the ice, and slid toward Connor, who stood under the stalagmite archway. I didn't make it that far. Calatin appeared out of the surrounding mist to block me. He held Tara by the hand. Her eyes looked strange, like she was away from herself or just too darn scared to do anything but look up at the man towering over her.

Calatin snapped his fingers, igniting the torches set into stone sconces carved into the chamber walls. Now, I could see that the chamber was circular, with four arched recesses plus the doorway to the antechamber.

Calatin held Tara in front of him. "Kieran, we have no intention of remaining banished to the void forever. Give me the sword, and I'll let these children go. Keep it, and she'll be the first to experience the worst of my wrath. A fever will ravage her body. She will experience pain in every bone. Every breath will be like breathing fire. She will linger for days, aware of all that is happening to her. Anyone who tries to help her will also become infected, but she will be the last to die."

"Brannon, give him the sword." Connor stepped up to stand beside me.

I needed to think. Where was Kieran? If I gave Calatin the sword, he would destroy it. The world would be plagued by him and his kind forever. There had to be another way. I pulled the sword from the sheath. The Lady's face flashed through my mind. "If you want the sword, you'll have to take it from me."

"He can't," Connor whispered. "None of the Fomorii can touch it.

"Even you?"

"If my Tuatha side is stronger, I might be protected."

"Connor, you are my heir and Fomorii through and through. You can't see that now, but one day, you will and I look forward to the day when you join us. Bring me the sword, great-grandson." Calatin's voice was compelling.

Connor looked more confused than ever. The blood call was strong. Would he be able to resist it?

"I'm happy to chat away the evening with you folks if that is what you prefer. As we speak, the seals are decaying. Soon my people will be free. Still, I'll need to destroy the sword. Connor, take it from Brannon and bring it to me. If you do, I promise you Tara will live. You'll be alright if you don't touch the eye or cut yourself on the blade."

"Give me the damn sword." Connor grabbed my wrist to wrestle the sword from me.

I wouldn't let him have it. Not without a fight.

Kieran stepped from behind a stalagmite. "Connor, he doesn't care about you. Calatin wants to destroy the sword, and he'll sacrifice your life to do so. If he succeeds, no one is safe."

With two hands, Connor grasped the hilt and glared at me with all the stubbornness of a mule.

"Let go," I hissed. "It could kill you." Connor's face contorted in pain, as he held on with a vise grip. Would the sword kill him if he didn't let go? Could I take another death on my soul? I released the sword, and Connor staggered toward Calatin. The sword sapped his strength as he struggled to hold it steady. Calatin was right. My cousin's Fomorii blood ran stronger than his human blood.

In one fluid motion, Connor thrust the sword at Calatin. Surprised, Calatin jumped back, releasing Tara and narrowly escaping the blade and certain death from the eye of the seahorse.

Kieran used this moment to grab Tara and pull her away from Calatin. "Like Lugh, Connor is also part Tuatha," he said. "Lugh defeated you once before."

"Look at him. Even I can see how he longs for the power that only his Fomorii heritage can give him. His loyalty to you is iced with disappointment." Calatin's eyes narrowed. "Connor, you'll ascend to your rightful place at my side. You'll learn to master your gifts. You will belong, be loved, and cherished."

With an incredible show of strength, Connor swung the sword again. I couldn't help but notice the tattoo around his wrist dripped blood. Calatin and his Fomorii companions pulled back to avoid the blade. With their spears ready to strike, two Fomorii engaged Connor while two more moved behind him.

"Watch your back," I yelled.

Kieran spun his torch into the air. It hit the back of a Fomorii, who went up in flames.

Calatin raised his hands and, with fingers crackling with power, caused stalactites to drop from the ceiling, narrowly missing Kieran and Connor.

I took Tara's hand and pulled her behind a nearby archway. Connor dropped to his knees. Kieran grabbed and hauled him to safety in the staircase recess, where he vomited.

The Answerer lay on the ice about six feet in front of Calatin. I slid across the ice to grab it. My heart was pounding. What to do? I focused on the sapphire. The talisman had helped me before. Would it now? A stream of light cut through the mist from a tiny spark at the tip of my sword. I turned and saw hundreds of cormorants flying above us.

"Well done, Brannon. You've proven stronger and braver than I anticipated," Calatin said.

I spun around. Calatin stood with a spear in his left hand. Around the length of the spear was a series of intricately carved symbols. The tip, a sharp bloodstone, sizzled. With a word that I didn't understand, Calatin threw the spear.

I deflected the blow with the sword, but the spears kept coming. I backed away and took cover behind the rocks.

Spears bounced off the chamber walls and hit the frozen ground, creating a spray of shattered ice. A spear impaled a Fomorii warrior. Calatin showed no sign of concern for his fallen comrade.

Kieran and Connor ducked to protect their heads from the deluge of shattered ice and spears. Out of the corner of my eye, I saw Kieran scooping ice fragments into his hand and skillfully arming his slingshot. Connor followed suit, and together, they flung shards in rapid succession, keeping the Fomorii warriors from attacking me from behind. The missiles ricocheted off the walls. Some ice chunks hit the cormorants, who uttered a cacophony of cries and flew up and swirled above our heads. One cormorant flew in front of Calatin and took a jab to the breast meant for me. Furious, Calatin spoke in the Fomorii tongue. I stumbled, and Connor threw his head back as though Calatin had punched him in the jaw. Connor fell against the cave wall while Kieran countered with his own magical words.

Tara, who sought safety behind a large stone near the chamber's entrance, grabbed a torch from the sconce above her and waved it before her to clear a space around us. The fire kept the seabirds away.

I ducked behind a stalagmite to catch my breath. A simple distraction was all I needed, and it looked like Tara could provide me with one. It was risky. If I failed, I knew Calatin would kill her. She appeared from around a stalagmite and tossed a burning torch at him. In the second it took for him to extinguish the torch, I raised the sword above my head and brought the blade down onto Calatin's left shoulder.

Calatin dropped his spear and fell to one knee. I could feel the sword draining his energy.

This was the moment I feared. If I was going to do it, it had to be now. I brought the sword's tip to rest on Calatin's throat. If Calatin moved, I'd sever his jugular. He deserved to die. He killed Peter. How easy it would be to kill him now. If I did, I wouldn't be any better than Calatin. Did I have the right to be his executioner? Did I want to be?

Less than a month ago, I rode my bike with Peter, went to school, enjoyed Yellowman, listened to Granda's stories, and drew pictures. Now, I stood with a sword poised for a deadly strike I didn't want to make.

"No," I heard Kieran shout.

Someone gripped my sword hand. I looked down and saw the sheepskin glove.

"Kill him," Faolan hissed and, with his hand over mine, pushed the sword's tip into Calatin's neck. It felt the same as gutting the fish, the crunch through the esophagus, the gush of blood, the foul smell of death, and Calatin's eyes dimming to a dark, stagnant pool. I released the sword into Faolan's hand. The sword dripped with blood. Red like Peter's. Red like my own blood.

Connor stood over Calatin with his head bowed. Tara turned away from the awful scene to hide her face in her sweater. Faolan dropped to his knees with the sword balanced across his thighs. A cold sweat trickled down my face. I tried to wipe the sweat away with a shaky hand—my sweat mixed with Calatin's blood.

When the three remaining Fomorii rushed forward, Faolan stood and said, "Are you as committed to Calatin in death as you were in life?" The warriors looked at each other and dropped their spears one by one.

"Easy now." Kieran placed a warm hand under my arm as my knees began to buckle beneath me.

I longed for the wind on my face and the smell of the sea rushing into my lungs. Kieran's face blurred as I felt myself pulling away from my body. Peter was calling me. "I'm coming," I tried to say but couldn't get the words out. Oh, how I wanted to ride my bike with Peter, but damn, someone was shaking me and shouting in my ear.

Damp, putrid air rushed into my lungs. I opened my eyes and saw Faolan standing over me with the sword. "The seals," he said. I took Manannan's sword, The Answerer, and placed it in the sheath at my side.

Chapter Thirty-One

Brannon

Kieran led us to the first of the four seals. "With the act of restoring the seals," he said, "the Fomorii will once again be exiled to the void. Brannon, Connor, and Tara, you must do this as one."

Each seal was embedded into the cave wall at the four compass points. Carved into each seal was the Ogham symbol for one of the four elements: earth to the north, fire to the south, water to the west, and air to the east.

"Secure each chamber with one of the elements," Kieran explained. "Call upon the element it represents and focus the energy through the sword. Let's begin with the element air."

I held the Ogham symbol for air in my mind as I called to my friend, the wind. The wind did not have a face. It was a feeling like love. The unpredictable wind behaved as it always did, unruly and reluctant to be controlled. It swirled about the chamber, blowing out one torch after another while Faolan relit them with a wave of his hand.

Tara stood beside me, humming the chant Kieran had taught her. Another voice, Connor's, hesitant at first, joined hers. It surprised me to hear my cranky cousin had a lovely singing voice. Kieran added a countermelody, and together we used music to bind the energy of air and focus it through the sword.

Beneath the chant, I heard voices pleading. "Listen." I raised my hand to silence the singing. The wind died down in the chamber. "Do you hear them?"

Do not banish us to this darkness for another thousand years. We're not all evil. Our punishment has gone on long enough. What of Orla loved by one of you?

"It is true," Faolan said. "They're not all evil. Orla was proof of that."

"Isn't this what you wanted? Isn't this what you came here year after year to do?" Connor spun to face Faolan with rage burning in his eyes.

"My fight has always been with Calatin for murdering my parents," Faolan said. "It has been my life's quest to search the world for ways to destroy him. I know you hate me for that, and I don't blame you. Still, I could never have been a father to you until I completed this task. Now, I see it's too late."

Calatin was as despised by us as much as by you. Many of us have suffered from his cruelty. He led Manannan to believe that every member of the Fomorii supported him so all the Fomorii would share his fate.

"The Fomorii often misled and mistreated the Tuatha, and they learned that they never honored their promises," Kieran said.

This can be said about all people. Some of us are true to our word. Others cheat and kill. Does that make us all bad? Should all be punished for the crimes of the few? For thousands of years, the Fomorii languished in a dark void, as cruel a fate as any, because of Calatin's tyranny. Haven't the innocent endured enough?

I balanced the sword in my hand. I needed answers. What was the right thing to do? Would The Lady tell me if I asked? I pictured her as I had seen her the day she rode Aonbharr, and she appeared before me. The Lady looked like a priestess with the sapphire hanging from a gold chain around her neck and the pearl, the eye of the seahorse, set into a ring on her finger.

"Brannon, what do you ask of me?" she said.

"I ask for you to decide the fate of the Fomorii," My voice sounded foreign, older, and deeper.

"You know what you've been called upon to do. You must banish the Fomorii." Her tone was stern.

"You said that even a god can make a mistake. In war, one does what one must to protect themselves and their family. Some of these people are innocent and as much victims of the war as the Tuatha. Lady, we have all feared what would happen if the Fomorii escaped the void, but is there any way to make peace?"

The Lady turned to Kieran. "What say you, foster son of Manannan? How do we undo what has been done and remain assured that the Fomorii will not seek to avenge themselves?

"Is there one among you who can speak for all?" Kieran asked.

One of the warriors stepped forward. "I am Elatha king of the Fomorii clan. We were under Calatin's spell, and his death has set us all free. Banish us if you must, but to a land rich in soil and full of light. Surely Manannan can grant this request. In return, we vow never to enter the realm of humans again or harm the Tuatha."

The Lady turned to me. "What the Tuatha has done, the Tuatha must mend. Open the seals."

Kieran instructed me to visualize each seal, its element, and its opposite element. With Tara standing on one side and Connor on the other, I touched the sword's tip to each seal and released the exiled Fomorii.

The Fomorii were tall, proud people with pale complexions and long fingers. Most had six fingers on each hand. One by one, they bowed to The Lady and then stood in a circle around us.

"Near Manannan's sacred isle is a small fertile island. Under the protection of Manannan, the Fomorii can live there in peace," The Lady said.

"How will we get there?" Elatha asked.

"Faolan," The Lady said, summoning him to her side. "You have seen Manannan's blessed isle. If you agree to take them on your boat, it will appear to you once more. When you are within rowing distance of the isle, the Fomorii will disembark and travel to their new world. But Faolan, you must not go with them, or you will be trapped in their land forever.

You are human, and no human can return from these isles. On the other hand, Connor is part Fomorii and one day can travel between worlds. Do you understand?"

Faolan nodded. "I would like Connor to accompany me on this journey to see his people relocated to their new homes. It is time I were a father to him."

Connor looked surprised but pleased. "I'd like that."

"People of the Fomorii? Do you accept these terms?" The Lady asked.

A soft murmur grew to fill the chamber. The Fomorii spoke in one voice, "We do."

"Well, now," Kieran said. "It is time we made our way out of this cave before the tide traps us."

Some of the Fomorii carried Calatin's body, while others picked up the two unconscious Fomorii. Kieran was right. Going back was easier. I smelled snow borne by the sea wind when we neared the entrance. As we stepped into the pale light of day, I saw snowflakes curled about the cliff. Cold, but not the deathly chill of the cave. A healthy cold.

Aonbharr waited for The Lady at the cave entrance, where the tide lapped up to its hooves. The Lady turned to me and smiled. "Brannon, your journey has just begun. We of the Tuatha could not be prouder. Keeping justice and mercy in balance has brought peace to an age-old war. Manannan has asked me to give you a gift. A gift offered only to those worthy of becoming a true knight of the Tuatha de Danann. Aonbharr has sired a filly who will grow to be a magnificent mare. She is yours if you want her when she is old enough."

"Japers." I gasped. "It's an honor. I don't know what to say. I've always wanted a horse. Yes, I do want her. Thank you."

"Connor, you have the blood of three races: human, Tuatha, and Fomorii. One day, you will be a light bearer for all three. Your gift." She took his hand and placed in his palm an emerald talisman—an amulet of his own.

The Lady took Tara's hand in hers. "Your harp will always be in tune, and you'll be able to sing any song requested of you. Your music will heal the land, and one day people will travel from far away to hear you play."

Kieran helped The Lady mount the steed, and I handed her the sword, which she attached to a sheath at the stallion's side. Ocean spray caught in her hair like pearls as Aonbharr waded into the surf, then, rising upon a crest, rode out as far as the eye could see. I squinted and saw a mighty wave envelop them in Manannan's arms.

Chapter Thirty-Two

Brannon

Without a cloud to blemish the day, the sky seemed to reach forever across the ocean. The wind was cold, but neither too strong nor too weak to launch The *Breath of Cerridwen*.

The crewmen were busy with last-minute preparations. The Fomorii hovered in the sky, having transformed into cormorants and razorbills. Some Fomorii clung to the rigging and masks, while those too weak to transform were housed in the lower cabins. The power to change shape fascinated me. Would Connor be able to shapeshift one day? Imagine being able to transform into a dolphin or swan and ride the waves or glide upon the wind.

I smiled as Faolan chewed out Rory for throwing a stone at a cormorant. Chastened and more than a little confused, the boy went about the rest of his duties nervously, watching Faolan out of the corner of his eye. Poor kid. He'd be busy cleaning bird poop off the teak deck for their entire journey. Blessed Manannan! And what would the boy think when he saw the Sacred Isles rising out of the mist in the west? He'd think the end had come for sure.

Faolan walked down the gangplank toward me. "We're ready to sail. Where's Connor?"

I shook my head. I'd seen him wandering around like a lost kitten. He asked me at least three times in the past hour if I'd seen Tara, so I suspected Connor was searching the camp and surrounding cliffs for some sign of her. "It's hard to say goodbye, even if only for a short time. It's even harder to say it when it could mean forever."

"Not forever. A year maybe," Faolan said. "There is so much I'd like to show Connor."

A crowd gathered to see them off on their journey. Polly and Seanán stepped up to say their goodbyes to Faolan. They had talked long into the night with Ma, and I wondered if she had found it in her heart to forgive her brother.

The quiet rumblings of the folks died down as Connor rode up on Malachy. His hands were shaking as he handed me the stallion's reigns. Still, he smiled and punched me good-naturedly on the arm. "Take good care of him."

The job of caring for the horses would be mine for as long as I stayed with the tinkers. It would be a while, as Ma and Da still had to find a new place for us. Besides, Kieran said he had plans for me. Connor spent the morning going over everything, and I hoped I'd have his unique gift with horses one day. "I'll do my best," I said.

My respect for my cousin had grown despite our differences, but I would never tell him. I didn't want to give him more reason to strut around like the most important stallion in the herd.

Connor paused before making his way to the gangplank and looked out over the field where the horses grazed. I knew he was looking for Tara who had not come to say goodbye. When Faolan called for everyone to board Connor gave a final wave and walked up the gangplank.

"Wait, Connor!" Seanán called out and pointed. "Look."

"All turned to see Tara sitting in Kieran's wagon. A plume of dirt trailed behind the wagon as it stopped beside the gang-plank. Tara scrambled out and met Connor on the shore. She pulled the sleeve of her sweater to her elbow to show him the bracelet he had made for her.

He traced the silver knot with his thumb. "But how? Where did you find it?"

"The round tower. I was playing my harp, and there it was, suspended in the morning sun."

Connor took her hand and led her away from all who strained to hear their words. Even the seabirds had ceased their plaintive cries. When the couple had finished their goodbyes, they strolled back to the boat.

"Can she come with me?" Connor asked Seanán with an impish grin.

"Get away with you now," Seanán said, placing his arm protectively around his daughter. "She'll not be going anywhere for a long time. Let's see what kind of man you are when you return. That's if you return."

"You know I will."

"If you don't, I'll come for you myself," Kieran said. "Now, isn't this a grand day, for standing before us are the descendants of the old folk? Connor, with the blood of three races, and Brannon, a prince of the Tuatha. Together, they have mended old wounds. Together they will be the future."

After the cheers died, Connor walked down the gangplank to the deck. Tears pooled in Tara's eyes. I gave her my handkerchief. "Hey, cousin," Connor waved his fist. "Don't get any ideas."

"You'd better be back then," I said, shaking my fist.

"Count on it." Connor looked wistfully over the group of people he had known for his entire life as two men removed the gangplank.

I watched The *Breath of Cerridwen* sail out of the harbor and into the open sea until all I could see on the surface of the water was a glistening sliver of silver on the horizon. Then I took Malachy, mounted him, and guided him to the road toward Ballycastle.

An orange tomcat sat on a section of the fence untouched by the fire that had leveled my house. "I hope Mary comes soon," I said to the cat.

An hour earlier, I had tapped on Mary's bedroom window. She mouthed the words to wait, so I went across the street to my house. After rummaging through the rubble, I found a few things worth keeping: Granda's favorite mug, an unopened bottle of Guinness, two spoons, and Ma's jewelry box, charred and empty. Strange that the looters hadn't found the bottle of Guinness.

The tomcat jumped off the fence and ran toward the side of the house. I looked up and saw Mary come around the side, wheeling my bike. "When I went back to McNeil's barn to look for you, you were gone, so I took your bike before someone else did." She propped it up against the fence.

"Thanks," I said, remembering how Granda had straightened the fender and oiled the brakes.

"So, I guess you know about Declan." She wrung her hands.

"I'm so sorry. I heard he drowned or something."

"Or something." She brushed a strand of hair from her eyes. It had escaped the ribbon that had come untied. She knows, I thought. Little Mary had always had the uncanny knack of knowing secret things she shouldn't. Poor wee one. Who would help her understand her gift?

"He was mean to me. He was mean to everyone, and I'd thought he'd killed you, too."

"Nah, it's hard to kill me. I'm like the old tomcat here. I've got nine lives."

"I wish Peter had nine lives."

"Me too." I opened my pack and took out one of Etain's shawls woven in soft greens and yellows. "This is for you."

She reached out to touch it. "Oh, it's so pretty and soft as a kitten."

When I placed it around her shoulders, I knocked the ribbon out of her hair. I picked it up and gave it back to her.

She tied the ribbon around my wrist. "To remember me."

"I'll never forget you, Mary." I took my bike and ran my hand over the handlebars before sitting on it. The seat felt too low. I looked down. The tires were still pumped. I rang the bell. The sound was as clear as ever, but somehow my bike didn't feel the same. I got off and leaned it back against the fence. "Darn it all and go to heck. It feels too small for me now. Please keep it. Besides, I have Malachy to ride now."

"When I see you again, I'll give it back to you."

The ends of the ribbon fluttered against my hand. "I might be gone for a long time."

"I know."

Malachy tried to nip the frayed ribbon around my wrist as I led the horse to the road. I mounted the stallion, and with Mary riding the bike beside me, we took the road out of town. When I could see the Bonamargy Friary in the distance, I halted Malachy. "You'd best be going back now."

Mary rang the bike's bell and headed back into town. I lost sight of her when she disappeared around a bend in the road with the bell still pinging through the air. I waited until the sound of the bell faded before pressing Malachy toward the friary.

After leaving the stallion to graze at the side of the road, I sat on the brick retaining wall. The apple tree where Peter and I had played was bare except for a dab of frost glistening on the tips of the branches. Out of my bag, I took a charcoal pencil and my sketchbook, which fell open to the unfinished portrait of Peter. I squinted into the midday light streaming through the branches and saw Peter leaning against the tree trunk, with a piece of grass hanging from his mouth. And, on the wind, I heard his laughter.

Glossary

People, Places & Irish Expressions

Pronunciation of Irish Character Names

Anrai [oin-ree]: The town silversmith.

Etain [ay-deen]: A tinker.

Faolan [fway-lawn]: Molly's brother.

Kieran [kee-ran]: A druid.

Seamus [shay-mus]: Friend of Granda.

Seanán [shan-awn]: Tara's father.

Geographical Places

Ballycastle: A small seaside town on the most north-easterly tip of Northern Ireland.

Ballintoy: A small town five miles west of Ballycastle.

Bonamargy Friary. [Bun- na-mirage]: A Third Order Franciscan Friary on the outskirts of Ballycastle. The friary is known for sightings of the nun Julie McQuillan, who slipped on the seventh stair and died. She made many predictions; some have come true.

Dolmen: Single-chamber megalithic tomb consisting of three or more upright stones supporting a large flat horizontal capstone. Also known as the druid's altar.

Knocklayde [knocklehid]: A mountain near Ballycastle.

Portrush: Seaside town in Northern Ireland.

Irish Terms and Expressions

Ach: Expression of annoyance, frustration.

Anam Cara: soul friend.

Aye: Yes.

Barmbrack. [bahr-een brack]: Traditional Irish Halloween cake. Yeasted fruit bread with fortune-telling objects baked inside, such as a ring, a small coin, or a stick.

Blootered: Drunk on liquor.

Bodhran: [bowran] Irish drum

Buzzie: A derogatory term for an Irish Tinker.

Cacks: Trousers.

Cakehole: Mouth.

Catch yourself on: Wise up.

Cowbeg: Naughty. Not a nice person.

Crabbit: Grumpy or bad-tempered.

Curragh. [kuhr-uh kh]: Irish rowboat used for fishing and transport.

Cutty knife: Bread knife.

Eejit: Stupid person.

Gack: Stupid person.

Ginny Ann: A sissy. A wimp.

Gob: Mouth.

Gobsmacked: Dumbfounded, shocked.

Gabshite: A person who talks about something he knows nothing about.

Granda: Grandfather.

Japers: Expression of surprise.

Napper: Head.

Narky: Cranky. Irritable.

Odd-as-get-out: Weird, strange person.

Ogham: [aw-guh m]: Ancient Celtic script composed of notches or lines placed along a central stem line.

Poteen: Irish moonshine.

Samhain. [sah-win]: Festival held between October 31 and November 1st. It is believed that the veil between this world and the next becomes thin on Samhain.

Skitter: Used affectionately when describing a child.

Tinker: Nomadic people of Ireland. Also called Travelers.

The Cause: To reunite all of Ireland and free it from the British.

Triquetra: [Trai-kwet-ra]: Triangle. Three-cornered knot.

Wellies: Wellingtons. Boots

Where're you to: Where are you going?

Mythological Names and Places

Answerer (The): Manannan's sword.

Aonbharr. [Ane-varr]: Manannan's horse.

Banshee: "Women of the Fairies." It is thought that the wailing of the banshee foretold death.

Calatin: A Fomorii Sorcerer.

Breath of Cerridwen: Faolan's schooner.

Firbolg. [feer-buhl-uh g]: They lived in Ireland before the Tuatha De Danann.

Fomorii: ([oh-mawr-ee]: Considered violent sea-gods who challenged the Firbolg and the Tuatha De Danann. They were often described as having one hand, foot, or eye. Other stories said they were beautiful to look upon.

Land of Youth: Land of eternal youth. Manannan's realm.

Lugh Lámhfada [Loo Lawvfada]: "Lugh of the Long Arm." A sun god and King of the Tuatha De Danann. Lugh was half Tuatha de Danann and half Fomorii. He was a skilled warrior and craftsman. With his slingshot, Lugh defeated the Fomorii leader Balor of the one eye and brought victory over the Fomorii.

Manannan Mac Lir: [mah-nuh-nahn]: Irish sea-god and ruler of Tir na nOg.

Pooka: [poo-kuh]: A shape-shifting fairy that appears most often as a black stallion.

Pooky Night: Halloween night.

Sidhe: [shee]: The fairy folk.

Tuatha de Danann. [too-uh-huh dey dah-nuh]: "People of the goddess Dana." The last generation of demigods to rule Ireland. They defeated the FirBolg and the Fomorii at the first and second battles of Magh Tuireadh [Moytirra]

Tir na nOg. [teer na nóg]: Land of Youth.

Wave Sweeper: Manannan's magical ship. It could move without oar or sail and could travel as easily over land as water.

Acknowledgements

Thank You

Eye of the Seahorse was originally conceived as a stage-play in my first screenwriting class. It was my instructor, Ian Weir (author, playwright, and screenwriter), who taught me the importance of three-act structure. The screenplay went on to become a novel in my fiction writing class taught by poet and author Brian Brett, whose gift with words was a constant source of inspiration. Finally, the novel took shape in my writing for children's class with author Glen Huser. Thank you, Ian, Brian, and Glen for your guidance.

I would also like to acknowledge Ray Hudson, Edna Hudson, and Zelda Frost, for their helpful comments and encouragement.

Most of all, I would like to acknowledge the love and support of my sister Mary-Lou, who read countless versions of the novel. Her enthusiasm sparked many discussions about Irish Mythology, character development, and plot points. I am grateful to have such a wise and patient soul in my life as it was her belief in me that made the creation of *Eye of the Seahorse* possible. She is my keystone.

Lastly, I must thank Cai, whose stories are laced throughout these pages, for where would a writer be without their muse.

Author
Virginia McCausland

Virginia McCausland is the author of the young adult contemporary fantasy, *Death's Ferryman Rides A Harley*. She is a musician and playwright. with a Bachelor of Music from Western University, an MFA in Creative Writing from the University of British Columbia, and a Publishing Certificate from Toronto Metropolitan University. She lives and writes in a small lakeside town in British Columbia. *Eye of the Seahorse* was inspired by her Irish heritage.